Black January

A SPECTRA Files Novel

By
Douglas Wynne

JournalStone

JOURNALSTONE

JournalStone books may be ordered through booksellers or by contacting:

JournalStone

www.journalstone.com

The views expressed in this work are solely those of the authors and do not necessarily reflect the views of the publisher, and the publisher hereby disclaims any responsibility for them.

ISBN: 978-1-945373-08-4   (sc)
ISBN: 978-1-945373-09-1   (ebook)

JournalStone rev. date: October 21, 2016

Library of Congress Control Number: 2016949891

Printed in the United States of America

Cover Art & Design, interior SPECTRA logos: Chuck Killorin
Images: A derivative of a photo by Stephen Arnold, Unsplash.com - A derivative of "Callanish Stones in summer 2012 (7).JPG" by Chmee2. CC BY-SA 3.0, wikimedia.org - A derivative of a photo by Lucas Gallone. CC0, unsplash.com - "Dragonfly Drone" by Jen Salt

Edited by: Vincenzo Bilof

This one's for you, Mom

Black January

"I call architecture frozen music."

–Johann Wolfgang von Goethe

Letter to Johann Peter Eckermann, March 23, 1829

"O, that this too solid flesh would melt, thaw, and resolve itself into a dew!"

–Hamlet Act 1 Scene 2

"Precisely by slicing out this moment and freezing it, all photographs testify to time's relentless melt."

–Susan Sontag

Prologue

NOVEMBER 2012
CONCORD, MASSACHUSETTS

By the time Maurice Ramirez found the witch house, the acid was starting to kick in. Maybe the shift in perception was *why* he finally found it. He had taken the commuter rail out of Boston first thing in the morning, knowing that he would need time to walk from the train station to Felton Street, aware that by all accounts the place would be hard to find and wanting to finish his business with the house before night fell. Walking the dusty road, he cursed himself for not undertaking the quest months ago, when the days were longer. But the research had led him down avenues almost as obscure as the one he was now pacing amid the brambles, false paths, and shifting shadows of the marshy valley.

The house was supposed to be perched atop a terraced hill, embowered with pine trees and overlooking a rolling meadow surrounded by new growth forest. The books were in agreement on the geography, but the handwritten accounts he'd consulted at the Boston Public Library suggested the address had possibly been changed in recent years, the road renamed and renumbered. And then there was the Internet lore—a hopeless tangle of urban legends in which a handful of accounts with the ring of truth here, or a telling detail there, were camouflaged.

Maurice hiked the dusty road north and south and north again, sweating in his olive trench coat. The coat had seemed vital against the chill wind of the morning, but had since become a burden. He almost wished he had a car to stow it in, but the deep pockets held a wide array of tools, and who knew what he might need once he found the place? He turned his mind to this inventory as he walked, and then to whatever other distractions he could think of. He recalled passages of poetry he'd memorized in college, and the recipes for meals he would cook if he could afford the ingredients. When he ran out of other distractions, he sang a White Stripes tune. Anything to keep his mind off of the house he was hunting.

All the literature agreed, whether in pixels or ink, that the place had used the years to hone its talent for hiding between planes, merging with the landscape, as if it were made of mirrors rather than timbers, stone and glass.

The trick to finding it was to catch it out of the corner of the eye, to detect its shape from an oblique angle, without grasping. The path to the pillar-flanked front steps had to be held lightly in the mind until you ran a gentle hand over the weathered porch railing and grasped the silver filigree doorknob.

The Wade House, built by renowned candle maker and rumored witch Caleb Wade in 1782, and known as the Concord Witch House since the 1920s, did not like to be seen.

Maurice took a deep breath of blue sky and felt the universe vibrate in and around him. He was not a regular user of psychedelics; those days were behind him. Entheogens had been useful stepping stones on his spiritual path but were mostly unnecessary once the faculties they introduced were established, and anyway, it had proven difficult to obtain a steady supply of lab-grade acid on the east coast after the Grateful Dead stopped touring. Nonetheless, he retained his appreciation for the value of viewing the world from a different angle now and then, and kept a few paper tabs printed with an eye in a triangle sequestered in one of his coat pockets with other emergency bits of kit.

After his fourth pass of Felton Street, he'd placed one of these on his tongue. On the fifth pass, he took a set of cardboard-framed red and blue 3D glasses and a tangerine from one of his deep pockets, placed the glasses on the bridge of his nose, and peeled the fruit as he walked. And on the sixth pass, with citrus sluicing like liquid sunshine down his throat, he caught a glimpse of the stately yellow and purple trimmed Victorian, and stopped dead in his tracks.

Shadows pulsed at the corners of his eyes. A sparrow flew over the road, blazing a prismatic trail across the sky. The house leaked streamers of blackness, flooding the fragrant valley with malevolence.

Maurice turned his head slowly, not looking at the crumbling mansion but holding it gently in his peripheral vision until it winked out of existence, then scanning back again until it flickered and returned. A silver path through high weeds wended up the slope to the front porch steps. He stepped onto it, whistling as he went.

In a moment the house towered over him, the harsh sunlight wavering on the windows as if the leaded glass pulsed with the beat of the house's dark heart.

Was it an organism camouflaged as a building?

He had yet to strike that theory from his list. And if it was alive, was it young or mature by its own time scale? Certainly it was old for the New World, and had shown its age in decay long before its reputation for haunting had left it abandoned. Maurice wasn't concerned with rumors of ghosts. Such anomalies were rare and seldom harmful side effects of greater forces. For him, the more vital mystery had to do with sentience in the structure and the possibility that it might be undergoing a growth spurt. All living things went through phases of volatility and—God help him—procreation. He didn't know if the house had a mind or a will, couldn't say whether it scrutinized trespassers, and he could only speculate about its criteria for allowing passage through its portals. But he knew what he had to do to put its innermost portal beyond reach.

He patted his chest and felt the leather pouch that hung from his neck. Hiding its contents here, so close to that damnable door was risky, for sure. And yet, for that very reason, it might be the safest place—a place where signals that would otherwise draw attention might blend into the background radiation bleeding through from the suns of other dimensions, converging and confusing the would-be seeker.

If the house itself was hard to find, many of its inner doors were even more elusive. Even if the Starry Wisdom cult traced Maurice's steps to Europe and New Hampshire, they'd never think to look for what he'd found in Paris beyond the threshold where he intended to hide it today. He might be regarded a lunatic among lunatics, but no one would think for a minute that he was *that* crazy.

At the door, he took a piece of chalk from his trench coat and inscribed the five-branched Elder Sign on the splintering oak boards. He turned the silver knob and the door swung inward without so much as a creak, as if eager to welcome him.

The staircase lay straight ahead across a threadbare Persian carpet, the banister topped with an iron lamp in the shape of Eris, goddess of chaos, holding aloft a glass apple. Hand-carved dark wood moldings and cornices flanked the entrances to a sitting room on the right and a dining room on the left. Weak sunlight filtered in through moth-eaten curtains lending the bubbled wallpaper an even deeper yellow hue than time had imbued it with. He glimpsed antique furnishings draped with sheets, the upholstery thick with dust where it peeked through.

Maurice licked his chapped lips and reminded himself to breathe. The sour smell of sweat permeated his coat as he placed a hand on the banister.

He caught motion out of the corner of his eye and whirled around as a table lamp crashed to the floor, the rotting shade practically disintegrating on impact, coughing out a spray of shattered glass at the vanishing tail of a small animal; a cat, or a rat.

Steadying his nerves, he set a scuffed boot on the bottommost step, eyes trained on the pulsing shadows above.

For a moment, he thought he might ascend to the second floor without incident. But just as he began to drop his guard, he detected a roiling motion in the deeper darkness of the upper staircase. He had just enough time to draw the laser pointer from his pocket as a mammoth centipede of oily black smoke rushed down the stairs, blotting out the light from the circular window over the landing and eclipsing his field of vision.

Maurice sidestepped and sliced the dusty air with the red beam, branding a ruby pentagram on the creature's mottled flank. The light sheared the smoke, and by the time the howling mouth curled around to snap its rings of teeth at him, the worm was vanishing in tatters of black vapor.

He pocketed the laser pointer, wiped his brow with a paisley bandana, and bellowed, "I ain't afraid of you motherfuckers. You hear?"

When nothing answered, he climbed the stairs to search the second floor.

After a quick tour of the master bedroom—which had a murder vibe—and the upper level of a two-story library well-stocked with moldering volumes he wished he had time to peruse, Moe found what he was looking for: a canvas draped piano in the center of a large empty room beneath a chandelier. He swept the cover aside, revealing a baby grand with an inverted white-on-black keyboard.

He used the piano bench as a step to climb onto the closed hood of the instrument, then fished a length of nylon cord with a carbon fiber grappling hook attached to one end out of his trench coat. It took three swings to get a feel for the hook's momentum and trajectory before he let it soar overhead, where it surprised him by wrapping around the chandelier on the first try. Maurice was not a small man, but fixtures had been built strong when this house was erected. He pulled at the rope, leaned back on his heels, and lifted his boots off the piano lid for a second. The chandelier creaked and rained dust, but it held.

He looked around the room for a stronger anchor point, but found nothing. The best bet might have been the staircase banister in the hall, but he had doubts about the length of the rope, and anyway, some of the rods had looked as crooked as bad teeth. Even the straight ones might be rotted. The chandelier would have to do.

He climbed down off the piano, rummaged in another of his trench coat pockets, and produced a folded square of paper. He shook out the folds and blew dust from the page—a handwritten musical score speckled with tea stains and smudged with ash at the corners. He removed his 3D glasses, stowed them in his pocket, and studied the page. It was a photocopy, but he could still see the spot where whorls of India ink preserved the composer's partial thumbprint, and for a moment he could picture the man dipping his quill by candlelight. The title of the piece, scrawled in bold calligraphy, read: *The Invisible Symphony*.

Maurice lifted the hinged music rack, set the page on it, placed his fingers on the keyboard, and struck a chord. In defiance of the laws of physics, the piano was perfectly in tune despite years of neglect. Unable to help himself, he followed the chord with a little trill and a descending blues lick. He smiled, popped his shoulders, and cracked his knuckles.

He ran his finger along the staff and came to a cadence of three chords circled in pencil. He played through the sequence carefully, pausing for a beat between each chord while his fingers climbed the keys and found the next position. He hadn't had access to an instrument for many years and now wished he'd sought one out in advance to brush up and reacquaint his fingers before it mattered. Even a cheap synthesizer at a Boston music shop would have been good enough. But he *hadn't* practiced and it was too late now and his ring finger hit the wrong key—a dissonant little slip on the last chord. He corrected it quickly but the quick-beating vibration of the errant note continued to clash in the air. The lid of the instrument bounced and a thick gray tentacle lashed out from under it, slicing the air just inches from his face and leaving an odor of sewage in its wake before vanishing again beneath the thumping lid.

Like a driver recoiling from the gas to hit the brake, Maurice jerked his foot off the sustain pedal, cutting the music short. He stared at the trail of ichor smeared across the varnished wood for a moment, then played the chords again, stepped on the pedal, and let the sound ring out while he raised the lid a few inches to peer inside.

In the shadowy interior, he found only hammers, strings, and the gilded soundboard. He set the lid back down, went to the stairs, and broke a carved oak rod from the railing. Back at the piano, he knelt on the floor and wedged the rod under and over the three pedals so that the one in the middle would stay down. Then, standing hunched over the keyboard, he struck the chords again. He shuffled around to the side of the instrument while the rigged pedal kept the notes ringing, lifted the lid, and caught his breath.

This time he found none of the mechanical components of a piano but only a yawning void redolent of ozone and sea breeze. He rested the piano lid on the hinged arm, tossed the coil of rope into the blackness, and climbed in after it, grateful for his fingerless rawhide gloves as he grasped the rope tight and put his weight on it.

High above, the chandelier groaned, lurched, and chimed. A flurry of plaster dust drifted down onto his afro as he lowered his bulk into the darkness, his hot cheeks caressed by the stirring air of a vast, open space.

Down and down he went through the chill air. Above, the piano-shaped window glowed pale and distant, doing nothing to illuminate the ground below. He grunted a sigh of relief when his foot finally found it.

With hands now free, he switched on his flashlight and swept the beam over the cracked hardpan, illuminating seashells, driftwood, and desiccated horseshoe crabs. At the farthest reaches of his beam, he glimpsed a shadow cage of ribs clawing at the sky—a wrecked wooden ship or the carcass of some beached leviathan. Now that he'd recovered from the descent, his own breath no longer rasping in his ears, he listened for the sound of rolling surf, but heard nothing, not even the cries of gulls.

He had read that the tides of this shore took years to cycle.

Maurice scanned the desolate seabed, decided that the wrecked boat—if that was what it was—would be the most obvious landmark for any investigator, and ruled it out right away. He walked a winding course across the hardpan, checking with the flashlight for footprints—especially his own—and concluded that the ground was too firm to take impressions.

When he felt he had reached an adequate distance from his touchdown point, he chose a random horseshoe crab shell and flipped it over. Worming a finger into the leather pouch at his chest, he worked it open and peered inside. Silver light spilled out, tracing watery sine waves across his forehead.

It was beautiful. A beautiful, terrible thing.

He slipped the cord over his head, cinched the bag shut and gave it a last squeeze, hoping he was doing the right thing when he nestled it between the two rows of claws on the dead crab's underside, then gently placed the shell facedown on the ground, just as he had found it.

Maurice lumbered back to the dangling rope, gave it a tug, and sighed. It had been a long day already. He was tired, and the rope was long. The knots he'd tied in it would provide footing for rest on the way up; but who could say what else might assail him as he fled the Wade House in the fading light.

He ran his gloved hand over his beard, appraising the rope with a grunt. "Shoulda quit those fuckin' Whoppers."

Chapter 1

Becca Philips adjusted the settings on her camera, then, letting it dangle from the strap, wrapped her legs around the aroeira bough and quietly shimmied out over the dark water of the Rio Cuiaba. With dusk still some ninety minutes off, the declining sun had withdrawn the harsh highlights from the trees, and the wildlife was stirring. It was her third trip to the Pantanal since she came to Brazil two years ago, and she felt well attuned to its rhythms. This evening she was stalking a jabiru—a red-necked white stork—and had spotted one perched on a neighboring tree. In January, the water level was low, the green reeds high, and she hoped to capture a shot of the bird leaving its perch to glide down to the river bank once it chose a spot for fishing. For now, the jabiru was busy grooming its feathers, seemingly unaware of the photographer next door.

Becca went out a little further. The branch swayed, leaves rustling. On the ground below, her dog, Django, whined. Between the two of them they were going to scare the bird off before she was in position to take the shot. Wrapping her left arm around the branch, she took the camera in her right, and trained it on the bird. Her thighs stung below her cargo shorts where the tree bark had raked her with scratches and scrapes, but the pain scarcely registered while her mind was on the shot. With only one hand to work with, she relied on the autofocus and pressed the shutter release. The light was gorgeous.

She took another shot, and then another. The bird had to be aware of her by now, but it hadn't flown off yet.

Could she reach the camera dials with her left hand and make a few adjustments? She was about to try when Django's anxious separation whine morphed into something else: a long drawn out growl culminating in two warning barks.

Becca looked down and almost dropped her camera at the sight of the crocodile, its snout and fore claws emerging from the muddy water, followed by an endless procession of ridges. It climbed the bank toward the trunk of the tree where Django sat guard, Becca's blood going colder with every inch until the tip of its tail was out of the water. It had to be 9 feet long. Her first instinct was to get a good shot of it, but the idea perished before it was fully formed, replaced by the urgent need to scare the monster away from her dog.

She did a quick mental inventory of objects she might throw at the crocodile, but the snacks and photo paraphernalia in her pockets were no substitute for rocks.

A buzzing sound caught her ear and she shot a glance back in the direction of the jabiru to find a dragonfly hovering in the air about a foot away from the bird. There was something slightly off about the insect's movement and Becca realized she had never heard the sound of a dragonfly before. With wings too delicate to be detected by human ears, they weren't supposed to buzz like bees. Was this some heightening of her senses brought on by panic?

Django barked again—aggressive bursts punctuating his droning growl. Becca couldn't see him from this angle but pictured his hackles up. She was sweating now from the physical strain of holding on to the branch, the mental strain of the threat below, and her inability to act quickly with arms and legs essentially tied. She searched the tree for fruit or a dead branch that she could break off, but there was nothing. It was either throw the camera or hope that yelling would be enough to scare the monster back into the water.

Scare a predator in its native environment? Unlikely. She should've left Django back at the cabana in Porto Jofre.

The dragonfly buzzed over to her tree now, hovering nearby as she inch-wormed back down its length to the trunk. Another insect scurried across her calf and she avoided looking, didn't even want to know what it was. But this dragonfly…there was something strange about it. It didn't belong here.

Now that it was close, she detected other sounds: clicking and whirring.

Becca squinted at the bug's faceted iridescent eyes.

The fucking thing was a drone. Suddenly, she didn't know whether to swat it out of the air, try to catch it, or ignore it altogether.

The jabiru took flight, soaring toward the far bank of the river. She'd forgotten about it for a second, and when its white wings unfolded and flashed in her eyes, and set the leaves of her branch trembling, she slipped, lost her grip, and found herself hanging from her thighs, camera dangling below her head as the crocodile turned away from the dog and fixed its ancient gaze on this new gift of dangling meat.

The mechanical dragonfly shot past Becca's face, and her gold scarab necklace slipped out from under her tank top as if to greet it as it passed. Django's barking shifted in tone again, taking on another kind of excitement before cutting off entirely as a gunshot rang out.

Becca's heart felt like it was giving in to gravity and tumbling into her throat, but she held on tight, crunched up, and hugged the branch. Below, the crocodile turned and slipped into the river as a second bullet plinked the muddy water. Muscles burning with fatigue, Becca reached the tree trunk, found her footing, and scrambled down to a branch low enough to jump from.

Upon landing, Django nuzzled her scraped thighs, whining. She crouched and soothed him; petting the ridge of raised fur along his spine and tucking the scarab back under her shirt with her other hand.

A man stood at the riverbank watching the crocodile retreat. The dragonfly drone hovered beside him as he holstered his weapon, and she knew him before he turned to look at her: Jason Brooks, SPECTRA agent and redheaded Boston homeboy. They had seen some shit together.

"Hey, Becca. Still doing your damnedest to die for a photo, huh?"

She tried not to smile and failed. Still, it was a wry grin that didn't last long. "And you've still got my back, huh?"

"Guess so. Django doesn't scare off the birds you're trying to shoot?"

"I've trained him not to. How long have you been following me with your robot bug?"

Brooks didn't answer. He didn't deny he'd been spying on her, either.

"Would you have stepped out if we weren't about to get eaten?"

"Hey, it ain't like that. You're lucky I found you." He raised his palm to the sky and the dragonfly landed on it. "And the toy is yours. I was just trying it out."

Becca crossed her arms. "It almost knocked me out of the tree. I think I'm fine without it."

"I think it was a bird that almost did *that.*"

"No, actually, it was your gunshot."

"Nah. Bird. Pretty sure I got a photo of it."

"On *that?*"

"Yup. Hi-res, too. Wanna see?"

"Seriously, Brooks, I almost let go when you fired that damn thing."

"I knew you wouldn't." Now he was the one grinning.

Becca shook her head.

"You didn't let go at Bunker Hill. C'mon, take a look." He held what looked like a phone out to her and swiped the glass. "There's your bird...and you...and the croc from above..."

He handed her the device. She took it, and was soon thumbing through shots and zooming in on details. The glass responded the way she expected it to, but the processor was light years ahead of any phone she'd ever tried shooting with. Her breath hitched in her chest at the clarity and detail. "Do you control the bug with this thing? It's the remote?"

"Yeah."

"And the dragonfly beams the pictures back instantly?"

"As you take them."

She cupped her hand over her mouth.

"The drone hovers on autopilot if you have to drop the remote into your pocket. That's why it didn't crash when I shot at the croc. You're welcome, by the way."

"Why are you here?" Now that the adrenaline had washed through her system and her heart rate was settled down, she found her innate skepticism returning. "You flew down here to give me a piece of classified tech because SPECTRA loves to share these things with nature photographers?"

"You're a nature photographer now? What happened to urban explorer? Art school student?"

"I think you know."

"Well, I guess you're still risking life and limb among amphibious beasts, so it can't be *that* different."

"At least I'm not risking my sanity down here."

They had strayed beyond the bounds of jest and for a moment neither of them spoke. A flock of birds took wing from the far bank, a tumult of black against the purpling sky. The boughs and reeds sighed in the breeze. Brooks swatted a mosquito on his neck, leaving a smear of blood.

"What do they want me to shoot with that thing?" Becca asked at last.

Brooks shrugged. "If we really knew that, I probably wouldn't be coming to you, but...probably monsters."

"Government's getting good at shooting things from a distance."

"What's that, an anti-war comment?"

Now it was Becca's turn to shrug. "What do they need *me* for?"

"Let's say you have an eye for the weird. And the case I'm on has personal relevance for you, if you care to hear about it. Even if you don't come back to the States with me, I figured I owed it to you to let you know."

"Know what?"

"Your father went missing."

Becca scoffed. "That's news? He went missing from *my* life a long time ago."

"I mean missing from…this dimension. Maybe." He swatted another mosquito, this one on his arm, and waved his hand in front of his face. "Becca, this isn't how I intended to have this conversation. I have a boat. Let me give you a ride back to your cabin and I'll tell you what I know."

She scratched Django's head. "What do you think, Django? Take a ride with Jason and hear him out? He *did* pay our way to Brazil, after all."

"Hey, I even brought a bag of marshmallows. You have a fire pit?"

"Django can't eat marshmallows."

Brooks rummaged in his field vest and brought out a thin package. He waved it in the air. "Beef jerky, buddy?"

Django sniffed the air, but didn't stray from his mistress' side.

* * *

Becca poked the fire with the carved tip of her stick and watched the sugar residue burn. Sparks drifted up toward the stars splashed across the sky. Beside her wood plank lounge chair, Django snored. "You said I have an eye for the weird," she said. "So do *you* last I checked. Or did you take that drug, Nepenthe, to make it go away?"

Brooks shook his head and took a pull on his beer bottle.

Her eyes fixed on the flames, Becca asked the question she feared most: "Have you seen anything in Boston since the equinox? Anything…"

"Fucked up? No."

The fire popped. The damp wood sizzled.

"How about you?" Brooks asked. "Seen anything since?"

"In São Paulo? No."

"Anywhere."

Becca bobbed her head side to side. "I thought I saw something once in the rain forest, but I couldn't be sure. I was spooked, so...might have been my own mind playing tricks on me."

"I wouldn't rule anything out. Brazil's been a hotspot for UFO activity since the 50s."

"You think what happened in Boston has something to do with aliens?"

"Well...not in the usual sense. They don't tell me everything, but I know there are people at SPECTRA who think UFOs aren't from other planets but from another dimension here on Earth. So...what did you see?"

"I don't know. And it was shortly after I got here, so maybe it was residual weirdness in my own head, my imagination acting up in a spooky place."

"What place?"

"Calçoene. It's a megalithic site in the north. Standing stones."

"I'll make a note of it. Might be worth looking at, eventually."

"Did you come here to tell me my father might have been abducted by a UFO? Because that'd be a real good excuse for him missing my birthday this year."

Brooks laughed, set the empty beer bottle down beside his chair, and leaned forward. "All right, here's the deal: the first weird thing we've seen since the black sun blew up over Boston."

"*We've* seen? Or *you've* seen? You're the only one besides me who still has the sight, right?"

"Far as I know, yes. And it's 'we' because *anyone* can see this. Everyone can."

Becca and Brooks didn't have much in common, but the special perception they shared set them apart. In September 2019, a radical member of the Starry Wisdom Church had set off a harmonic bomb on a subway train. The technology, cobbled together from a boom box and a 3D printed, lab grown larynx known as The Voice Box of the Gods, enabled the pronunciation of ancient spells and mantras the human voice was no longer capable of producing. Brooks was on the train at the time, was one of the only survivors, and was exposed to frequencies that altered his perception, enabling him to occupy the same plane of reality as the trans-dimensional entities evoked by the event. And anyone who could see the entities could also be hunted by them.

Becca had become entangled in the situation—first as a suspect when her infrared photos started picking up traces of the same incursion, and later as an ally in the fight against the cultists and their dark gods. She was uniquely positioned to make a difference because of family secrets kept by her late grandmother, a professor at Miskatonic University and authority on the occult. In a sense, it was a war she had been born into, and her grandmother had left her an heirloom to aid her in the fight to turn the tide.

After first resisting the lure of secrets that had torn her family apart, Becca, in a moment of peril, had embraced her role, exposing herself to mantras chanted by the Black Pharaoh himself during an attack on Boston's Christian Science Center in broad daylight. In the aftermath of the crisis, unlike the other civilians exposed, Becca had refused the drug that shut down the extra dimensional perception. Brooks had advocated to grant her that right, making the case that she was an unsung hero in an invisible war. He understood that she, like him, wanted to retain an early warning system in case the incursion wasn't really over. In case the monsters came back.

"You know how those of us who were exposed could see the black sun and the tendrils that dropped down on locations where there was a manifestation? Well, we think this might be some kind of fallout from when your scarab blew it up. There's black snow falling over Boston now, like ash. There were isolated reports of it around Christmas last year, or I guess you could say since the winter solstice. Then nothing. But now it's back and gathering intensity."

"And the people reporting it weren't exposed in '19?"

"No. Like I said, *everyone* can see it in the sky. You don't watch the news, huh?"

"I avoid the Internet altogether unless I'm in contact with a client."

"What kind of clients do you get?"

"Too few, but living here is cheap. Go on."

"We didn't know what it was. Still don't. But we had a breakthrough when we realized the black snow is gathering at a specific location. It's the weirdest fucking thing. When you map it, it literally looks like iron filings drawn to a giant magnet."

"What's the magnet?"

"It's a house. An abandoned mansion west of Boston, in Concord. It had a reputation for being haunted even before the black snow, but hey, it *is* an old abandoned mansion, why wouldn't it? Anyway, we've cordoned off the site, locked it down. Everyone on the scene can see the black snow. Of course, the neighbors saw it first. Publicly, they're calling it an environmental disaster cleanup site. Even set up a shell company we can sue for toxic emissions at an old factory in Waltham. That's the official explanation for the fallout."

"People are buying that?"

"Managing the press has been…tricky. Fortunately, what the neighbors can't see—and this place can be hard to see *at all* from the road—is that most of the black snow is being sucked down the chimney. The hill around the place is still covered with it, but it seems to want to go in. The house is definitely an attractor."

"What does this have to do with my father?"

"When we first arrived, we found a motorcycle registered to him parked on the property."

"And you haven't found him."

"No. Not at his last known address, not in the house or the surrounding towns. We even ran his picture on TV for a little while—with a fake name so people wouldn't associate it with *your* five minutes of Beantown fame. No leads."

"And obviously you didn't find him in the house."

"Yeah, no. Here's the thing, though: this house, well, you know how mirrored surfaces and pools of water acted as portals to let things through? Well, the house hasn't let anything *out* into our world yet—that we know of—but it may be letting people pass through into whatever world those things came from."

Something cold wormed in Becca's stomach. A knot popped in the campfire. "You think my father went into the house and got lost in another dimension?"

"Maybe. It's possible. The place is strange. Its architecture changes. Passages and doors appear where they weren't before. Other things too, little things like the number of steps in a staircase, the number of panes in a window. It's all in flux, up for grabs. That's the other reason they want your help; to explore it."

Becca splayed her fingers. "Whoa, hold up. Not likely."

"Not only would you have a drone camera you can safely maneuver into any questionable space you want to photograph, but you've already trained yourself in urban exploration. Abandoned buildings are your thing, right?"

"They don't need me. *You* have the sight. And I'm sure they have military guys who can get around in a derelict mansion."

"This is no ordinary mansion, Becca. And you're no ordinary photographer. We need to document this. And…I thought you'd want to find your father."

She crossed her arms. "You thought wrong."

Brooks stood. "All right then. I told them I'd give it a shot, but I kind of figured Boston in January would be a hard sell for you. I'm glad you're happy here." He fished his phone out of his pocket to call for extraction.

Staring into the fire, Becca said, "Why would he go looking for the sort of trouble he ran away from? The stuff my grandmother was into…he wanted nothing to do with it."

"I don't know. I'll tell you if we find anything. If you care."

The dragonfly was perched on the arm of Becca's chair, as if sleeping. It really was a fascinating piece of machinery; so intricate. She ran a fingertip between its aluminum lace wings, stroking it from head to tail, then picked it up and offered it to Brooks.

"We have a few fragments of info to get us started, so it's not like it's hopeless. The most promising stuff is from the journals of Maurice Ramirez. He visited the house about a decade ago."

"Moe was involved in this, too?"

Brooks nodded.

"His stuff is always hard to decipher, but the geeks are working on it. He was a little more coherent before you met him."

Moe Ramirez had been a homeless occultist living in an abandoned textile mill by the Charles River when Becca met him in 2019. Ranting about the apocalypse, writing on the walls, and performing banishing rituals with a Burger King crown on his head. It still seemed strange that the government considered him a reputable authority on the nature of reality, but then he *had* been right about that apocalypse.

"I wonder if my dad ever met him."

"Dunno. Didn't you think Ramirez might have been a student of your grandmother at one point?"

Becca shrugged. "Just a hunch. They studied a lot of the same rare books."

"I could check Miskatonic's records, if you're curious."

"I'm more curious about what my father was looking for in that house."

"I have a theory," Brooks said, dropping his phone back into his pocket but not taking the dragonfly from Becca.

She raised an inquiring eyebrow.

"You," he said.

She closed her fingers around the tiny drone.

Chapter 2

The SPECTRA jet touched down at Hanscom Air Force Base in Bedford, Massachusetts, a short drive from Concord, where the Wade House was located. Becca had dressed for Boston winter before boarding the plane, but it still came as a shock and she found herself rubbing her arms through her army jacket as she descended the steps to the tarmac. The sky was a shade of dirty pewter and the wind whipped her hair. Brooks led her to a black Ford sedan waiting nearby. An attendant put their bags in the trunk. Brooks opened the passenger door for Becca, followed by the rear door for the dog. As he settled into his own seat and turned the key in the ignition, he pointed at the digital temperature gauge on the dashboard. "Hey look: it's 48. Unseasonably warm."

"Sure as hell doesn't feel like it," Becca said. She tucked her chin into the upturned collar of her jacket and pulled the zipper up to her nose. Django, still zonked out on Benadryl to take the edge off of flying, was already falling asleep in the backseat.

"That's because it was summer where you came from. You've had your share of Boston winters; for January, this is nice."

By the time they hit the highway, Becca's face emerged from her jacket like a turtle from its shell and Brooks turned down the blasting heat. She saw him reach for the radio and change his mind. Maybe he was remembering the Tool t-shirt she'd been wearing on the day they'd met, the day SPECTRA abducted her with a black helicopter and a bag over her head. Maybe he was familiar with her entire music collection from the days the agency had spent sifting through her computers, and knew he would be unlikely to find anything on the radio to satisfy her. She stared out the window at melting snow banks dusted with diesel soot, barren gray tree limbs flashing by.

"I shouldn't have come back," she said.

"Why is that?"

"I thought I might be over it. I'm not."

"Over what? Rafael's death?"

She cast a withering glance at him. "How could I get over that? I was talking about Seasonal Affective Disorder. It was strange breaking the cycle; living in the southern hemisphere when my body said it should be winter. I felt pretty level the whole time I was there. I still had bad days, but it wasn't like the drowning feeling I always had in Boston or Arkham for half the year."

"But there was nothing to test you down there. Why would you think you were over it?"

Becca drew a rayed sun in the condensation on the window with her finger. "This will sound crazy, but *everything* that happened that fall was crazy. I thought maybe the scarab, once it had the ruby in its pinchers again...I thought maybe...maybe it healed me. But just looking at this place, I know it didn't."

"There's no reason you can't go back to Brazil after this job. They'll fly you back if that's what you want. Your bank account will be replenished. You can get on with living the good life."

"You know much about my bank account, Brooks?"

"I wish you'd call me Jason."

"Have you been keeping tabs on me this whole time, *Jason*?"

"I worried about you."

"You needn't have. My share from the sale of my grandmother's house goes a long way in a place like Brazil. And I'm starting to sell photos."

"Yeah? That's great. Who to?"

"You sure you don't already know?"

He kept his thumbs hooked on the steering wheel but splayed his fingers and bobbed his head toward them. "I wouldn't ask if I knew."

"Nature conservation groups, rare butterfly and bird enthusiasts. I'm trying to break into nature magazines."

"Butterfly enthusiasts?"

"Yeah. Who knew, right? There are people who don't want to visit a location until I've scouted it out and sent photographic proof that it hosts the species they're looking for."

"So what's the coolest butterfly you've photographed?"

"You know a lot about butterflies, Brooks?"

"Jason."

"My favorite was the Blue Morpho, but it's not rare. You ever seen one?"

"I don't know. What's it look like?"

"The undersides of the wings are mottled brown and gray, like foliage with circles that look like owl eyes, to keep predators away. When the wings are folded up, that's what you see. But when it's flying, the other side is this brilliant shade of metallic blue. Flying, it looks like it's flickering in and out of existence between camouflage and that blue radiance."

"Sounds cool."

"I learned a bit about them, and apparently their eyes are really good at detecting UV light. They reminded me a little bit of myself. Reading about them, I could almost believe that the things we saw in Boston were part of the natural world, the natural order, not signs of some malignant chaos underlying everything."

"Back up a sec. Why did the butterfly remind you of yourself?"

"Wishful thinking, I guess. They look blue, right? But they're not, not really. The blue color isn't pigmentation. It's just iridescence from the angle of the scales on their wings. They're just really good at reflecting blue light. It got me thinking, *hoping,* that maybe my own blues are like that, that maybe depression isn't something that was tattooed onto me when I was a kid. Maybe it has more to do with my environment, or the angle of the light."

Brooks nodded. "Maybe you're right." He flipped the blinker for the Concord exit. "This is us."

*   *   *

Becca saw the black snowflakes swirling in the sky before the car took the bend at the base of the hill. She pressed her finger to the windshield and the condensation around it melted, but the flakes on the outside didn't. Soon they were accumulating. "Aren't you gonna turn on the wipers?"

"Nah. We'll be there in a minute. The wipers just smear that shit around like ink."

They turned onto a gravel road that wound up a terraced hill surrounded by threadbare woods. The ground appeared to be covered with a dusting of ash, in some places heaped in piles. The flakes swirled in eddies as the car passed.

The base of the hill was wrapped in a 10-foot electrified fence topped with razor wire. Brooks took a holographic card from a clip on the visor, rolled the window down as the car rolled up to a guard booth, and passed the card to an armed security officer in gray fatigues with a SPECTRA shoulder patch. The guard examined the card, tilting it this way and that and briefly holding it under a UV light before passing it back. He pressed his thumb onto a fingerprint reader and set the motorized gate trundling open on side-rolling wheels. Becca noticed an assault rifle propped in the corner of the booth as they passed. A second guard, with a matching rifle, was stationed under a rain shelter inside the gate.

Climbing the hill, the first structure to rise from the blackened landscape was a large corrugated Quonset hut.

"What's that?" Becca asked.

"We call it 'Base Camp.'"

"Wow. Do I get a Sherpa to carry my stuff?"

"No, but you get your own bedroom in the mansion."

"We're not sleeping in the hut?"

"The hut is where you'll be briefed on the mission. It houses our support staff."

"The house isn't big enough for them too?"

"Oh, it's big enough. Take a look."

The day had grown warmer, the shrouded silver sun drawing a curtain of mist from the marshy ground, but gazing up the slope at the Wade House, Becca felt cold even in the heated car. It loomed out of the fog like the prow of a black ship, and for a moment she felt as if she were in a lifeboat on a limitless sea, falling under the baleful shadow of a vessel that promised no shelter, only menace and terrors to make those of the deep a preferable refuge.

"We're sleeping in *that?*"

Brooks didn't answer.

As they moved through the mist and came nearer to the structure, the impression of a ship passed and the house seemed to shift, as if turning to admire itself in a mirror from a different angle. Even though she knew it was the car that was turning, Becca stopped breathing for a second, sure that something grotesque would be revealed as the details emerged: the mossy foundation stones and the weathered textures of scalloped shingles, the ornate lace of the trim skirting the sloping Mansard roof and towering turrets. She felt certain she was watching a living, breathing thing that had not been built but had grown like a tumor from the earth, and now, having attained a dark sentience, was straining to *mimic* the shape of a house.

It made her head ache to look at it. Regaining her breath, she looked away and focused on the gleaming metallic siding of the Quonset hut and the cars parked around it. The contrast was enough to make her stomach lurch, but it broke the spell and she realized she had been thinking in mixed metaphors—trying to reconcile the Wade House into some category, when in fact it was a place beyond category and comparison. She settled her gaze on her hands, afraid that one more glance at what should be merely a slouching, many-winged mansion would instead reveal a glimpse of a cold-blooded predator costumed in the rotting lace, hoops, and straps of a Victorian gown.

Brooks put the car in park and killed the engine. "The boss wants the support staff to maintain an objective distance from the house so the anomalies don't affect the computers. Or the minds of the operators."

"So they're scared."

"You could say that."

"Who's the boss?"

"Daniel Northrup. You're gonna meet him in a minute, I believe."

"And what effect do they expect this place to have on our minds, exactly?"

"Hallucinations, nightmares, *shared* hallucinations, *shared* nightmares, murderous rage, the usual."

"Great."

"It's the interest in shared dreams that calls for the expedition team to shack up in there."

They walked through frost-crusted mud amid a scattering of vehicles, all of them strewn haphazardly between the hut and the house: a Humvee, a white van, and a black Porsche SUV. Leaving the luggage in the trunk for now, Brooks led Becca to the gray door of the hut, slid his magnetic card through a slot in the doorknob mount, and ushered her into what looked like an airplane hangar that had been converted to an NSA surveillance center.

The curved ceiling was bisected by a grid of white LED lights that cast cold illumination down on cubicles furnished with computer workstations and folding Army cots. Thick cables snaked between the cubicles, feeding banks of blinking servers, and converging on a central conference table outfitted with a horseshoe array of widescreen LCD monitors. The sound of a gas generator droned through the corrugated wall at the far end of the building. Becca followed Brooks to the central table.

A handsome man in a charcoal suit with black hair frosted at the temples looked over the shoulder of a younger man in short sleeves and a tie marking up blueprints with a pencil. Both men glanced up at their approach. The one in the suit gave Becca a curt but firm handshake while studying her eyes. "Rebecca Philips," he said. "Thank you for joining us."

"Just Becca, please."

Brooks chimed in, "Becca, our director, Daniel Northrup."

"Becca, meet Dick Hanson," Northrup said. The seated man tucked his pencil behind his ear and shook her hand with a disarming smile.

"Dick was a consultant with us during the Boston crisis. Now he's full time SPECTRA. Background in applied physics." Northrup scanned the milling bodies and said, "We also have a marine biologist and a reverend of the Starry Wisdom Church around here somewhere. I think you've met him before, actually. As you can see, we're approaching the problem from multiple angles with a variety of disciplines."

"How many of us are exploring the house?" Becca asked.

"Only those I mentioned. A team of five, including you."

She looked at Brooks. "Are you the fifth?"

He nodded. "Team leader, charged with keeping the rest of you alive."

Northrup addressed Brooks, "Have you shown her the drone?"

"She has it."

"My camera's in the car," Becca said. "Will I need it? I don't know how to fly this other thing."

"The dragonfly is equipped with infrared sensors, but yes, you should also carry whatever equipment you're most familiar with. We'll set you up with a training session on the drone first thing."

"I'm curious: Why does it look like a dragonfly?"

"Two reasons. Natural selection is a far better designer than man, and we've repurposed a device originally built for discreet surveillance."

"Thought so."

"There's an empty barn down the hill where you can get a feel for flying the drone through a structure. I'll have Mark take you down there and show you the ropes."

Northrup put two fingers in his mouth and whistled. A hush fell over the busy space and heads turned. He called out, "Burns!" and waved a young man over: lanky with spiky dirty-blond hair and stubble, dressed in black jeans and a navy blue thermal shirt.

"Burns, this is Becca Philips, the urbex photographer. She'll be documenting everything on-site. Photo, audio, and video."

Another quick handshake. "Hey, I'm Mark."

"Burns is the biologist," Northrup said. "Take her down to the barn and train her on the dragonfly. Be back at eighteen-hundred for a pow-wow."

Mark Burns nodded toward the door. Becca followed him through the bustle, back out into the quiet of a January afternoon on a sleepy wooded lane, past the vehicles and away from the electrified fence. Near the house they picked up a trail that led down the side of the hill, branching off from the gravel path that continued to the veranda and front door. Night was falling early, and the hazy effect of low light was augmented by the black snow sailing in lazy flurries around the mansion, making it little more than a silhouette as they passed. No lights shone in the windows. Not even a porch light had been illuminated. Her guide seemed intent on passing the house as quickly as possible, but Becca looked back, training her eye on the chimneys where black flakes gathered and streamed in, like fireplace ash flowing in reverse, or a swarm of mutant moths drawn to darkness rather than light.

"Your jacket's a little light," Mark said, "but I see you've got good boots. You'll need them for this next bit. We'll cross over a creek. Messy, but it beats having to go through security checkpoints, and it's more direct than walking on the road."

Becca followed, stepping sideways down a gentle ravine. She scooped up a few flakes in her fingers and rubbed her thumb across them. They felt as cold as snow, but didn't melt in her hand. Rather, they smudged, just as Brooks said they would, leaving a grainy residue, and a faint aroma of swampy decay.

Feeling naked without her camera bag, she wished for her headlamp as she wiped her hand on her jeans in the deepening dark. A moment later, Burns produced a small LED flashlight, and guided her through brittle brown reeds to a place where a fallen tree bridged a shallow creek of black ice. Following him across with her arms out for balance, Becca felt like a little kid. On the other side, she saw the barn—a slouching mossy wreck nestled in a shoulder of the hill, skirted with ash and frost.

Mark slid the door aside and flicked a switch that flooded the cobwebbed rafters with harsh light from a pair of halogen tripods.

"Let's have it," he said.

Becca took the dragonfly and remote from her jacket pocket and handed them to him gingerly.

"Don't worry," he said. "You don't have to be delicate with it. It was built for the field. I've seen it take quite a beating and keep going."

"This same one? I thought you were a *marine* biologist."

"Yeah."

"What do dragonflies have to do with the ocean?"

"This was one of the first models that worked. I've used it to observe arctic animals. It's surprisingly reliable in cold weather, even waterproof. So's the remote. I don't know how the nano gears don't get jammed up with ice, but they don't. Some new formula of metal. They eventually gave me a submarine version, but the controls are almost the same."

"Submarine? Let me guess: Does it look like a little fish?"

"Yeah, actually. A minnow. Blends right in." Mark switched on the handheld unit and tossed the dragonfly into the air. Its wings hummed to life as the screen in his hand lit with amber wheels and grids. The drone rotated on its axis a foot away from Becca's face.

"When you first switch it on, it does a sonar scan of the room you're in." He swiped the glass and the control grids were replaced by a 3D model of the barn, including rough renderings of the tripod lights and moldy bales of hay piled against the walls. "Of course, it can only model the space it can see, so we won't get adjacent rooms, or in this case the hayloft, unless we send it up there. You can also set it to infrared to pick up heat signatures from people and animals. Navy SEALs have used it to map out rooms before doing a raid."

"I always figured they had something like this, but to actually see it…it's pretty incredible."

"It is."

"And a little creepy. Don't you think?"

Mark gave her a sidelong glance with a smile. "Yeah, people used to worry about 'bugs' in their phones. Now my husband is paranoid about bugs in the air. Thinks I'm spying on him."

"Have you been married long?" Becca asked.

"Almost five years. I'm kidding though, mostly. He's not *too* paranoid for someone married to a spook."

"So how *does* a marine biologist get involved with a covert agency?"

"How does an art photographer?"

"That's a long story."

"I've heard some of it. They need all kinds of experts, right? And, I mean, it's hard to say no to the money. I've seen some of your photos. When Boston happened they wanted me to compare the tentacle shapes that were turning up in your infrared shots with actual cephalopod anatomy."

"How *did* they compare?"

"Well, obviously the patterns you found had fractal repetition in them. Even though sometimes fractals look like trees or what have you, living organisms don't replicate patterns exactly like that. Northrup wanted to know if those early photos of yours were the result of something you did with the optics, or if they were capturing something organic beyond the visible spectrum. We ruled out optics right away. And then when actual creatures became visible to people who were tuned to perceive them, well…then we knew we were dealing with something from another dimension. But I still don't know why so much of the anatomy matches marine life. I guess their dimension is some kind of oceanic realm, but they don't suffocate when they emerge here."

Becca nodded. Her mouth had gone dry while he rattled on with geeky enthusiasm, and for a few seconds she worried that a panic attack might be coming on. She had experienced occasional flashbacks to the crisis during her first months in Brazil, and expected one to slam her now, but it didn't come. She focused on her breath, deliberately slowing and deepening it until the moment passed. If Mark noticed her distress, he didn't comment on it.

Grasping for a mundane topic to shift the conversation away from monsters, Becca said, "Did you want to be a marine biologist since you were a kid?"

Now *he* took a deep breath before answering. "No, actually. I was afraid of the ocean as a child after my mother drowned."

"Oh... Jeez, I'm sorry."

Mark waved her sympathy away. "Eventually, I decided that studying it might make it less frightening, less mysterious. Turns out the more you study the ocean, the *more* mysterious it gets. It's like outer space that way."

"Did it get less frightening?"

He shook his head, eyes on her boots. "Marine life remains both beautiful and terrifying," he said with a wry grin.

"Especially when it's found thriving on dry land."

"True."

She thought of telling him she'd lost her own mother at a young age, but something about that felt like pandering. She let the moment pass.

He had switched the device back to the control display and was sliding his thumb around a wheel of light, causing the dragonfly to circle the barn and weave through the rafters. "I'm honestly stumped about the nature of the creatures you encountered in Boston, but I'm still on the payroll. Northrup seems to think I may get a chance to study them firsthand here at the house."

Becca's voice wavered when she spoke: "Careful what you wish for. No one in their right mind would deliberately open the door to those things."

"I know. I mean...I *don't* know, but I've read the reports. Sorry, I can't really imagine what you've been through, but you asked, and that's why I'm here."

"Show me how it works," Becca said, nodding at the remote. Her skin was flushed and prickling, and she was eager to change the subject.

Mark passed the remote back to her. "This wheel controls the vertical axis, altitude. This is lateral motion, and this rotates it. You can view it as a third person icon, or through its eyes, which is what you'll want for taking photos. You play video games at all?"

"No."

"That's okay, you'll pick it up quick. Just watch out for—"

The dragonfly shuddered to a halt, frozen in the intersection of a pair of rafters.

"Cobwebs?"

"Here—use the pincers to cut the web," Mark said. "It can be a mean little fucker when you need it to be."

Once Becca had the hang of basic maneuvers, Mark left her to practice with a promise to keep an eye on her watch and make the meeting at 7 o'clock.

By 6:45 she had crashed the drone enough times to admire its resilience. She'd also learned how to free it of the thickest webs. For her last circuit of the barn, Becca turned the drone's headlight on and killed the halogen lamps to practice flying in the dark.

Enswathed in cold light and careening shadows, she felt a tingle of fear at the prospect of walking past the Wade House alone with only the glowing bug to light her way. Distracted, she crashed the drone into a wall and watched it tumble onto one of the canvas-draped pieces of farm equipment—or so she assumed—that lay scattered around the outer edges of the dirt floor.

In her haste to leave the barn and get back up the hill on time, Becca plucked the dragonfly from the dusty tarp without noting the contours of the object it concealed, and so failed to find what her father had left behind.

Chapter 3

They gathered around an oval conference table in the center of the Quonset hut. Most of the support staff had left for dinner in town, leaving a quieter environment for Director Northrup and the five members of the exploration team: Becca Philips, Jason Brooks, Mark Burns, Dick Hanson, and Reverend John Proctor.

Becca had met the reverend briefly the previous year when she photographed a birdbath in the courtyard of an abandoned asylum that turned out to be a sacred site for the Starry Wisdom Church. Proctor had been performing prayers and prostrations at the asylum in observance of a holy day, and for a moment Becca had feared he might try to smash her camera. She had since been in bloody confrontations with members of his congregation and the deities they worshipped, but had not seen the reverend himself since that day. He looked weathered, as if he had aged more than a couple years. He still wore the same dusty black frock and miter cap, but now the tattoos on his forehead and temples— letters of the Lengian alphabet—contrasted more sharply against his sallow complexion. When he reached for a glass of water, Becca noticed scars on his arms that she hadn't seen before. She tried not to stare, focusing on the others at the table, and letting her eyes glance over him. She hadn't expected to see him again, and the sight of him made her skin crawl. He reminded her too much of the awful institution where they'd met, where her grandfather had rotted away in confinement, where her friend and lover Rafael Moreno had died.

"Early investigations of the house confirm that it does appear to change shape," Northrup was saying when Becca tuned back in to his voice. "So far, our measurements of the first floor remain consistent, as do the number of windows, closets, and doors on the first floor. These elements are *variable* above and below the ground floor. For this reason, we are assigning each of you to a first floor room for sleeping and essentially camping out. There are enough of them for some degree of privacy, even though they aren't all bedrooms. Ms. Philips, as the only female member of the team, will get a bedroom with a door. Agent Brooks, as the only field agent, will carry the only gun. We don't know what effect the environment will have on your minds, so we are limiting weapons to Brooks in his capacity as team security officer."

"Hold on," the reverend said. "I thought my job was to provide *spiritual* protection. What about knives? I can't cast the proper wards without a ritual dagger."

Northrup's eyes darted to Brooks. "It's just a symbolic tool, right? You don't need to bleed goats with it?"

"A symbol, yes, of the discerning mind. A tool for carving sigils in the astral to keep the forces of chaos at bay."

"I thought you *worshipped* the forces of chaos," Brooks interjected. "I can't imagine why anyone would trust you with a knife in a place like that house."

Northrup held up his hand. "You can have a dagger with a dull blade. We'll grind the edge off."

"Not just any knife will do," Proctor said. "The blade must be the proper kind to project energy; a three-sided spike, like a Tibetan *phurba*. I brought one with me."

Northrup drew on his cigarette. "An agent will inspect it."

Brooks scoffed and sat back in his seat.

Proctor hunched forward, scowling at Brooks. "I was not involved in the attacks on Boston. You know that. I am no radical. And unless you've studied my religion, don't presume to tell me what I worship."

"He cooperated with the investigation—" Northrup said.

"After you tortured him."

"—or he wouldn't be here."

"He was their *leader*."

Northrup stared Brooks down. "Everyone here has a motivation to cooperate. And you're out of your depth without him. You're going to need someone who knows the lay of the land. You think we could do anything in Syria or Afghanistan without help from the locals? Think of Reverend Proctor as a citizen of the astral, the borderland between our world and the dimension those creatures come from. He's been vetted."

Brooks examined a pen he'd picked up, his jaw tense. It was clear the discussion was over. Northrup addressed the group. "Tonight you'll sleep here at Base Camp. Tomorrow we turn the house's utilities back on. They were shut down while we ran the scans and needed to keep electrical interference to a minimum. Now that you're all here, you can move in tomorrow morning. Is anyone allergic to dogs?"

No one spoke.

"Good," Northrup continued, "Philips will keep hers in the house. There's reason to believe that cats are better at detecting these phenomena, but who knows, maybe he'll serve as an early warning system."

"Where I go, he goes," Becca said. "But you're not using him as a canary in a coal mine. I won't send him anywhere you wouldn't send me."

"That's what the drone is for," Northrup said.

"What are we looking for, exactly?"

"Clearly, the black snow is attracted to the house and seems to be returning to the dimension it came from through any crack it can find," Northrup said. "Our top priority is to make sure nothing is going in the *other* direction, leaking into our world."

"Do you even know what that stuff is?" Becca asked.

Northrup stamped his cigarette out. "I could show you the chemical composition, but it wouldn't mean much. What we do know is where it came from: the destruction of the black orb over

Boston. The flakes seem to be the last remnants of that incursion into our world, and now they're being drawn back to their own."

"Brooks said the snow didn't appear until a year after the Red Equinox," Becca said. "Why is that?"

"The theory is that the black fallout was not perceptible until it found a pathway to the other side, at which point it gained some kind of energy," Northrup said. "The house itself may have become more visible at that time as well, more substantial. And if matter can pass through the house in one direction...might it not go both ways? If there's a breach in there, we need to find it and seal it."

"Any idea how?" Brooks tossed the pen he'd been clicking onto the tabletop to keep himself from fiddling with it. He stared at the reverend.

"I have some ideas," Proctor said.

"What about my father?" Becca said. "I thought we were looking for him. Brooks said he might be trapped in there."

Northrup glared at Brooks.

"What?" Becca said.

"I hope you didn't promise her anything," Northrup said.

"Hold on," Becca said. "Was that just to get me here? Is he not a priority?"

"If you can find him," Northrup said, "we'll try to extract him. It's a big *if*."

Dick Hanson cleared his throat and leaned in. "We don't know much about how sound and light travel in and out of the structure." It was the first thing the physicist had contributed to the conversation and all eyes turned to him. "It's possible that sound may carry through the walls and floors, even when a portal isn't available."

"What does that mean?" Becca scratched at her arm absently, thinking she might know.

"I'm saying you might hear him. You're the only one of us who would recognize his voice. And if you do hear him and you call back, we may be able to find a place where we can bring him through. A portal, a door."

"And if we *don't* find him? If we only find a portal he isn't on the other side of? Then what? Are you planning to 'seal the breach' anyway? Trap him inside forever?" Becca had felt cold despite the cranked electric heater beside the table, but now she was flushed with heat from within as a new thought occurred to her and tumbled out of her lips. "Is he the reason why you haven't brought a wrecking ball up here, or is he not even a factor in that decision? What's stopping you from burning the place down?"

"We don't think it's that simple," Hanson said.

"We don't know what destroying the house would do," Northrup said. "It might open a bigger portal, more permanent than the ones that are blinking in and out of existence in there right now."

Brooks leaned forward and met Becca's eyes. "Blowing up the gates of Hell is the last resort, kiddo. Lest they end up throwing them wide open."

SPECIAL PHYSICS EMERGENT COUNTER TERROR RECON AGENCY
NORTHEAST REGIONAL OFFICE. BOSTON, MA.

September 20, 2019

TO: ███████ █████████
FROM: ███████ █████████

MEMORANDUM: INTERROGATION SUMMARY

SUBJECT: REV. JOHN PROCTOR
INTERROGATOR: ██████ ███████
LOCATION: ███ █████████████ ████████

Reverend John Proctor, leader of the Back Bay Starry Wisdom Church was detained in a joint FBI/SPECTRA raid on the Church at 1105 Boylston Street after the attack by Darius Marlowe on the Redline train at Harvard Square. Proctor was a mentor to Marlowe, as Marlowe was an active member of his congregation. Undercover agent ███████ █████ has attested that the relationship between the radical Marlowe and the apparently more moderate Proctor has become increasingly antagonistic in recent months.

Due to the urgent nature of the evolving crisis, I engaged the subject from a position of keeping all possibilities open. It is my opinion that the alleged tensions between mentor and acolyte do not necessarily indicate a divergence of opinion on the matter of terrorist attacks, but may have any number of explanations, including: disagreement with regard to methods, timing, suitable accomplices, etc.

Nor have I ruled out the possibility that agent ████████'s cover may have been compromised, the antagonistic scenes staged for ████ benefit. I have therefore handled Proctor as I would any dangerous conspirator potentially withholding actionable intelligence regarding imminent attacks. My team has employed a variety of the enhanced interrogation techniques at our disposal, as outlined in the ████ manual.

SPECIAL PHYSICS EMERGENT COUNTER TERROR RECON AGENCY

INITIAL ASSESMENT OF SUBJECT'S PSYCHOLOGICAL STATE:
Proctor is endowed with the conviction of the devout. He is difficult to intimidate or rattle, and concerns for his own safety and freedom seem secondary to his concern for the continuing operation of his church. He exhibits high tolerance for threats and coercion.

PAIN THRESHOLD: High.

ORIENTATION AT SESSION START: Subject claims to have had no knowledge of Marlowe's plans in advance of the attack. Also denies knowledge of technology employed, ██████████████████, and potential accomplices still at large.

TECHNIQUES EMPLOYED: Verbal threats of death penalty and consequences for family members abroad via our back channel leverage with the ████████ and █████ governments, isolation, sleep deprivation, low-level electric shock applied to ███████ ███ ████████, and ██████████████████

DURATION: █████████████

ORIENTATION POST INTERROGATION: Subject continues to deny knowledge of or complicity in any and all terror attacks past, present, and future.

If innocent, his detention may serve to further alienate him from the more radical elements of his flock, but his deep knowledge of their practices could make him a valuable asset if we can identify effective pressure points.

Please advise.

SPECIAL PHYSICS EMERGENT COUNTER TERROR RECON AGENCY

Chapter 4

In the morning, Becca followed the smell of coffee until she found a station with a carafe and a box of donuts. She poured a cup, snagged the plainest looking donut she could find, and took Django out for a walk around the grounds with her camera hanging from its strap and the dragonfly stowed in her jacket pocket.

The previous evening, leading Django from the car to the hut, the dog had shown a cursory interest in the black flakes but was more interested in where she was leading him, sniffing out the structure to determine whether or not he needed to protect Becca from the people inside. That was a question she hadn't fully answered for herself, she realized, but Django had settled in and accepted their company quickly. Now, roaming the hillside and marking the terrain, he sniffed at the ashy flakes but stopped short of tasting them.

There was little else in the way of animal life on the property to help her assess the toxicity of the environment. Only when they had walked some distance from the house did she begin to notice signs of birds and squirrels. Granted, it was winter and only the cawing of crows marred the silent morning, but as Brooks had pointed out, it was unseasonably warm for January.

Becca wondered at what temperature the black flakes would melt. They were cold to the touch, but body heat didn't affect them the same way it did snow.

She led Django around the house and peered up at its blank gray windows. The place exuded an aura of disquiet. She wondered how much she was projecting onto it based on what she'd heard, and how much had to do with the environment. Psychologically, the shorter days crushed her, and had since she was a teenager—although medication helped. Even in Brazil she'd been afraid to stop taking it. But the dark part of the year could be dazzlingly bright when it snowed, and she'd always appreciated how the white crystals reflected and amplified what little sunlight there was. This black stuff, however, seemed custom ordered to darken her spirits, and it cast scant light at the windows that watched over her. She soon felt uneasy walking in the shadow of the house. She led Django down the path Mark had shown her the previous night, to the barn beyond the creek.

The creek had been frozen when she'd last crossed it on the fallen tree, but today she heard the trickle of water before she reached it. In the morning light, she could see the cloudy ice near the banks pierced through by reed stalks fading to black ice, which gave way to a channel of rushing water in the center of the creek. Spindly, leafless branches forked off the fallen tree trunk and disappeared below the surface. Becca stopped dead in her tracks. A blue heron that had no business in Massachusetts in January stood perched on one of the gnarled branches, head cocked, eyes fixed on the water, hunting for breakfast.

Despite the warm temperatures, Becca figured all the frogs and small fish were long gone and this fellow should have made his way south with the others months ago. As she watched, the bird stalked across the branch bending its long stilt legs slowly and deliberately, head ticking from one angle to another as it regarded reflections in the stream.

Becca switched on her camera and focused it on the bird, wishing for the telephoto lens she'd left in her bag back at the hut. Django had long ago grown accustomed to watching her stalk predators as they stalked their own prey, and when she dropped his leash, he snuffled in the tall dead grass along the bank, paying the bird no heed. In turn, it ignored him.

Becca took a few shots of the heron, checked them in the LCD, and adjusted her settings. The bird had its back to her, its blue-gray feathers almost silvery in the diffuse light of the overcast morning. She was framing another shot, crouching and moving in, feeling her boot sink into the soggy ground, when the bird raised its right wing and stretched it out to the side with a long slow jab, as if pointing toward the woods behind the house.

Becca caught the gesture with her camera. She felt the little thrill of knowing that it was a good shot without needing to check, and fast on its heels, a pang of regret at leaving the rainforest behind to return to barren Massachusetts in the dead of the year. But if she could find a blue heron in a black January, maybe things weren't all bad. The contrast of the silvery plumage against the black snow granted the composition a peculiar beauty that she knew she would find nowhere else on earth.

For a moment she stared at the bird, forgetting the camera and slipping into an almost meditative zone for the first time since she'd arrived at the Wade House. If she had learned anything in the past year, it was that nature had a soothing effect on her. She wondered again why she had spent so many years living in the city. Art school had lured her to Boston from Arkham, but even when she'd called the city her home, she'd made a study of the abandoned places where she could find nature's fingers clawing their way back in.

A harsh cawing sound startled her out of her reverie and she almost dropped her camera on the thin ice. The heron extended its wing again and this time stretched its long neck as well with a low, groaning croak that sounded to Becca like someone slow scratching a vinyl record of a human voice: *HHAAATE... HAAATE...*

She thought of all the times she had seen faces in water stains or the mold growing on concrete. She thought about the human talent for pattern recognition, the ability to find eyes and hear words where there was only chaos and noise. The bird wasn't really talking to her any more than stretching its wing meant it was pointing at something. But then, there had been a time when the patterns in her photos turned out to be more than chaos mimicking order. A time when she'd seen tentacles in brick walls.

HAATE...HAATE...RAAAGE...HAATE...HAATE...RAAGE... RAAGE...

As if the bird were adding a synonym to hammer the point home.

But a speaker of another language might hear a different word. And even another English speaker might interpret the squawking differently. The same sounds could be "wait" and "age." Or "wade" as in The Wade House, also known as The Witch House to locals and students of occult legend and lore. And if ever there was a creek beside a house where a bird might speak a warning...

The sound was horrid, even without taking the apparent words into account. The gray morning suddenly felt darker. Django returned to Becca's side, his hair up along his spine, a low, barely audible growl percolating in his throat. The birdcall was almost as deep as his growl and considerably louder.

Becca felt cold, as if the blood had withdrawn from her extremities, and with the chill came the certainty that the world itself had gone bad as a rotten egg, and would never be right again. And the more the bird repeated the sounds and gestures, the harder it was to pretend she was imposing sinister meaning on something ordinary and natural, if a little out of season.

She scanned the hill for anyone else who might be out walking, but she was alone. The heron turned its head and stared at her over its wing with glassy black eyes.

It cawed again, and this time she had the impression that each word was accompanied by a jab in a different direction: *HAAATE* with the wing pointed at the house on the hill, and *RAAAGE* with a jab at a different angle, toward the woods. She watched for several cycles more, concerned that the animal might be sick and suffering, but more afraid that it wasn't, that the only sickness was in the land and the house that had been built upon it, the house where she would soon be living.

The pattern was consistent. The wing moved back and forth with each vocalization. Becca tried to follow the line of the wing when it stretched toward the woods. She stood up and took a few steps back, away from the creek. Had she really been worried about scaring the bird away just a few minutes ago? It had been doing its best to scare *her* off ever since. Or did it want her to follow the line of its wing? She picked up Django's leash and set off in the indicated direction, searching the spare trees for some structure or landmark but finding nothing.

Becca trundled up the hill at an angle, her boots crunching in the dead grass, the cuffs of her jeans already stained black from the inky flakes. It felt good to be moving away from the house. Its diminishing presence at her back was like a weight lifting off her shoulders. She wondered if this little excursion wasn't just a way to avoid confronting the place. But even if not for the bird, she would have been curious about the grounds and likely would've explored them before the house itself. No one had given her reason to believe that she wouldn't be allowed to venture outside at will, and yet it felt as if she were taking a last look at the outside world for a while.

Django did his part to keep track of their path by marking a tree every few yards. Becca unclipped the leash and let him roam, urging him on with the occasional whistle, but it wasn't long before he was trotting ahead and waiting for her to catch up.

Just when she was thinking of turning back, she caught sight of stone slabs juxtaposed against the rough bark: monolithic standing stones glimpsed between the trees.

"What do we have here?" she said to Django, stepping off the path and cutting through a patch of brambles to a clearing marked with a starburst of scorched black ground surrounded by a ring of lichen-speckled granite slabs, twice her height, reaching for the sky at odd angles.

It took her a moment to realize that the black snow — which had thinned out in the forest, gathering in random drifts scattered here and there—was completely absent in the circle, despite the open sky offering a clear path to the ground.

"Django, wait," she said.

The dog heeled and let her clip the leash to his collar. Finding a fallen tree, she looped the handle of the leash over a broken branch to keep Django from following her. He whined as she moved around the outer edge of the circle of stones, but she spoke to him soothingly, telling him to sit and wait. It was a routine he knew well, and eventually he settled. She couldn't say why, but she didn't want him crossing the boundary of the circle.

Becca snapped a few photos of the stone slabs with her Nikon before taking the dragonfly from her jacket pocket. She switched the drone on and watched it hover in the air while she brought up the controls on the remote.

Looking across to the inward facing side of the farthest stone, she saw that it was carved with crescents and sigils. She set her thumbs on the amber dials on the screen and sent the dragonfly buzzing between two of the slabs, into the center of the circle. Nothing happened to it when it crossed the invisible boundary, and the tension in her shoulders eased a little. She divided the screen and sent the drone on a lap around the inner perimeter, recording the full set of symbols with its digital eyes as it flew.

Becca took a breath and stepped into the circle, expecting some sensation upon crossing the threshold; at the very least, a low vibration like the hum of a poorly grounded appliance. But there was nothing, only silent wind through leafless trees. Turning on her heel, rotating clockwise while the drone continued to revolve counter, she gazed out at the stones and walked backwards toward the center.

Distracted from the screen, she miscalculated an adjustment of the controls and sent the drone crashing into one of the granite slabs. It fell to the ground buzzing and twitching. Becca thumbed the reset button on the remote, picked the dragonfly up, and blew clotted dirt out of its aluminum lace wings before setting it to flight again.

At the center of the circle, she brought the drone slowly up, high above her head, to hover over the tops of the standing stones. It felt strange to be looking at her own head from above, and she could spot Django sitting flat on the ground as close to the circle as his leash would allow, his nose on his paws. These stones were more refined than the megalithic slabs she had seen at Calçoene in Brazil. Those had seemed older, more irregular in shape, and lacking any iconography or symbols. These were more like pillars, still roughhewn granite, but carefully spaced and elaborately graven. Nevertheless, standing in the center of the circle, she felt rocked by a wave of dreadful déjà vu.

She hadn't told Brooks much about her experience at Calçoene. Just the bare minimum, really. She had intended to answer his question honestly without getting dragged into details. She trusted *him*, but was still unsure of what SPECTRA wanted from her. She couldn't let go of the nagging suspicion that the reasons they'd brought her back to Massachusetts were not all on the table. In fact, if there was one thing she felt certain of, it was that SPECTRA was an agency that *never* laid all of its cards on the table.

Had they monitored her email while she was living in Brazil? Had they followed her, perhaps with this very drone, on her excursion to the standing stones known as Amazon Stonehenge? In Brazil, mechanical dragonflies hadn't been on her radar. Or might they even have orchestrated the trip, posing as the client who'd requested the photos for a book on recent archaeological discoveries? If they *had* put her there, and were now placing her here, was there a connection between that site and this one?

Heat rose at her collar, flushing her neck, prickling at her hairline.

Don't go getting paranoid or there'll be no end to it.

Becca put her hand to her chest and touched the scarab beetle through her shirt. In Boston, when she had faced the entity known as the Haunter of the Dark, she had tapped the power of the amulet with a two-word incantation recalled at the moment of crisis. In Brazil, she had attempted to repeat the feat, to awaken the ruby in the scarab's pincers, the Fire of Cairo, to no avail. Alone in the jungle, beneath the stars of the southern hemisphere, she had tried every way of pronouncing those sacred words: *Yehi Aur*. Let there be light. She had whispered, chanted, sung, and screamed them. But no light had arisen in the dark gem. That had been in the south, near the falls where they had scattered Rafael's ashes. She had wondered at the time if the power could only be awakened on certain days of the calendar, such as the equinox, the one time she had seen it happen before.

But then, at Calçoene, the scarab *had* stirred, fluttering its wings, tickling and startling her long after she'd given up hope of it ever showing signs of life again. She had been too paralyzed with dread at the time to think of the incantation, too eager to get away from the place to linger and experiment. Hope had swelled within her for a moment, but the scarab hadn't so much as twitched since, and she'd begun to wonder if what she hoped was an awakening was more akin to final death throes.

Had she spent all the magic she possessed at the Red Equinox? The dragonfly with its nano gears and microchips might be a small miracle of technology, but the beetle was once a wonder of a different order. One she could no longer rely on.

Becca brought the drone to rest on her upraised palm, switched it off, and tucked it away.

She had tried not to think too much about what she'd seen at Calçoene. Now, the memory welled up and towered over her like a tidal wave, shortening her breath.

The stones there hadn't been graven with letters or glyphs, hadn't appeared as precisely placed, but their teetering angles had unnerved her. And there had been one precise carving: a circle cut through a single slab, like a porthole.

Had she been drawn to it? Had she pressed her face to the cold stone and gazed through that ancient aperture on the winter solstice?

Resisting, remembering, a tremor began in her boots and grew to a shuddering vibration. It climbed her body and thundered in her head, rattling her teeth with a blinding flash. She fell to her knees, the forest eclipsed by the flashback, replaced by a Brazilian meadow. Oily black limbs glistened in the air around her, like ribbons of kelp twisting in dark water. Teeth gnashed in lipless orifices, raw wounds in piebald flesh. A concussion of sound, as if the earth were a drum, and she was cast out, thrown between the jagged slabs onto the dry grass by an invisible blast that sent dust flying at its crest.

From outside the perimeter, the circle had appeared empty but for the circular hole in the rock through which a giant curdled-milk eye stared out, rolling endlessly like a planet spinning on a diagonal axis, its black hourglass pupil undulating to the rhythm of the maddening pulse in her head until she blacked out.

* * *

Brooks parked his black Taurus behind the Wayside Convenience store, just a few miles from the Wade House on Lexington Road. He was on his way back from a supermarket run in Concord. His excuse for the trip into town was that he needed a few ingredients for the meal he had offered to cook for the exploration team on their first night. The house cupboards and fridge were well stocked by SPECTRA runners, and he could have sent one to pick up the spices he wanted. Instead, he'd stressed needing to see the bottles on the shelves to trigger his memory. That much was true enough, but he didn't want any passing agency personnel to notice his car parked in front of the convenience store while he was making his second stop on the way back.

At the counter he asked for the cheapest pre-paid cell phone they had, and tried not to stare at the rip-rolls of shiny, glittering scratch cards while the cashier picked it for him. A wad of cash was burning in his wallet and the cards were calling to him. They'd had some scratch cards with the cigarette cartons at the supermarket, too, but it had been a minimal showing; nothing like the extravagance on display here.

It was ironic, he knew, that anticipating his ex-wife's presence on site had him itching to gamble when the habit was the reason she'd left him in the first place. Well, one of them, anyway. He hadn't reformed many of his failings since Nina had moved out, but he *had* made GA meetings a priority. It had been 14 months since his last lapse. He'd lost the house before the wife and had dropped the habit before SPECTRA could drop him. For some reason, the possibility of getting fired hadn't occurred to him until one of his first partners, a veteran named Joseph Talley, who had a few years on him, spelled it out.

"Our masters will indulge a hankering for booze better than they will one for cards, James."

"Why is that?" Brooks had asked, after tossing back a shot of the former and setting his glass down.

"Because booze helps some men do the job. But a man in deep debt is a wildcard. Not to be trusted. Sooner or later, his mind will turn to trading in secrets."

Brooks had been grateful for the warning and had taken it—like all advice from Talley, whose eyes seemed to brim with all manner of horrors both cosmic and mundane—quite seriously.

The job, when it was risky enough, when it rode the razor's edge of survival and madness, gave him everything he needed to satisfy his gambler's itch.

Work had been quiet for a while now, but he could feel that changing. He worried about the world in which his daughter lived, a world in which men like himself, fallible men grasping at straws, kept real monsters at bay. And in the absence of a close relationship with Heather, he worried about Becca. He couldn't foresee the consequences of bringing her back to Massachusetts, didn't know if they would be damaging or even fatal to her in the long run. And hadn't she done enough already? He helped her to leave the darkness behind after Boston, and now he'd dragged her back into it. Maybe she would find her father, and maybe that would bring her something other than sorrow. But maybe was a thin thread.

Action scratched the itch, but worry only aggravated it. And Brooks worried about all the people he had dragged to the edge of the abyss by virtue of their connection to him and his work. Work he could never be fully open about. He wasn't afraid for himself because he knew he'd already lost most of the things that mattered in his life, things he had won on a miraculous streak of luck when he was younger. He worried about Nina and Becca and even Becca's damned dog because of how much it mattered to her. And he worried about Tom Petrie, a bystander at the opening act of the apocalypse, whose first child was born after the Red Equinox. Tom who didn't remember much about his time in SPECTRA's custody after he'd been exposed to brain altering harmonics in a terror attack, but who remembered enough to not fully trust the agency.

But Tom did trust Brooks. He had reached out and left a short, cryptic message saying he wanted to talk, using a keyword Brooks had given him the last time he'd paid a visit to the man's home to check in on him.

Brooks left the scratch cards at the counter, their loud names and foil letters clamoring around in his mind's eye as he sat in his car and cut through the burner phone's packaging with a Swiss Army knife he kept in the glove box. RED HOT CASH, WHEEL OF LUCK, YELLOW KING CROWNS. He looked through the grimy, ash streaked windshield for the dumpster behind the store and was glad to find it lacking a chain. He would toss the packaging in there before he left.

In his wallet, he found a folded slip of paper with Tom's number scribbled on it. He punched it into the cheap keypad and waited for it to ring. When Tom answered his voice was little more than a whisper, as if he didn't want to disturb his napping child.

"Tom, it's me. I got your message. About the plants." Brooks left his name out of it and hoped Tom would, too. Just because his burner phone wasn't being monitored didn't mean Tom's line wasn't. "How's the family?"

"Okay…" Tom said. There was a pause long enough to make Brooks wonder if Tom had hung up. He listened for the telltale clicks of surveillance and didn't hear them. At last Tom said, "Noah's episodes are acting up."

"I see."

"We're thinking a change of scenery might help. Could you drop in and water the plants?"

A car pulled up slowly beside the parked Taurus. Brooks watched it pass and noted it was clean. Too clean? Recently washed? No black residue… *Don't be paranoid.* "I'll see what I can do. It's a little hard to get away right now."

"You're the only one we trust in the house."

"Okay. Hang in there, buddy."

A buzzing vibration caught his attention and Brooks watched his secure work phone judder across the dashboard, throwing icy light at the grimy windshield. He picked it up and saw a text from Base Camp.

Northrup: Is Philips with you? We can't find her.

"Tom? I have to go."

Chapter 5

Becca regained consciousness to the sound of Django whining. Someone was carrying her, arms under her knees and shoulders, her body rocking side to side with each step. Somehow she knew it was Brooks before opening her eyes. Stark trees swayed above his head reaching for the ashen sky, leaves crunched beneath his feet. Django, trotting alongside, licked her dangling hand.

"Put me down," she said.

He stopped walking, set her feet on the ground, and said, "Are you sure you can stand?"

"Yeah."

He let go of her and she wobbled, put her hand against a tree, and held the other one up to keep him from grabbing her again. "I'm fine. Just give me a minute."

"Have you eaten anything today? You passed out back there in the stone circle."

"I...yeah, had a donut. What is that place?"

"We don't know yet. One theory is that Caleb Wade erected it when he built the house. Another is he might have chosen the location to be near it."

"Anyone else ever pass out in it?"

"Not since we took over the site. What happened to you in there? Did you see something?"

She shook her head. "I think I had a flashback. I've had a few since…Boston. How did you find me?"

"I heard Django barking. We moved into the house. When you didn't show, they sent me looking. There's a doctor on standby at the hut. I think he should take a look at you."

"Told you, I'm fine. Nothing happened that didn't already happen."

"What does that mean?"

"Nothing. I just need to lie down for a bit. Let's go to the house."

"You're sure you can walk?"

"I'm sure."

"Follow me."

Black flakes swirled at the edge of the woods. Becca pulled her hood over her head and followed Brooks around the north wing of the house to the front steps; a crew was running cables over the porch and across the field to the Quonset hut.

After the stone circle, the house appeared benign, just a neglected mansion crawling with technicians. The fog was absent today, and for a moment, Becca felt like an actress on the set of a horror movie, reassured by the daylight, the company of a working crew, and the ubiquitous technology. The supernatural, the deeply weird would be out of place here.

She climbed the decrepit front steps without trepidation and passed over the oak threshold without ceremony. No chill passed down her spine, no shadow over her heart. She was exhausted from the flashback in the woods, drained of her usual curiosity. She only wanted someone to show her to her room so she could rest and gather her wits before exploring anything else.

Before she could ask for directions, Django had scented her bags, and following him down a hall off the foyer, she found a high-ceilinged bedroom covered in bubbling blue and gold wallpaper with badly scratched hardwood floors, an ebony bureau, and a four-poster bed frame with a stained mattress. Her bags and a clean pillow had been left on an Army cot over which a new sleeping bag was spread.

Brooks came up behind her in the doorway and cocked his elbow against the frame. "Figured you wouldn't want to sleep on the bed anyway, but just so you know, we have orders to not move any of the furniture unless it's necessary for the investigation."

"Why? Are there monsters under the beds?" Becca arched an eyebrow to let him know she was feeling well enough to joke.

Brooks didn't smile. "There could be. In the closets and cupboards, too."

"Where's your room?"

"I'm in the pantry off the kitchen. You gonna crash for a bit?"

"Yeah."

"Okay. But when you get up, remember: no venturing upstairs or down without a partner."

"Got it."

As Brooks moved to close the door, Django's ears pricked forward. He crouched and growled, then sprang through the gap before the door reached the frame, lunging past Brooks and tearing down the hall, claws scrabbling for traction on the floorboards.

"*Django!*" Becca shot off the cot and Brooks stepped aside, but by the time she'd cleared the doorway, the dog's bushy tail was disappearing into the parlor at the end of the corridor.

"What was that?" she called to Brooks without looking back as she hurried after Django.

"A cat, I think."

Now she did turn to gape at him. "*What* cat?"

Brooks shrugged. "A black and white cat. Must've wandered in from the street."

Becca came reeling around the corner at the grandfather clock expecting to find a fight in progress and found...nothing. The room was empty, its austere furnishings untouched. Not so much as a lampshade wobbled to suggest the passing of animals in full flight.

And yet there were no exits from the room apart from the one she occupied. She turned to Brooks. "He's gone. Where did he go?"

Brooks pushed past her. "What do you mean *gone?*"

Becca put her fingers to her lips, trying not to panic as Brooks tossed cushions from an embroidered sofa, then took a knee and peered under its frilly skirt.

"I thought you trained him not to chase animals," Brooks said.

Becca sighed in frustration. "We didn't run into any *house cats* in the rainforest. He's fine around—"

A bark rang out from the kitchen and Becca hurried toward it, but when it was followed a second later by another, the sound seemed to issue from the bedroom down the hall. She spun on her heel to find Django poking his head out of the room they'd started in, smiling and panting.

Becca exhaled.

They searched the house for a good ten minutes, but there was no further sign of the cat. For his part, Django wasn't any the worse for wear, lacking so much as a claw sheath embedded in his nose or a clump of white fur in his lips to attest to the feral trespasser's existence. Eventually, Brooks left Becca and her dog to settle in, with the weak injunction to "give a shout if you need me."

Becca cleared her bags from the cot and lay down on it. Django settled beside her, his nose on her stomach. She stroked his fur and stared at the cracked, water-stained ceiling, expecting her body to shut down and fall into a nap after the stresses of the morning. But caffeine and adrenaline still buzzed in her veins, and she soon found her thoughts turning to her father as sleep evaded her restless mind.

She reached for her jacket, and dug a worn 3 x 5 photo out of a zippered pocket. Printed on matte photo stock by a pharmacy photo lab, it was the best shot she had ever taken of her parents, during her first mad spree of photography at age 8 when they'd deemed her old enough for a digital camera, but too young for a smart phone.

Her parents looked so young and happy, with sunlight in their entangled, windblown hair and a rippling lake in the background. Lonesome Lake, in New Hampshire, near Mt. Lincoln where they used to camp. Her mother wore sunglasses. Her father's eyes were the same deep blue as her own.

Why would he have come here, to this house? The place had a reputation for exactly the sort of occult phenomena that Becca's grandmother, Professor Catherine Philips, had devoted her life to studying. Luke had run off, leaving Becca in her care, after the dark forces Catherine dabbled with drove Becca's mother to suicide. So what was it about this place that could possibly draw him out of hiding after all these years? The last Becca had heard, her father was holed up in a cabin in the White Mountains when he wasn't off on cross-country motorcycle tours. Could Brooks be right that he had come here looking for her?

She wondered what kind of network her father was connected to for information. He'd never been computer savvy and it was hard to picture him getting on the Internet, even at a public library, to research the Wade House, but she supposed it was possible he had heard something from Catherine about the place when he was young. Who knew what conversations her grandparents had at the dinner table when Catherine was at the peak of her career at Miskatonic University, traveling frequently and gathering data on obscure cults, their practices, artifacts, and sacred sites? But even without computer access, her dad probably had a TV. While the public would never learn most of what had happened, or Becca's precise role in it during those few weeks in September when Boston was hunkered down under terror attacks by members of the Starry Wisdom Church, she had briefly been connected to those events in the public eye.

Had Luke tried to get in touch with her when the dust settled? By then she had relocated out of the country. He would've had no chance of finding her. Had he simply straddled his Harley and followed the falling black snow?

What were you looking for? Was it me? Or was it something else? Something hidden in this house?

Becca ran her fingers over the wall beside her cot. *Fleur de lis* crumbled away from the wallpaper like moss from a tree at her touch. Was her father really lost in these walls? And if he was, how much did he know about what was going on here? She wanted to believe he'd stumbled unwittingly into it, looking for her. But turning that possibility over in her mind, she couldn't help feeling it was counterfeit.

Eventually, she dozed off. Before adrenaline-charged adventures had entered her life, she'd been the queen of the short nap, the long nap, and the fuck it, let's hibernate until springtime sleep marathon. If depression was good for anything, it was getting plenty of sleep. But these days, sleep came in shorter, shallower doses for her.

* * *

Becca woke to the smell of garlic, her stomach groaning as she sat up. Django swished his tail back and forth at her rising and laid his head in her lap. She scratched behind his ears and kissed him on the temple as he licked her face.

"You must be hungry, too," she said. "Let's get you fed."

Following the dog down the long hall to the dining room, she stubbed her toe against the wall molding and pressed her hand against the wall to absorb the pain. When she could walk again, she came to a doorway draped with a heavy velvet curtain. Here, the smell of incense mingled with the food aromas drifting down the hall, making a sickly blend that almost quelled her appetite. The baritone drone of a chanted mantra reached her ears through the curtain, the rhythm repetitious, the content unintelligible. Django sniffed at the hem of the curtain and growled. Becca nudged him on down the hall and rolled the already aching toe under her foot with another misplaced step.

"*Fuck!*"

The chant wavered at her curse.

She squeezed her toe in her fist while it throbbed, then set her foot down and limped the rest of the way to the kitchen, the walls tilting around her like an amusement park funhouse, every angle conspiring to mess with her senses of proximity and perspective.

Night had fallen, though it wasn't yet 5 P.M. by the grandfather clock she passed in the parlor. She found the others in the dining room seated around a long dark wood table with two unoccupied place settings. A ceramic bowl of pasta sat between a larger wooden bowl of salad and a baking pan on a trivet steaming with the aromas of garlic, tomato, and whatever melted cheeses were baked on top. Brooks waved at her with the oven mitt still on his hand.

"Is that clock in the parlor accurate?" Becca asked.

Dick Hanson nodded, piling salad onto his plate with a set of tongs. "I set it this afternoon." He watched her limp around the table with a mirthless grin.

"Slept longer than I realized. Sorry."

"I was gonna wake you in a minute for dinner," Brooks said. He pulled a chair out and gestured at the gold-trimmed white china and silverware.

"Smells good," Becca said. "But is it—"

"Meat? No, Eggplant Parm. You're veg, right?"

"Yeah. You remembered." Becca went to the cupboard where she'd stowed a bag of kibble earlier, dumped a scoop into Django's bowl, and set it down in a corner away from the table after making him sit. As she settled into her chair, Hanson passed her the bowl of pasta, and Mark flashed her a friendly smile.

"Stub your toe?" Mark asked.

"Yeah."

"That makes two of us. Hanson walked into a doorframe."

"I thought the first floor was supposed to be stable," Becca said. "Not prone to shifts."

"That doesn't mean it isn't...a little off," Hanson offered. "They say we'll get used to it."

Brooks took the seat at the head of the table. "Dig in, everybody. I figured I'd start us off with a group meal for our first night. After this, we can fend for ourselves, but there should be plenty you can eat. The pantry and fridge are well stocked."

"No plate for the reverend?" Becca asked.

"The rev says he's fasting to prepare."

Becca recognized the tense jawline that meant Brooks was restraining himself.

"Chanting, too," Burns added, pouring a glass of red wine and offering the bottle to Becca. "We gave him the library as a bedroom for privacy. I think he's turned it into a temple."

Becca took the bottle, sniffed it, and poured herself half a glass. "So…do you think he can protect us?"

"*Can?* Yes." Brooks said. "*Will?* Can't say I'm confident. Personally, I have more faith in my sidearm."

They ate for a while in silence. Becca had taken only a small portion and was soon picking at her salad and nursing her wine. Setting her fork down, she said, "What's the plan, now that we're all here?"

Brooks burped into his napkin. "After dinner we fetch his holiness and go upstairs, take a tour of the second story."

"Are we looking for anything particular?"

"No…but I don't think we'll have any doubt if we find it."

"The first team they sent in," Becca said, "I know they got inconsistent measurements, but did they see anything weird?"

"They weren't equipped to explore," Dick Hanson said. "They only set up the surveying equipment and then retreated to check the data from the hut. The lasers read different measurements at night than in the daytime. Activity seems to increase after the sun goes down."

"But no one's been upstairs at night before us?" Becca asked.

"Not since we claimed the site," Brooks said. "They didn't want techs getting caught off guard or triggering something they couldn't cope with. You could say it's virgin territory up above."

"And below," Mark said, pointing downward with his fork.

"The cellar," Becca said. "What's down there?"

"We'll find out when we explore," Brooks said. "According to the floor plan, it's a boiler room and workshop. Caleb Wade was a candle maker back when candles and oil lamps were the only sources of indoor light. It's hard to think of it as a lucrative business now, but he built this mansion on the profits of what was basically a local utility at the time. He had some blacksmithing and glassblowing skills, too. Made all sorts of lamps for the fuel he sold. When his sons inherited the house they installed electricity, but the old man wouldn't allow it as long as he lived here. Claimed he didn't care for the color of the light."

"As a photographer I can relate," Becca said. "Electric light sucks."

"How's it going with the drone?" Mark asked. "You getting the hang of it?"

Becca took another sip of wine. It was warming her up and helping her to relax. "Actually, no. It's a finicky little bitch. Good thing it's built strong because I'm good at crashing it."

"You'll get the hang of it."

The conversation diminished with the food, and soon Becca busied herself with cleanup to avoid the discomfort of small talk with strangers. Hanson left the room while Burns wiped down the table. He returned a moment later with a roll of blueprints, which he spread over the table, pinning the corners with salt-and-pepper shakers and clean utensils.

"This is the floor we're on," Hanson said. "You've all seen most of it, and we don't expect it to change, so I won't dwell on it. The Reverend's bedroom is the library, Becca's is at the end of the hall, Mark and I are in the billiard room, and Brooks has the pantry." He jabbed his finger at a door marked with an X in red pencil. "This is the cellar door, off the kitchen. No one goes down there without a partner."

Brooks cut in: "And just because the doors don't change where they lead to on this floor doesn't mean that it's a normal zone. Neutral, maybe, but not normal. And we're not just talking stubbed toes and bruised shoulders."

"What do you mean?" Becca asked.

"It has its own wild cards up its sleeves, but the geeks figure it can only deal them while you're sleeping—in the form of dreams."

"I thought no one has spent a night here since SPECTRA claimed it," Mark said.

"True, but there's a lot of Internet literature, accounts written by people who have slept in the house on a dare. Even an amateur parapsychology club. You'll find journals and pens in with your pillows and blankets. We're all expected to keep dream journals for comparison, to see if there are common themes, or…messages."

"Whoa, wait a minute," Becca said. "Who's going to read them? Cause if you think for a second I'm going to be transparent with a black government agency—" She scoffed.

"Nina," Brooks said. "Nina will read them."

"Who's Nina?" Mark asked.

Becca and Brooks spoke over each other:

"His ex."

"Her shrink."

"How'd *that* happen?" Mark asked.

"Coincidence," Brooks said. "But she's qualified to look for patterns while keeping our confidentiality."

"She's working for SPECTRA now?" Becca asked. "Or was she always? Are you two back together?"

"No, we're not. She's staying nearby. She'll be on call. And you don't have to worry about her sharing anything with me."

Becca laughed. "How do *you* feel about your ex-wife reading your dream journal? No one thinks there's a conflict of interest there?"

Brooks sighed. "Actually, I argued against it, but Northrup wanted her because she knows two of us well enough to sift between subconscious material and images from…elsewhere. Since you and I are the only ones on the team with EDEP, they'll be looking more closely at our dreams."

"What's EDEP?" Mark asked.

"Extra Dimensional Entity Perception," Hanson replied.

"And you're telling me *Proctor* doesn't have it?"

"He wasn't exposed in the attacks," Brooks said.

"But they were carried out by members of his congregation. He didn't want to be exposed to his own gods?"

"The device was built by a radical who kept it secret from the church leadership," Hanson explained. "He thought the reverend was too conservative to endorse ushering in the apocalypse. We took Proctor into custody when we raided the church after the first attack, so he was out of play early."

"So those spells and mantras he's chanting," Mark said, "he can't even see the entities they're supposed to protect us from?"

Brooks shook his head.

"Nor can he invoke them," Hanson said. "The human voice lacks the necessary harmonics. But ritual gestures combined with his clerical voice training might offer some protection."

"Is it true that they castrate them before puberty?" Mark asked. "I heard that from a trans hooker in P-town who—"

"Yes, it's true." Proctor had appeared at the end of the hall. He looked sweaty in his heavy black garment, despite the chilly atmosphere of the old house, but it looked to Becca like the sweat of exertion, not anxiety. If anything, he exuded the meditative calm of a man in his element.

"Don't worry, I can hit the high notes," Proctor said. "And your lives may soon depend upon it." His thumb caressed the antique silver pommel of a dagger sheathed in his belt. "So…are we ready to venture upstairs?"

Brooks, leaning against the sink, knocked back the rest of his wine. "All right, everybody. Get your gear."

Chapter 6

They gathered in the vestibule at the foot of the stairs. The light from a cast-iron statue of a woman holding an illuminated apple extended to just beyond the first landing, after which the yellow walls darkened to absolute shadow. Above, the second floor was perfectly silent. Brooks called Base Camp on his walkie and announced that they were about to make the first ascent. Becca, her hair up in a ponytail, felt the back of her neck prickle as she set her hand on the black oak banister and made her first physical connection to the realm that awaited above. She had dressed in a single layer—a black thermal shirt and cargo pants—but felt over warm even in the drafty stairwell.

She held the dragonfly aloft and set it flying. When it reached the landing, she tapped the remote. An ultra bright LED on the bug's head cast a beam of cold light over the decaying Persian carpet runners and threw spokes of shadow across the wall through the banister rods.

Flanked by the others, Becca set her boot on the bottom step, feeling that she was committing to something irrevocable, pushing past the internal resistance before fear took hold of her and made her hesitate. She followed the drone up the stairs, concentrating more on the bug and its flight path than on the shadowy architecture and furnishings around her. The stairs, firm under her feet, didn't even creak. At the top of the stairs, she brought up the camera view on her handheld and counted the doors the drone passed on its flight to the end of the hall: 3 chambers on each side. The hallway ended at a set of bookshelves built into an alcove made of a bay where it seemed there should have been a window instead, and she wondered how much light reached this floor in the daytime.

The drone hovered like a hummingbird, wobbling slightly and turning on its axis, sending drunken shadows careening up the walls and bobbing over the spines of worm-eaten cloth volumes, lending the reading alcove the appearance of a cabin on a sinking ship, darkness undulating like a rising waterline.

The small group of explorers stood outside the circle of light at the top of the stairs. They seemed to be holding their collective breath until Brooks found a switch plate and, with a click, threw the entire second story into stark and shocking incandescence.

The hall was furnished with antique bench seats, one on either side, topped with dusty velvet cushions. A wide canvas depicting a landscape hung in a baroque gold frame, the only adornment apart from the iron lighting fixtures to break the monotony of the faded, burgundy wallpaper.

Moving down the hall between Brooks and John Proctor, Becca passed two closed doors before coming to a wide doorframe accented with a hand-carved leaf motif that let onto a large chamber with a gold brocade sofa, a grand piano, and a fallen chandelier lying amid a scattering of broken crystal fragments.

The light from the hallway spilled into the music room, but when Brooks tried the wall switch nothing happened. The broken electric chandelier had apparently been the only light fixture in the room. He drew a flashlight from his belt, switched it on and swept the beam across the floor, sending a spray of little rainbows fanning out from the prismatic shards.

Becca sent the drone in and hung it high in a corner of the room where it augmented the flashlight, granting each person who entered a double shadow.

Dick Hanson walked to the piano and lifted the keyboard lid, revealing inverted keys, white on black. He struck one and a note wavered and trembled in the air. When it diminished, he stepped away and Brooks shone his flashlight at the piano bench. He raised the cushioned seat and peered into the compartment where sheet music would typically be stored. Finding it empty, he dropped the lid.

Mark passed through a doorway beyond the piano and must have found another light switch because the adjacent room lit up; Becca could see a patch of wooden slats through crumbling horsehair plaster where the wall had been damaged, reminding her of an open wound.

"Wait up," Brooks said, following Mark into the chamber with the rest of the group coalescing around him.

Becca entered the room last. Her first thought was that a TV had been left on, tuned to a dead channel. A storm of black and white static swarmed in a square near the floor. But on second glance, she saw that it was a fireplace, not a screen, the cold dance of light a result of the black snowflakes rushing into the house through the chimney, energized by their collisions as they vanished into a bed of ash clogging an iron grate.

Mark had walked past the fireplace. He stood poised before a door in a corner of the hexagonal room where one of the short walls formed a closet.

"Can you hear it?" he said, pressing his palm against the wood. Becca couldn't tell if he was trying to feel a vibration in the door, or keep it from opening, and now she detected a sound: the irregular rhythm of a buoy bell clanging as waves rocked it side to side. It sounded close, despite the reverberation that enveloped it, and she caught herself searching the floor in front of the door for water spilling through, but the boards were dry.

Proctor pushed past her, drawing his dagger.

Brooks drew his gun, pointed it at the floor, and stepped to the opposite side of the closet. Becca wondered if he meant to bring his weapon up on the reverend or on whatever might lie on the other side of the door, and realized he was probably positioning himself for either option. Only Hanson hung back and watched the scene unfold. Becca summoned the dragonfly and positioned it over Mark's shoulder, ready to send it through for reconnaissance when he opened the door, if it should turn out to reveal more than dusty shelves.

Mark turned the knob and the latch clicked. He opened the door just a crack. Nothing emerged, but the sound of the buoy bell grew louder and clearer. Such a lonely sound. Salty humidity laced the air, wafting on a cool breeze that jostled the hovering dragonfly and caused the sleet of static in the hearth to flare up momentarily. Letting go of the knob, Mark took a step back and allowed the door to swing open.

A corridor of rough-hewn stone weeping sluggish tears of algae-congested slime yawned away beyond the possible boundaries of the house before diminishing to a distant black rectangle.

Becca tasted a fetid undertone on the air, a dank putrescence blooming into the room. She put the back of her hand to her mouth and took a retreating step just as Mark set foot in the mouth of the passage. The stone slabs joined the doorframe where they met, so Becca knew the corridor couldn't have dimensions that differed from the frame, but when Mark stepped into it he suddenly appeared smaller, the walls and ceiling dwarfing him. When Brooks reached to seize his shoulder and pull him back, he came up short.

"Burns, *wait!*" Brooks shouted teetering on the threshold. "Get back. We send the drone in first."

"Yeah… Okay."

Becca strained her eyes to look beyond Mark, forgetting for a second that she could see more by sending the dragonfly down the shaft like Brooks was saying. Was something writhing in the darkness at the end? Was the wall covered with snakes? "What the…"

Mark turned to face his companions. The blood seemed to drain from his skin at the sight of the gulf already stretched between them. He looked at the ground beneath his feet like he expected to find a conveyor belt where there was only stone glistening with strands of green seaweed.

Django barked loud and sharp, setting hearts jumping and nerves buzzing, putting the team on edge for what was coming. In the near silence following the dog's warning, they heard it: a low churning rumble.

The black rectangle at the end of the passage flashed white, leaving a tangle of violet tentacles imprinted on Becca's retinas. As the flash faded, a thunder of percussion shook the floor. A surge of whitewater foam and agitated photons crashed over and around Burns, pushing him toward the doorway for a heartbeat before sucking him back and erasing him under the receding wave.

Becca screamed.

Proctor lunged forward, but Brooks body checked him aside and slammed the closet door shut, knocking the drone out of the air, and sending it skittering across the floorboards. But the dragonfly was built tough; it righted itself and got back on its feet before the reverend could do the same. He lay on his hip, his cloak pooled around him, his ceremonial dagger a few feet away, still spinning like the dial of a board game. It came to rest finally, pointing at Hanson, who hadn't moved since the closet door had swung open.

Proctor shot a black look at Brooks—equal parts fear and hatred. He looked like a kicked dog. Becca helped him up, but as soon as he was standing, he spat on the floor at Brooks' feet.

Brooks cocked his head and scowled. "Jesus, buddy. I probably just saved your life. I'm not losing two on the first night. Not to the first door we open, no way."

"You can't just leave him in there," Becca said. She moved for the door, but Brooks put the heel of his hand in the hollow of her shoulder. His gun was holstered again, but she felt his hand twitch toward it as Proctor bent and retrieved his dagger from the floor. Then, he too sheathed his weapon and the tension dissipated.

"Open the door," Becca said. "Open the damn door and let me look for him. You can tie a rope around my waist."

"Yeah, *that'll* help if something in there wants you."

"Then let me send the drone in at least. Maybe just opening the door will bring another wave and wash him back."

Brooks didn't answer. The clanging bell rolled on, now fainter, farther away.

"Let *me* go in," Proctor said. "It's what I'm here for. I can protect him."

Brooks shook his head. "You're here to help against anything that comes *out*. And to seal breaches like this one."

"You're not sealing anything with Mark still in there," Becca said.

Proctor turned away from the door. To Hanson, he said, "I don't know why you brought me here if you don't trust me to do what I'm here for."

Brooks focused on Becca. "We'll take steps to get him out, but we have to think it through. Just don't anybody do anything—"

Becca shot her arm past him and yanked the door open.

"—rash."

The stone passage was gone, replaced with an empty closet: four dusty shelves and all the silence of a cupboard. No bell, no surf, and no sign that Mark Burns had ever been there.

"The *fuck*, Becca," Brooks said. "If you can't follow my command you're out. I'll take opinions when we strategize, but in a crisis, you will obey my command. That is not negotiable."

"Did he go to the same place as my father?"

Brooks squeezed his eyes shut and pinched the bridge of his nose. "I don't know."

She nodded at the reverend. "You said he's here to seal the breach. Like how Moe used to talk about 'sealing the cracks.' So when does that happen? When exactly do you decide you can't get them out and move on to sealing them in?"

"Back to the hall," Brooks said. "Everybody. Out of the room and back downstairs. Don't touch anything on the way back, and do not open any doors."

They stared at him, each waiting to see if another would defy the order.

"*Come on.* We need to call this in and plan our next step or we could be putting Burns in even greater danger. I won't let this escalate. Let's go. Downstairs."

Hanson moved first. Becca wound up her foot to kick the drone across the floor in frustration, but stopped short at the last instant as Django shot down the hall in a cacophony of claws. Becca snatched the drone up and ran after him, bumping Hanson aside and catching sight of Proctor's black frock swirling around the corner of a bedroom doorframe after Django's tail. In an instant Becca was rounding the same doorway, her heart pounding in her chest, her ears filled with canine snarls, a piercing feline squall, and the incongruous, authoritative drone of the reverend's sonorous incantations.

Was he attacking Django?

Becca reached out to shove the reverend aside, but coming up behind him she saw that he wasn't touching her dog. He waved his gleaming dagger in the air, slashing geometric figures with it and trailing ghosts of blue light, hurling waves of energy that Becca could actually see into the corner where Django had trapped the black and white cat.

Was it a cat, or something masquerading as a cat, revealing monstrous alterations in a fit of fury?

The air wavered and for a moment she was seeing the skirmish as if through layers of reflective glass stretching down a long corridor—a kaleidoscope of fang and claw, fur and blood.

Proctor inhaled deeply and the illusion smeared toward him. He reared back and then thrust the dagger forward beside his spear-fingered left hand, a current of energy rippling over him, crackling from the tips of his fingers and blade, carrying his incantation down the tunnel like a depth charge. "*PHI-THETA-SOE! THIAF! ABRASAX!*"

The cat creature shrieked and recoiled as the mirror corridor collapsed, leaving Django staggering back, whimpering, and drizzling blood on the scuffed boards. Becca lunged past Proctor and fell to her knees, clutching the dog in a fierce embrace.

* * *

When she had cleaned Django's wounds well enough to know that he would need stitches, Becca turned him over to a SPECTRA runner who promised to get him swiftly to a veterinarian the agency had on call. Blood-smeared and exhausted, she finally joined the others in the first floor parlor where they fidgeted in a half circle of antique sofas and chairs. Brooks paced the carpet, waiting for Northrup to arrive.

Northrup entered without a knock and found his way down the hall. He clicked on a digital recorder, set it down on the coffee table, and folded his arms over his chest. "What happened?"

Brooks gave a complete account of the first excursion, with Becca chiming in to add details.

"Unbelievable," Northrup said. "You can't even get through the first night without letting the house swallow one of your team?"

Brooks glared at him.

"It all happened so fast," Becca said.

"Nothing came out, right?" Northrup said. "Nothing came out of that door? Not so much as a slug or a spider?"

Becca looked around the room. No one answered. "There was a cat," she said. "Django chased it into another room and it attacked him in the corner."

Northrup cocked an eyebrow. "A *cat?* Where did it come from? The closet Burns went into?"

"No. I don't think so."

"It wasn't a cat," Proctor said. "Not *just* a cat."

Northrup looked at the reverend. "Where did it come from? What was it?"

"It was Caleb Wade's companion."

"You're telling me this cat is from 1782?" Northrup said.

"It was his familiar," Proctor said. "Maybe it's something else on the other side. Here it's a cat. It roams secret passages outside of time and space."

"Did you kill the thing?" Becca asked Proctor. "Whatever it was?"

Proctor shook his head. "Wounded and banished it is all."

"Did you catch it on video?" Northrup said.

Becca fished the remote from her pocket. "I don't know. Maybe a glimpse. I was chasing after Django before I even saw it. But I got everything that happened when Mark opened the closet. Here, check it on a big screen."

Northrup took the device from her and switched off his audio recorder. He slipped both into a leather valise, sighed and ran his hand through his wavy black hair. "I should pull you all out of here tonight and rethink this. We thought it might take weeks to detect activity, but...I don't know. Maybe the house is becoming unstable, more volatile."

"Pulling out would be a mistake," Brooks said. "You need eyes and ears in here. Any clue one of us picks up could be the key to finding him. Even something from a dream, right?"

Northrup nodded. "Okay. You'll stay the night and we'll reconvene in the morning. But nobody leaves the first floor. I'll be back at sunrise. Maybe by then we'll know more about what we're dealing with from the video."

* * *

Becca couldn't rest until she knew Django was okay. She waited at Base Camp until the runner returned with him. One ear was bandaged and his fur was shaved in a few spots where they'd stitched him up. He was loopy from the painkillers, unable to walk straight for more than a few feet, but he perked up at the smell of her, and soon she was snuggling him under a blanket on the floor of her bedroom.

She woke on the hard wood in the night, muscles aching, and moved to the cot. It wasn't much of an improvement, and she tossed and turned for a while before popping two tabs of Klonopin to take the edge off and help her sleep. Her emotional exhaustion made the pills more effective than usual. Oddly enough, the murmured mantras drifting down the hall from the library also helped to wind her down. Django paced for a while, then settled on the blanket between Becca and the door, his nose pointed at the crack to detect any threat that might approach while she slept.

When she woke, shortly after 3 A.M., her first cycle of dreamless sleep had burned off the fatigue, and she was instantly alert to the sounds of the dog's pacing, whining, and scratching. Not at the door to the hall, but at her closet. She sat up in the dark and groped for the headlamp she'd been reading by before falling asleep. Slipping the elastic over her head, she clicked the light on. It was still on the red setting she preferred when using it as a reading light, washing the room in a bloody hue that did little to ease her apprehension when she slipped out the side of the sleeping bag in her boxers and t-shirt, and set her feet on the cold floorboards.

The hair on her arms rose as she approached the closet door. She thought of picking up a weapon, but she had none, and realized it was a lack she might need to correct after tonight, if only with an iron fire poker filched from the parlor. Nonetheless, she swept her head side to side, scanning the corners with the red blob of light, searching for something, anything, heavy and blunt, but coming up empty.

Django's fangs would have to suffice if it came to it, but he wasn't growling at whatever he had detected. She took another step toward the door he was sniffing at, wondering if she should call for Brooks.

She set her ear to the door and detected a high-pitched whining sound, like the buzzing of a mosquito, or the ringing of her own ears after a concert. She moved her jaw to try and clear them, but the sound continued. The more she listened, the more she could make out textures shifting below the ringing: sloshing fluid and a scraping that reminded her of bricks sliding against each other.

She crouched and examined the crack between door and floor, her fingertips glowing red in the light from the headlamp as she touched the wood and found it dry, dusty even. Her heart raced as she lowered her head and sniffed, searching for whatever Django was picking up. Something complex and overly sweet with strains of rot at the core. It reminded her of exotic flowers and fruit gone bad; a chest filled with spices exhumed from a shipwreck.

Did she hear raspy breathing through the crack?

"Becca..."

Had she heard that right? Had someone whispered her name through the door?

"Dad?" she croaked.

The door shuddered in its frame, sending a jolt of fear through her body, but the doorknob didn't rattle or even twitch, and it occurred to her that maybe the doorknob didn't exist at all on the other side of the door and the only way for whoever was inside to get out was for her to open it.

She did.

Something cold and clammy fell out of the closet and dragged her to the floor with a thud. Django yelped and skittered out from under her, then launched into full-throated barking, sounding the alarm. Becca felt a wash of brackish water pooling around her and soaking through her t-shirt. The body of Mark Burns, unmoving, pinned her to the floor. She didn't know if he was alive or dead as she struggled to look past his shoulder and see what lay beyond the threshold—a closet, or another world? But her eyes found only gray darkness lacking depth. No moving air stirred in the room or chilled her wet skin with a breeze from beyond. Nonetheless, she stretched her foot out and used it to slam the door.

Lying on the wet floor of the red-washed room, Becca felt a vibration and realized that Mark's teeth were chattering. She pushed him off her until she could see his face beneath a fringe of dripping hair. His eyes, wide and crazed, shone like blood-dipped coins, and she realized with mounting horror that the vibration wasn't only his teeth chattering from the cold; the deeper shaking, in his bones, was laughter.

SPECIAL PHYSICS EMERGENT COUNTER TERROR RECON AGENCY
NORTHEAST REGIONAL OFFICE, BOSTON, MA.

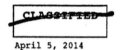
PROJECT
WADEHOUSE

April 5, 2014

TO: ███ ███ ███
FROM: ███ ███████
THROUGH: ASST. DIR. Daniel Northrup

SUBJECT: WADE HOUSE SPACE/TIME ANOMALY

In late 2013 NSA notified SPECTRA of cluster hits containing key words of interest to the agency found on a private message board on the intranet of a UMASS Lowell student organization. Keywords included: WADE HOUSE, ████, NON-EUCLIDIAN, ███ ████, TIME LOOP, and STARRY WISDOM.

With assistance from ECHELON and █████, SPECTRA intercepted emails, text, and other SIGINT identifying the members of a student paranormal investigation club operating under the moniker, The Hub Paranormal Society.

SPECTRA asset ████ █████ was assigned to infiltrate the club. She joined right away, and by March 2014 had established a trusted position in the group. Fortunately, the Wade House excursion was delayed by numerous snowstorms and illnesses and was not carried out until ████ ██████ had already accompanied the team on two similar excursions to sites of reputed paranormal activity, enabling her to acquire familiarity with the protocols and psychological dynamics of the group. Of the 4 members of the Wade House exploration team (not including our asset), only ████ █████ was a likely hysteric prone to obvious self-delusion.

On Saturday, March 29th 2014 the HPS drove from Lowell to Concord with sleeping bags, flashlights, takeout food, a variety of inexpensive digital audio recorders and a Go Pro video camera.

Exploration was limited to the first and second floors, and the group made camp in the first floor parlor. According to ████

SPECIAL PHYSICS EMERGENT COUNTER TERROR RECON AGENCY

████, all members were "too freaked out to venture into the basement or attic."

An effort by ████ ████, the designated cartographer, to map the floor plan on graph paper resulted in excessive erasures, arguments with████ ████, and ultimate abandonment of the effort.

With one notable exception* no entities were observed or captured on the video. The evening eventually devolved into a debate about the one fluctuating phenomena the entire group could observe, record, and compare discrepancies for: the number of stairs in the staircase. No two 'investigators' counted the same number of steps. Counts varied between 19 and 27. Ultimately, ██ ████ labeled the steps with masking tape and a permanent marker (1 on the lowest step to 24 on the topmost), but on the next count, ██ ████ and ████ ████ found the number tags to be scrambled in non-sequential order with some numbers missing.

The group bedded down in sleeping bags at 2:10 a.m.

At 3:40 a.m. ████ ████, an avowed light sleeper, woke to the sound of the defunct grandfather clock 'tick-tocking.' Upon waking, he saw the white-tipped tail of an animal passing out of view around the parlor entrance into the hall. ██ ████ followed without waking the others and used his flashlight to pursue what turned out to be a black-and-white cat to the second floor where the animal entered an empty bedroom chamber.

██ ████ closed the bedroom door behind the cat and returned to the parlor. He woke ██ ████ and asked ██ to accompany him to the second floor bedroom. Once there, they opened the door but found no cat in the empty room. 'On a hunch,' ██ ████ closed and opened the door again. The same black-and-white cat was now present in the room again, arching its back and rubbing up against an iron radiator on the far wall. ████ ████ guarded the door to keep the cat from escaping the room while ██ ████ checked the room to make sure the cat could not have hidden behind said radiator or in some other niche such as a closet. But no suitable hiding places were found. The single closet door remained firmly shut.

Joking that they had found Shrodinger's Cat, ██ ████ left the room and closed the door behind her. When they opened it again, the cat had again vanished. It did not reappear on any subsequent opening of the door that night or in the morning.

Note: see case file #WH-140405B for asset's dream record.

SPECIAL PHYSICS EMERGENT COUNTER TERROR RECON AGENCY

Chapter 7

Becca lay curled in the same stuffed chair she'd claimed the first time they gathered in the parlor, bundled in flannel pants and a hoodie with Django at her feet. The sky was a dirty shade of pink watercolor under a black sketch of reeds in the bay window beside her. Mark Burns sat opposite, wrapped in an army blanket, his right foot bandaged with gauze through which a dim bloodstain had swelled. He'd rinsed in the shower, but the miasma of low tide still clung to him.

Dick Hanson tinkered in the liquor cabinet for a moment, then handed Mark a brandy on the rocks. "For your nerves," he said.

Mark took the glass and managed to hold it without dropping it, but he didn't drink.

Reverend Proctor hovered at the threshold of the room, eyeing Mark with what Becca thought might be envious fascination.

Brooks took a dark wood chair from its place along the wainscoting, carried it to the center of the room, and set it down facing Burns. He sat, hunched forward, and tried to make eye contact. Becca hardly recognized the man wrapped in the blanket. Since their first meeting, Mark had seemed calm and composed in the face of the unknown—maybe too much so, considering what they expected to find in the Wade House. But now, after becoming the first to confront it, he was twitchy and restless, his eyes darting to the corners of the room, his unwrapped foot bobbing on the carpet. He looked at Brooks for half a second, then sniffled and looked away, ended up gazing at the floor, swinging his head from side to side, lip quivering.

"Have a sip of your drink," Brooks said.

Mark raised the glass to his lips. The ice rattled. He took a sip and set it on the end table beside his chair.

"Do you remember stepping through the doorway upstairs?" Brooks asked. "Do you remember that?"

Mark shook his head.

"Do you remember anything that happened to you before you fell out of Becca's closet?"

His eyes widened and he worked his jaw, but no words came out.

"Do you remember a wave carrying you away?"

He nodded.

"Okay, let's back up a bit. State your full name. Can you do that?"

"Mark Burns."

"Good. Can you tell me your birthday?"

"May 9th, 1987"

"What's your husband's name?"

"M…um…Michael."

"Do you know who the president is?"

"Uh…Clinton? No. Nereus Charobim?" He laughed. It took a while for him to stop.

Brooks shot a look at Hanson. Charobim was the name of a mentor to the terrorists of the Starry Wisdom Church. It wasn't a name known to the public, and he was believed to be dead, if he could ever have been said to be alive. The Book Breakers, SPECTRA's occult scholars and tome sifters, called him an "avatar of Nyarlathotep," whatever the hell that meant.

"Was that a joke, Mark? Look at me," Brooks said. "Was that supposed to be a joke?"

"No."

"Where did you hear that name?"

Mark composed himself, shook his head, and swallowed. "Sorry, I don't know. I don't know where I heard it. There's lots of new stuff in my head."

"It's okay. You've been a little scrambled by your journey through the house, but you're gonna be okay. Just try to relax. It will help you remember."

Mark took another sip of his brandy.

Brooks gave him a moment and then said, "You went into a stone passage. There was a bell. A wave came and washed you away. Then what happened?"

"I...I was washed through halls of granite, like a... labyrinth I think. It washed me out to a place like a shore. But the sky...the *sky*...it was the strangest yellow. I've never seen a yellow like that. There was a mound of black and gray sand, like a spiral. It was like a temple with carved columns going up to that mustard gas sky..."

Brooks gave him time to go on, but nothing more came. He prompted: "What else did you see? Was there life?"

Mark scratched his chest and nodded, his upper lip curling into a grimace. "Northern stargazers. In the sand."

"People? There were people?"

"No, it's a fish. *Astroscopus guttatus...the one who aims at the stars*. Faces in the sand...eyes on their foreheads. I didn't see them. Stepped on one. They zap you with electricity, then get you with needle teeth. Fucker got me good." He curled the toes of his bandaged foot.

"What else? Were there other creatures?"

Mark shuddered. He stared at a blank space on the wall and nodded. "Tall, slender ones in black robes. Not people. They had pale faces like the bellies of fish. Scales and no hair. Mouths, but no ears. I thought they had no eyes, but when they opened their mouths to chant, I saw it: one eye where the tongue should be, ringed by sharp teeth, like...seashell shards. They chittered and chanted and struck their clawed fingers together for percussion. Such a sick sound. And then the northern stargazers—but they weren't really, they were too big, too *awake* to really be stargazers, but they were something like them, something more *evolved*—they sang the bass notes, and the sand buzzed around their half-buried faces and made patterns. It was like they were communicating through the shapes, signaling to something in the sky that could read the patterns in the sand, and…and…"

"And what? Did you see something in the sky?"

Mark shook his head vigorously. Becca couldn't tell if he was answering *no* or refusing to describe what he had seen, or teetering on the edge of a seizure.

"What did you see?" Brooks asked again. "What did you see in the yellow sky?"

Mark's jaw worked and his brow knotted, but the only sound to escape his lips was a guttural groan like a death rattle.

"Stop it," Becca said. "You're stressing him too much."

Brooks leaned forward and squeezed Mark's shoulder. "It's okay. You're gonna be okay." He stood up and approached Proctor. "You recognize what he described. I can see it on your face. What are they?"

"The Twilight Choir. They gather the tides of the astral ocean and usher currents into the dreams of sensitives on the terrestrial plane."

"Speak English," Brooks said.

"They are keepers of the borderlands between dimensions. Heralds of the Great Old Ones. Their songs can cross the membrane between worlds and flood the dreams of artists, mystics, and lunatics. But they cannot physically pass into this world. Not without a breach like the ones Darius caused in Boston."

"You sure about that?" Brooks squatted, positioning his face in front of Mark's unblinking eyes. The biologist had finished his drink, and was crunching an ice cube in his teeth. The sound grated on Becca's nerves. "How did you get out? How did you find the door? Did they try to follow you?"

"I don't know what happened. Another wave came. I was carried on a current. I told you what I remember, but some things don't fit the words I have. I'm sorry."

Brooks sighed. "Okay. You may remember more with time, or find a way to tell it. The important thing is you made it back, we thought we lost you in there."

"Mark," Becca said. "Did you see a man? A man with long hair and a reddish beard?"

Mark shook his head and swallowed.

The sound of the front door opening traveled down the hall. A moment later, Northrup entered the parlor carrying a metal attaché case, accompanied by a petite woman in a gray overcoat smudged with black flakes that matched her short hair: Nina Rothkopf. Becca made eye contact and Nina gave her a curt nod, then settled in the chair her ex-husband had just vacated, facing Burns.

"Hello Mark, I'm Nina. I'm a psychiatrist. Dr. Matheson is on his way to give you a complete physical. But I'm here to check a few things first. I'm going to shine my penlight in your eyes, okay? I'd like you to track it as it moves."

Mark nodded. When he had done as she asked, she tucked her penlight away, apparently satisfied. Hanson had taken Northrup aside and presented him with a vial of cloudy liquid that reminded Becca of a urine sample. "I squeezed this out of his clothes," Hanson said. "Let me know what the chemists find."

Northrup pocketed the vial, then knelt beside Mark and undid the clasps of the attaché case. Becca drifted closer and looked over Nina's shoulder. Inside the case a small stone idol occupied a cavity cut to size in a bed of black foam rubber. Northrup carefully removed the figure and handed it to Nina. She held it up in front of the dazed biologist, who reacted to it with a snap to attention.

"What do you see, Mark?" she asked.

"A statue."

"Describe it."

"It's like a monster, standing on a stone block carved with runes."

"Very good. Does it have a color?"

"The base is greenish brown but the figure is sort of blue."

"How much detail can you see? Describe the figure to me as if my eyes are closed."

"It uh...looks like a warrior, like a man with rows of crab claws running up his sides and crustacean armor plates and a tail like a stingray. Its face is flayed open like something on a dissection table, with flaps of flesh spread out in a diamond where the face should be, a fang at the tip of each flap, and in the middle a rictus of square teeth. It's horrible. And it's holding a weapon that looks like a harpoon, but nastier."

Becca saw the same thing, though no one asked her. He had described it perfectly.

"Lung Crawthok," the Reverend Proctor whispered in awe.

Nina studied him. "Do *you* see it, too?"

"No, I see a broken base with no figure, but that's what he described. Lung Crawthok, the guardian."

"Why can't *he* see it?" Brooks asked Nina. Becca thought he already knew the answer but wanted confirmation.

"Extra Dimensional Entity Perception," Nina said. She passed her hand through the solid figure as if it were a candle flame or a hologram. "I can't see it either," she said, "or feel it. Becca, you try."

Becca extended her fingers toward the revolting figure and was not entirely surprised when they stopped at solid, carved stone.

"Those of you who have been exposed to the harmonics—Becca, James, and now Mark—can interact with things that originate on the other side. You can see, hear, smell, touch and be touched by...dare I say taste and be tasted by...*them.*"

Becca withdrew her hand and suppressed a shudder. "But it's a statue, not an entity. It's not alive. Is it?"

Nina looked to Hanson. "Not exactly," he said. "I mean it's not organic. But as far as we can tell, it's been imbued with enough energy to exist in both dimensions for those who have the ability to see it."

"How?" Becca asked.

"Probably from being the focus of worship for so long. It's very old. Certain practices may have endowed it with some of the properties of the god it represents. We're not sure. We're still studying it, but it makes a good litmus test for EDEP, if nothing else."

"And when *you* look at it, you only see the base?" Becca asked.

"Right," Hanson said. "You see the fault line above the creature's feet?"

"Yeah."

"It ends there for me. We think the astral form you can see was left behind when the physical statue broke off and was lost. By then, it had become real enough that the image of the god lingered on some level."

Becca glanced at Proctor. He was staring hard at the stone pedestal in Nina's hand, drinking up every moment it was out of the case, as if staring hard and long enough would grant him a glimpse of the idol. She felt a pang of sadness for the man, alienated from his own gods. Gods he now claimed to renounce for the sake of his fellow man.

Nina, perhaps sensing his scrutiny, put the statue back in the case and closed the lid.

"You called it *the guardian*," Becca said to Proctor. "What does it guard?"

"The inmost gate, of which Yog Sothoth is the key."

"What's beyond the gate?" Brooks asked.

"The Island Out of Time. The city of the gods."

* * *

The team dispersed to their private rooms, aimless and anxious while Norhtrup and Nina escorted Mark Burns to the hut for a full medical exam and psych evaluation. The unexpected return of their lost teammate had woken the house in the early hours of the morning, and Becca knew she would need a nap to recover before she could function and focus on whatever the next step was. But before showering off the brine and returning to her cot, she led Django to the kitchen and gave him an antibiotic the vet had provided, with a bowl of kibble.

While she was bending over to set the bowl on the floor, the scarab slipped out of her tank top. When she rose, she found Proctor in the doorway staring at it.

Her hand moved reflexively to her chest to conceal the pendant, but she stopped herself and watched him until he met her eyes.

"You didn't try to use it," Proctor said. "When your dog was attacked."

"Well, you had it under control. Thanks."

"It's what I'm here for."

Becca didn't know what else to say. A beat of silence passed and then she let the words on her mind slip out: "Is it? What you're here for? Don't you want them to come back, your gods?"

He licked his lips and she wondered if he was considering lying. "Not at such a cost. Humanity is not without its merits. And who knows? Maybe they'll take me, if they want me. Anyway, my congregation doesn't."

"Why not?"

His eyes returned to the golden scarab clutching the scarlet gem. "After my interrogation, they didn't trust me."

Now she touched the scarab, but didn't hide it. "It doesn't work anymore, anyway. I've tried."

Brooks shouldered past Proctor, knocking him aside. He looked at Becca standing frozen in the middle of the kitchen, her fingertip on the jewel, then back at the Reverend with a withering gaze. "The fuck are you looking at, Padre? Why don't you go polish your stiletto?"

Proctor's nostrils flared. He whirled away, leaving Brooks looking at Becca.

"What?"

"Jesus, Brooks, I already have a guard dog."

She stepped around him, started down the hall, then turned back. "You said the first floor was supposed to be stable, but he came out of my closet. Do I need to barricade it? Should I be worried about *every* door?"

Brooks shrugged. They'd been in the house just one night and he already looked haggard. "I don't know, Becca. I thought we understood more than we do, thought we had a safe zone, but... Just use your head. Try not to close or open doors. And I wouldn't trust windows or mirrors, either. I wouldn't count on finding what you expect in them."

"Okay. I need to crash for a while. I'll leave my door open a crack."

"Good."

* * *

Becca dreamed she was sitting at a kitchen table, writing in the dream journal SPECTRA had left on her cot. At first she thought it was her grandmother's kitchen in the house where she'd grown up in Arkham, but the light was strange. Being acutely attuned to light, this was unlike any she recognized at first, a murky green ambience. She was recording a dream she'd had about one of the deities of the Starry Wisdom Church, the one with the dragon wings and tentacles. Darius Marlowe had transformed into a child of that dark god at the equinox, and Becca had sent him to his death down the central shaft of the Bunker Hill obelisk.

Darius had been a mere minion of the gods, but his devotion had been sufficient to transform his anatomy, to make him a trespasser between worlds. What had she dreamt about the octopus god, whose offspring she had wrestled, following that transformation? She struggled to read her own notes, but they looked more like math than language, like something Darius, an engineering student at MIT, might have dreamed: graphs charting sine waves, lists of numbers in kilohertz and angstroms.

The pages fluttered in the breeze through the kitchen window. Although she had studied light's basic properties at art school, she was no physicist, and the words in the journal were beyond her understanding. The air was sluggish, the pages resistant as she flattened them down against the book again. She knew then that it wasn't a breeze but a current.

Looking around the kitchen, she found it was the galley of a ship. Fronds of seaweed danced beyond the porthole window.

Becca stood and felt her stomach sink with unease. She lifted her hand from the page, and vaguely noticed the book floating away in her peripheral vision as she walked to the end of the gallery and opened a steel door with rounded corners. It resisted and groaned when she forced it against the rust and barnacles, a noise that was somehow loud even underwater, just as she could somehow breathe underwater. She put her hand to her neck, thinking that she must have gills. But her flesh was smooth. She felt only the chain from which her scarab dangled.

She stepped through the doorway expecting to fall out of a closet, but she was still walking underwater, tethered by loose gravity to the deck of a sunken ship. She kept her gaze tightly focused for fear that if she looked up the surface of the water would be far too far away. Or something on the ocean floor would be too big for her to stomach. Sometimes looking up was as bad as looking down when some titanic thing reminded you of how small you were. Walking on the docks of Boston harbor as a child when the tall ships visited, she knew the sensation of vertigo that came from looking up at their towering masts. But how deep could she be if light was reaching her through the water, limning the sunken objects strewn about the deck of the ship: her grandmother's rocking chair, a painting by her dead friend Rafael Moreno, her father's motorcycle enswathed in seaweed as if it had lain here for ages.

She found herself at the railing and gripped it. Barnacles chewed into the palms of her hands. Here at the edge of the deck, she couldn't help looking out across the seabed. A jagged trench dropped into darkness a few meters out. On the other side of the rift, a massive structure climbed from the ocean floor, monolithic forms listing at odd angles, forms that could have been carvings in stone, or the bones of Triassic beasts picked clean by the eons. At the pinnacle of the structure, rising ribbons of kelp undulated in the cold currents. Or were they something else? Fronds of torpid flesh.

A sound rolled over the seabed from the structure, sending a cloud of powdered sand across the chasm. The crest reached Becca, stinging her with grains, compressing her eardrums through the water. And the sound had a shape. Through the bowel-shaking drone, she heard a word: *TUTULUUU.*

Something moved in her peripheral vision—a shadow swinging like a pendulum. A bell chimed, a buoy rocking and ringing. Suddenly, as if the spell that had sustained her in these hostile environs had broken, her chest was crushed under the pressure of the icy water. She gazed up at the surface and woke.

Chapter 8

The angle of the gray light stretching across the floor beside the cot told her it was afternoon. Becca rolled over and looked up at the carved molding that framed the cracked and stained ceiling.

A distant bell rang through the house from the second floor. No—a piano note. She glanced at the journal she'd been provided and considered jotting down a note about the already fading dream, just a few key words to trigger her memory later, but the chiming sound called for investigation now and the journal could wait. She followed the sound through the house, past the library where the chanting droned on and the incense spiced the air, past the parlor where they had convened in the morning, now empty. Along the way, she peered into each makeshift bedroom she passed, but saw no one.

Django followed, his tail swishing at the walls of the hallway. He cut into the kitchen while Becca headed for the staircase. She heard him lapping at his water dish for a moment. By the time she had set her foot on the bottom step and started her ascent toward the circular rose window on the landing, he had caught up and bounded past her, his gait still out of balance, head tilted to one side, as if the meds weren't done messing with him.

She hesitated for a moment, wondering if she should go across the lawn to Base Camp instead. But with no one else on the ground floor and the piano clearly being played by someone upstairs, it was obvious she wouldn't be alone up there.

The second floor was silent except for the now bright and clear piano notes echoing through the empty rooms. The shades of paint and wallpaper looked brighter than they had at night, but the clarity of the cobwebs, grime and water stains more than made up for any levity granted by the less austere pallet.

She found Brooks and Hanson in the music room. Hanson was seated at the grand piano, plunking at the keys and shuffling through papers laid out in a manila folder on the music rack. The piano's top board was propped open. Brooks sat in a red and gold upholstered chair in the corner, a broom propped against the wall at his side, a pile of crystal shards and dust forming a neat mound in front of him. Both men looked up at Becca's entrance.

"Hey," she said, "what are you doing?"

"A little experiment," Brooks said.

"With a piano?"

"We've found some notes in Moe Ramirez's journals that suggest the piano could be an important portal."

"How?"

"The lid might be another doorway. But only if the right sequence of keys is played."

She circled around to Hanson and looked over his shoulder at the sheet music. It wasn't notated in Maurice's chaotic hand but looked professionally printed, if fragmentary. "Where did you get the music?"

"SPECTRA's code breakers ran some permutations through their computers and printed these variations based on Ramirez's notes and cryptic allusions. He never comes out and says what notes to play, or if he ever did, those pages are missing."

"Do you play, like for real?"

Hanson cleared his throat. "My parents made me take lessons to prepare my brain for math." He laughed and played a little classical sequence to demonstrate. The piano was impossibly in tune.

"Any luck yet opening the door you're looking for?"

"We're just getting started," Brooks said.

"Have you tried any closets?"

"We did. None of them are active. Maybe because it's daylight hours, I don't know. But we're not just looking for *any* point of entry. Ramirez's notes suggest he intended to hide a power object in one of the zones reached through this piano. Whatever it was, he didn't want cultists to find it."

"You think it could be a weapon against them, like the Fire of Cairo?"

"We don't know," Brooks said.

"You don't know much, huh?"

"Finding it would be a start. For now, it's one of the only leads we have to go on to make sense of this place and its purpose."

Becca thought about it for a moment. "If what he brought here could be used to seal the leaks from the other side, wouldn't he have done it himself? What if it's something better left unfound? Something cultists could use to make the breach worse."

Brooks shook his head. "I don't think so. It would be too risky to hide something like that right on their doorstep."

Hanson slid out from the bench and lowered the top board. "The working theory is that each chord sequence is a key to a different zone on the borderland of the other dimension. We expect some won't work at all; when we open the lid, we'll just see the soundboard and strings. But others—if the geeks at Government Center got it right—should align the house with points of entry that we can start mapping. It's better than opening doors at random. We can start mapping which sequences lead to which types of terrain. If we see anything that matches the Ramirez notes, we mark it down to revisit when we're ready to explore."

"Okay," Becca said. "I'll get the drone. We can send it through for pictures, right?"

"That's what it's for," Hanson said.

On her way out of the room, Brooks called after her. "Becca, grab your headlamp and climbing gear, too. Just in case."

Gathering her equipment, Becca felt unexpectedly energized, as if she'd taken a shot of caffeine. Part of it was fear, a low-level current that had been with her ever since she laid eyes on the Wade House, surging up to a more perceptible level. But more of it was the anticipation of *doing* something, having an objective. It was better than waiting around for something to happen, waiting to be the next victim of a malign environment. She had been called here for her skill set, after all, and now that she could finally take action without Brooks holding her back, wringing his hands about how unpredictable the dangers were, maybe she could get a hand on the tiller and steer the ship toward looking for her father. That, after all, was the other reason she was here.

Back upstairs with her rucksack, she padded into the room to the sound of a fading, dissonant chord. Brooks opened the piano slowly and peered inside.

"Nothing," he said.

Hanson turned a page on the music stand and found the next chord fingering while Brooks set the lid back down and Becca put on her gloves and harness. The gloves, fingerless leather, would spare her rope burns while still allowing access to the drone camera's touch screen.

"What are you doing?" Brooks asked her.

"You said to get my gear."

"Just in case, I said. I'm not planning on sending you down."

"Well, I'll be ready just in case, then."

Hanson tried another chord progression, but again Brooks found only the guts of the piano under the lacquered board. Becca was beginning to wonder if there would be anything to do after all when she heard the stairs creaking. A moment later, Proctor entered the room, swinging a censer on a chain and trailing fragrant clouds of smoke. He nodded at her, crossed the room, and bowed his head to listen to the music from an unobtrusive vantage point. She noticed his ceremonial dagger in his belt.

Hanson looked up from the keyboard and eyed the reverend suspiciously for a moment before focusing on the printed music again. He rifled back through the pages in the manila folder, took a stubby pencil from behind his ear, and scribbled something on the staff.

"What are you doing?" Brooks asked, "Changing it?"

Hanson nodded. "I want to try something. The guys who came up with these...well, they're not musicians, they're occult scholars. Music is just another symbol set to them. It's a little like using computer software to restore a damaged painting rather than having an artist do it. Not that I'm an artist when it comes to music, but I've studied enough to know that these fragments are modal and the endings they've tried aren't."

"Modal?"

"The modes are evocative *flavors* of scales, defined by characteristic notes. They're named after the Greek islands. There's one I played a little while ago that resonates the piano in a weird way. I thought for sure you'd see something when you opened the lid. It's close to the Locrian mode. And if I just change one note at the end..."

Hanson struck the keys, producing a thunderous cadence that left the air beating with a nauseating pulse as the sound faded.

Brooks raised the lid a crack and cold vapor drifted into the room, mingling with the milky light of the declining sun. Becca held the silver dragonfly aloft, activated it, and sent it buzzing into the fog with its headlight on. She leaned over the edge of the open piano and watched the ball of light descend into a foggy darkness that she knew shouldn't coexist with the space in which shadows cast by the piano legs stretched across the floor through dry air laden with dust motes. As the whine of the mechanical wings diminished, Becca focused on the screen in her hand. Brooks leaned in to watch while Hanson maintained his position at the keyboard. The video feed reminded Becca of footage she'd seen from submarine cameras passing through murky water heavy with silt. The fog stirred in swirls and eddies at the dragonfly's approach. For a while, it was all gray on gray with no reference points to steer by. She selected a preset flight pattern, a descending spiral, trusting the program to gently bring the drone down to whatever floor, if any, might lie below and prevent it from drifting too far from the piano-shaped portal.

At length, the dark shapes of spindly silhouettes came into view: bare winter trees, dead limbs intertwined in the mist, groping at the void above. The dragonfly crashed into one and fell to the ground. The screen went blind with static for a second, flickering in and out while Becca held her breath and waited for the little twitching machine to reset and right itself. Her stomach fluttered as she wondered if it would ever fly right again.

From the drone's vantage point on the ground, all they could see at first were the trunks of scrawny trees layered with gilled shelves of pallid fungus. The ground turned out to be a floor of hexagonal tiles, cracked and crumbling everywhere the tree trunks had grown through. Becca gently brought the drone into the air, let it hover at about the height of a man, and set it rotating on its axis to capture a panoramic view of the room. She exhaled. For all its tiny parts, the thing was built with military-grade durability.

At this height, she saw that the trees were candelabra. Each branch terminated in a small spike upon which a thick, cylindrical candle was impaled. Becca sent the drone to investigate one of these, following rivulets of frozen wax past something dark like a peach pit at the core, to a blackened wick ensconced in a crater at the top. "Candles," she said to Brooks. "Trees holding candles. A whole little forest of them."

"And they look to have been lit at least once," he said. "Fly it between the trees if you can. I want to see how far it goes."

"What if I lose it?"

"Don't worry. You can use the auto return if you have to and it'll find its way back to the remote."

She found a central path and sent the dragonfly soaring between the black limbs toward whatever limit it might find. Finally the trees gave way to a subterranean lagoon where the drone illuminated its own reflection on the surface of the still, black water.

"Bring it back," Brooks said.

Becca traced a swirl on the glass and soon the camera was moving between the trees again.

"It's not supposed to be a forest," Hanson said. "Ramirez described a shoreline, a beach."

"There's an underground lake," Brooks said.

"That's not the same. The key I used brought us somewhere else. We should get out and try again."

"How do we know the trees didn't grow after he was there?" Brooks asked.

"It's only been a few years. Trees don't grow that fast. And they don't grow on beaches."

"Not in *our* world. Maybe in this one they do."

"Is there sand on the ground?" Hanson asked. "Sea shells?"

"No," Becca said. "Tiles. There's a cracked tile floor."

"It's not the zone we're looking for," Hanson said. "We don't know what could be down there."

"My father could be down there."

"It's unlikely," Hanson said.

Becca leaned into the piano and called through the cavernous space, *"LUKE PHILIPS!"*

Brooks grabbed her shoulder and pulled her back. "You don't want to go announcing us. He's right, we don't know what might live down there, what you might stir."

"We're already flying a light around. I want to go down and have a look. The drone's no substitute for a pair of eyes. Who knows what we're missing?"

Brooks shook his head. "Bring it back up, Becca. Let's quit while we're ahead. I'm not sending you down for less than our objective. You could come back shell shocked like Burns, or not at all."

She looked him straight in the eyes and said, "There was something in the candle. We should take a sample. And the bug can't do it."

"What do you mean? What's in the candle?"

"Something dark hidden in the wax. Didn't you see it when I went in close? Maybe it's what you're looking for. Maybe Maurice hid whatever he hid in a candle, and hid that one in a forest of candles."

Brooks looked at Hanson, a vein twitching at his temple. Finally, to Becca, he said, "Show me."

Becca soon found that focusing on a precise close up was harder than general exploration. Eventually, she had the drone hovering a few inches from the candle, shining its piercing light into the depths of the wax. The candle was speckled with dim stripes, layers of some dusty substance embedded in the wax. A dark spot marred the center.

"Make sure you save the high-res photos," Brooks said.

"Caleb Wade was a candle maker," Hanson said. "He probably made these and placed them there."

Brooks scratched at the stubble on his cheek, coming to a decision. "She could go down and grab the one candle. First sign of trouble, we pull her out."

Hanson nodded agreement.

"Okay," Brooks said to Becca. "But if we have a reason to pull you out, you come without question. No resistance."

Becca took a coil of nylon rope from her pack. She clipped one end to her harness while Brooks tied the other securely around one of the piano legs. It was weird as hell to be anchoring her rope to the same object that represented the abyss she was about to rappel into. She tried not to think too much about it.

While she checked her buckles and adjusted her headlamp, the drone flew out of the piano, following its homing signal, and settled on the floor beside the remote. Becca sat on the edge of the piano and swung her leg over. Brooks situated himself next to the instrument, holding a few coils of rope. Fortunately, he had at least 50 pounds on her. Nonetheless, he called Proctor over to don a pair of gloves and put additional weight on the rope behind him. With tension established, Becca leaned back and braced herself against the inside of the piano with her knees. "Good to go," she said.

Brooks and Proctor lowered her into the hole. Sitting astride the piano, she hadn't feared the height. But now, moving through what felt like open air, her lip quivered from more than the cold. She clutched the rope tight despite the harness, descending down and down through darkness for what felt like too long before her boots scraped the floor.

"I'm down!" she called. Brooks tossed a few extra yards of rope into the piano, giving her enough slack to walk among the trees near her landing point. He shouted down, "Everything okay?"

"Yeah." She rubbed her prickled forearms. "It's so cold down here."

Becca's headlamp illuminated a small circle around her, misted with her breath, little more than the drone had covered. But as her eyes adjusted, she could see farther into the darkness than the camera could, and she quickly established a more continuous mental image of the space than she'd been able to compile through the glass. The dim shapes of stalactites confirmed what her echoing voice had suggested—that this was a cave. And yet, in keeping with the tile fragments beneath her boots, certain details of topography implied a man-made space: carved stone arches and ornamented pillars glimpsed dimly through the trees at the edge of the subterranean lake.

Now she could see that all of the candles contained the same shadow at their cores. Impulsively, and without calling up to consult Brooks, she fished a plastic cigarette lighter out of her shoulder bag, flicked it, and lit the nearest wick. She gasped as the entire forest of candle-laden branches ignited around her.

"What did you do?" Brooks yelled. "Did you do that?"

Becca turned slowly, surveying the forest of flames. She touched a branch of the nearest tree, expecting it to feel cold as iron, but her fingertips met the rough texture of bark. She walked the winding path between the glowing trees to the black lake, hearing the gently lapping water more than she could see it beyond the glow of the candles, their light coming up short of the bank. She listened for other sounds beyond the lapping water, the squeal of bats or the moaning of the wind through cavernous spaces high above, but the air was uncannily still. She turned her back to the water and gazed over the field of flickering flames, surmising that what little wind passed among them was derived from her passing.

"Becca?" Brooks called. "You okay?"

"I'm fine," she called back, feeling that the echo of her voice marred the hallowed silence like boot treads across virgin snow.

She squinted into the blackness again and detected a sound she had missed before: water dripping into water at long, lazy intervals. She aimed the white flood in the direction of the sound, squinting at its perimeter. The light described the contours of a circular marble platform in the center of the lagoon, either polished to a high gloss, or wet. Another droplet fell from the high ceiling and exploded in a spray like sparks from a struck anvil in the light cast from her crown.

"*Luke?*" she called, her voice cracking, the word enveloped in echo, undeliverable, returned to sender.

"Focus on what you came for," she said under her breath. "Take a candle and go."

She had reached the limit of her tether. The little tug reassured her that she was not alone, not cut off from the others down here in the dark. Something about the marble platform was deeply unsettling, and yet hard to look away from.

A scent reached her brain, complex and exotic, not entirely unpleasant. Something about it was stimulating, and she wondered if it was responsible for the buzzing sensation awakening at her third eye, beneath the elastic band of the headlamp. She searched for the source and saw that the candles had burned down to the first strata of dust frozen in their cores, releasing it to sizzle in the liquefied wax and unfurl in wisps of purple smoke. She watched, entranced as the vapor floated on a subterranean draft toward the gold-veined green marble dais. It coalesced in a spiral around the slow dripping water, and Becca felt suddenly that she was not alone. Her skin, clammy in the damp air, prickled at the certainty. The polar opposite of the umbilical connection she'd felt to her companions above via the nylon cord, this was an overpowering sense of icy intimacy with something alien.

She backed away from the lake.

Now she could hear more drops falling behind and around her—wax dripping on the cracked tiles like rain—as she retreated up the path, gathering the excess rope in her hands, afraid of breaking into a run and tripping on it but still feeling the urge to flee. The dark seeds at the candle cores were visible now: speckled eggs from which the wicks grew like veiny roots. Becca didn't want to be down here when those eggs hatched and spilled their contents. What had she set in motion? She had only wanted a little more light.

Looking up, she found the piano hole in the calcified ceiling, the curved shape illuminating the fog she had passed through to reach the cavern floor. She tugged on the rope. "Bring me up!"

The eggs sizzled. A shiver ran through her body and her throat constricted under the pressure of her pulse. "What did I do? *Shit. What did I do?*"

The rope zipped through her gloved hands, then snapped taut and tugged at her harness.

The eggs popped all at once, unspooling ribbons of light, tongues of green fire. They wriggled through the smoky air toward the lagoon; shoaling, swooping and turning as one body until they were spiraling around the dripping water on the marble dais, merging into the coherent form of a single being, something dancing, swirling, trailing skirts of luminous flesh, something female, abominable.

Becca's heart thundered. Her boots left the ground. She focused on the pale light above and the rope pulling her toward it until she was passing through the wood frame to the sound of Django barking. Brooks grabbed hold of her, hauled her out of the piano, and together they spilled to the floor.

"Close it," she cried, scrambling. "Close it before it gets out!"

Chapter 9

"What was it? What did I see down there?" The four of them sat at the kitchen table. Becca warmed her hands with a cup of tea Brooks had made for her. She had just described the formation of the creature on the marble disc in the black lake, and if anyone could tell her what she'd seen, it was Proctor. She asked again, "Do you know?"

"Shabat Cycloth," the reverend said. He seemed stunned by her description.

"What's that?" Brooks asked.

"The consort of Lung Crawthok."

Brooks pulled a chair out and sat down across from Proctor, elbows braced on the tabletop, fingers steepled under his chin. "I think it's time you told us what this house means to the Starry Wisdom Church. I feel like we're poking a nest and we don't even know what species made it. What are we dealing with?"

"Some scholars believe the house itself is a garment of Yog Sothoth, the gate and the key."

"You're talking gibberish again," Brooks said. "What does that mean?"

"Think of the house as a hermit crab shell. Curled around the core of it is a god that is itself a doorway to the realm of the gods."

"And this god is named Yog Sothoth?" Brooks asked.

"Yes."

"What about the other gods you mentioned; Crawdaddy and Cyclone or whatever the fuck? What are they?"

"Lung Crawthok is the guardian. He dwells on the threshold and keeps the unworthy out. His consort, Shabat Cycloth, is the Lady of a Thousand Hooks. They copulate on the threshold of the beyond, and she spawns the fishers of men, the eels that pierce the flesh and drag their prey to the feeding of Yog Sothoth."

Brooks squeezed his eyes shut and pinched the bridge of his nose. "He's speaking English, right? He's speaking English and I feel like I need a translator."

Hanson cleared his throat. "Let's not get too carried away with cosmology. The bottom line is the music opens different zones on the borderland. The one we found today is not the one Ramirez used. So we keep trying until we find the place he described."

"But you don't even know what he hid down there," Becca said. "You don't know what you're looking for."

Brooks looked at Proctor. "We're hoping it's a weapon. Something that can be used against an incursion."

Proctor nodded. "It may be."

"And we need to find it so no one else ever does," Brooks finished.

Becca rubbed her arms, the chill of her first descent still clinging to her. "No matter what we stir up in the process?"

"Can you think of a better plan?" Hanson asked. "Are we supposed to leave the house alone and wait for it to stir on its own? We have to take some action, even if it involves risk."

"So you're going to keep trying different combinations on the keyboard until we stumble on the right one?"

"I don't think that will be necessary." Northrup spoke from the entryway where he had crept up on their conversation. "Hanson, come with me."

At the west end of the first floor, Northrup ushered Hanson into a room Becca had only peered into once, the game room. Waiting in the hall with Brooks and Proctor, she could hear a clacking sound, like pebbles being dropped in a pile, accompanied by a wavering voice humming softly. She craned her neck into the doorframe and watched Hanson take a seat on the sidewall, careful not to disturb the strange exercise in progress at the center of the room.

Nina sat cross-legged on the floral carpet next to Mark Burns. A wooden backgammon set lay nearby, the board neglected while Mark stacked the black and white game pieces in perfect little towers. He used more black than white, and the combination put Becca in mind of the inverse keyboard on the piano upstairs. The association gave her a little thrill of recognition at what he was doing, but her sense of rising hope was tempered by Mark's disheveled state: his eyes were glassy, his hair — usually meticulous — was chaotic, and his chin was raw, irritated from wiping off drool. He licked his chapped lips compulsively, and hummed a low dirge. An untouched glass of water occupied a coaster on a nearby end table. Becca got the idea that Nina would have offered it to him, if not for fear of breaking his concentration. She sat stone still, holding a voice recorder in her lap.

"I don't get it," Brooks said.

Nina shot him a reproachful glance and Becca shushed him.

"He's communicating in music," Becca whispered. "They represent black and white keys."

Hanson held his hand up to Northrup's ear and whispered something. Northrup left the room, hurried down the hall, and returned a moment later with Hanson's sheet music folder under his arm and a pencil in his hand. He passed these to Hanson and took a seat in the corner. Hanson shuffled through the papers, found a blank sheet of staff paper, and began transcribing.

For a time, everyone seemed to be holding their breath, as if a toppled stack of backgammon chips would bring the house down around them. Mark seemed completely oblivious to their presence until he laid a final black piece down and spread his hands above his creation, eyes wide with delight. He looked like a magician about to perform a trick guaranteed to draw gasps of awe. The humming had ceased, and now he laughed, a wild outburst of private amusement brimming from deep in his chest.

Hanson made a quick erasure on the page, brushed the leavings aside with his pinky, and resumed his quick notations, rushing to get it down before the chips fell or his memory of the chords evaporated. At last he set the pencil down and exhaled.

As if on cue, the four black and white stacks collapsed, and the spell was broken.

Mark dragged the back of his wrist across his chin, blinked and looked around at his silent audience. "What's everybody looking at me for?"

* * *

Becca needed air. The veranda wrapped around the front of the house in a U shape with doors leading onto it from many rooms. She found the nearest of these through an ugly sitting room with pink wallpaper that reminded her of vomit, cranked on the handle and pushed through the door. She took a deep, icy breath, looking out over the dead lawn, a flurry of snowflakes swirling down off of the overhanging roof, stinging her hot cheeks and catching in her hair.

The sight of snow, actual white snow, shocked her, and she realized she had become accustomed to the black ash flakes that covered the fields surrounding the house. Now black and white mingled in the air, just as they had in Mark's trembling fingers moments ago. But, as if in mimicry of the dreadful piano that lay in wait on the second floor, the black remained dominant.

She leaned over the railing and looked up at the house. The deck boards seemed to lurch beneath her feet as she surveyed the façade from this new angle. Then the door clicked open behind her and Nina stepped out, pulling her coat tight around her throat against the cold, and laying a hand on Becca's back.

"Are you okay?" Nina asked. "You shouldn't be out here without a proper jacket. You'll catch a cold."

"I just needed some air. This place is a bit much, that's all." Becca ran her hand through her hair and exhaled sharply. "Even out here...it's like the angles are all wrong."

"They are," Nina said. "There were a couple of studies conducted here in the 70s on the effects of asymmetrical manmade environments on the human psyche. I've been looking them over, and it's true, the place causes distress and nausea. Not as extreme as what some people experience in places like the MIT Stata Center, with its really wild angles, but nothing in this place was done according to the standard building codes your body is accustomed to. The Wade House was designed to be off balance in almost every dimension. It's mostly subtle, but all of those little misalignments add up."

"*Now* you tell me," Becca said. "I'm over sensitive to things like that."

"I know. I also know how hard winter can be for you. You've shown incredible resilience in coming back here to help."

Becca looked up at the sky and shook her head. "Fucking January."

Nina drummed her fingers on the railing. "You know, it's named for the Roman god, Janus, the two-faced lord of beginnings and endings, gateways and doors."

"Huh. Sounds like what the reverend was talking about." Becca took a pillbox from the pocket of her hoodie. She plucked a small, round tablet from the assortment, swallowed it dry, and snapped the lid shut.

"Klonopin?" Nina asked.

"Dramamine. Mark gave me some for seasickness."

Nina swept her gaze over the lines of the house. "That bad, huh?"

Becca nodded. "So, why was the house built at odd angles?"

"The architecture is based on a mathematical pattern. Like the golden ratio. You're familiar with it?"

"Sure. They teach it in composition class."

"Well, like the golden ratio, found in countless natural patterns from the nautilus shell to the proportions of the human face, there are other occult patterns, far less pleasing by our *human* standards. Patterns that resonate with another world, where life evolved along *different* lines."

"Were you always such an expert on this stuff, and it just never came up in our sessions?" Becca said. "How long have you been working for SPECTRA?"

"Not long, honestly. I've learned a lot since that autumn two years ago."

Becca brushed a snowflake out of her hair and watched it melt on her finger. "I don't know if I can stay here. They don't need me. Brooks has the sight, and now Mark does, too. At this rate, the reverend will have it next."

"If you haven't noticed, Mark isn't exactly of sound mind after passing through the shadow side of the house."

"And I should keep meddling with this stuff so I can end up the same?"

"I'm not telling you that you should, but you do have a way of looking at things, a way of exposing the nature of things."

"Everyone keeps saying that. I don't know why."

"Not everyone in your position would have rappelled down into that place and lit a candle."

"All that makes me is reckless. Seems like that would be a liability, given how volatile this whole situation is."

"But you intuitively did exactly what was needed to reveal the nature of that zone. We know more about what we're dealing with because of the action you took, and no one was hurt."

"*Yet.*"

"That's the kind of progress we're depending on. It's what this whole operation is about."

"Proctor was the one who knew what hatched and formed down there. Not me. I was just poking in the dark."

"Success depends on the team, Becca. Different strengths. Yours is intuition."

"I'm not risking my sanity because my shrink—who turns out to be in bed with a spy agency—likes how I score on a Myers-Briggs test."

"Hey...that's not fair."

"Maybe what's not fair is leading me into this by trying to make it personal."

"What's that supposed to mean?"

"When Jason came to Brazil, he said my father might be trapped or lost in the house. Did you tell him that would hook me?"

Nina looked down at her hands on the railing. "I thought you would want to know."

"Did they really find his motorcycle here? Is that even true?"

"It's true," Brooks said from between the double doors behind them. "Give Nina a break. It was my idea to bring you in. You wanna see the bike?"

Becca nodded.

"C'mon. It's in the barn."

* * *

Becca hesitated at the barn door while Brooks stepped inside and turned on the lights.

"You coming?"

"Yeah. I just..." She squeezed the fingertips of one gloved hand with the other. "The last time I was here was with Mark. Before what happened to him."

"Right."

"He uh...decided to study the ocean because his mother drowned when he was young, and now he probably doesn't even remember her."

Brooks walked past what looked like a rusting antique wood lathe, swept a tarp aside and threw it atop a stack of baled hay, revealing a motorcycle Becca hadn't seen in years but recognized at once: a late 90s Harley Davidson. Black and chrome, nothing fancy, but it still had the same studded leather saddlebags she remembered.

The walk down the hill and across the creek had provided some relief from the psychological pressure of the house. But seeing her father's bike and knowing that he could be trapped in the folds of that awful place—shattered like Mark, whose sanity had been blasted away by revelation—brought the full weight of it crashing down on her again as if she'd never set foot outside.

And she was twelve again.

Luke had mounted this bike and lit out for the hills in the wake of his wife's suicide, leaving his daughter in the care of his mother, despite the woman's obsessive devotion to the study of dark arts that Becca only dimly understood to be connected to the loss they had suffered.

Why come back after all these years? Why come to a place that was effectively ground zero for the forces he'd fled?

Brooks gave Becca space and watched as she stepped forward, running her hand over the cold metal of the gas tank, the worn leather of the seat. It seemed for a moment that the barn doors had opened on another time. She was back in the garage of her grandmother's house in Arkham, where they lived before the black tide of puberty had drowned her in hormones, grief, and depression.

Her hands moved idly over the sleek contours of the machine with an agenda of their own, and before she paused to think about what she was doing, she unbuckled the straps and was opening the nearest saddlebag.

"They photographed and logged that stuff and then put it back how it was before we brought the bike to the barn," Brooks said. "He doesn't seem to have left anything else behind on the property or in the house. Nothing we can identify as his, anyway, except for a few spent cigarettes."

Becca rummaged through the sparse contents of the pouch: an oil stained rag, a pack of Marlboro Lights, a fat, white piece of worn-down sidewalk chalk, and a single Lincoln log. She sensed Brooks' scrutiny from the corner of the barn where he stood with his hands in his pockets.

"What do you suppose the chalk is for?" Becca asked.

Brooks shifted in her peripheral vision. "You've seen chalk before in places like this."

"You mean the circle and symbols we found in my Gran's secret basement?"

"That's one example, sure."

"Did you find any chalk markings in the house when you first scoped it out?"

"Not inside. But there were protective symbols on the outside doors done in chalk. Probably *that* chalk. I think rain might have washed them off while I was bringing you back from Brazil."

"What kind of protective symbols?"

"The Elder Sign and some Enochian letters, names of angels."

"Sounds like the wards Maurice used to spray paint in abandoned buildings on the waterfront."

"Yeah. Same symbols. I don't know how much they help, but we have a team working on how to draw them with the proper incantations, as a precaution or a last resort, depending on how you want to look at it."

"He never wanted anything to do with magic."

"When's the last time you saw him?"

Becca sighed. "My grandfather's funeral. He got into a fight with Catherine and stormed off on this bike."

"So you don't know what he's gotten into since then."

She walked around the motorcycle and unbuckled the other saddlebag: empty except for a guitar pick. "Was there anything in here they didn't put back?"

"Half a sandwich and a deck of tarot cards they're still studying. So much for Dad shunning the occult, huh?"

Becca put the guitar pick in her pocket. Brooks didn't stop her.

"I notice you didn't ask about the Lincoln log," Brooks said.

"Huh?"

"You asked why he would have a piece of chalk, but not a Lincoln log. Does it mean something to you?"

She shook her head. "No, I don't know."

"It just seems like such a random item to carry around. We can't figure it out."

"Like you said, I don't know what he's into. Maybe it's just the right size for some kind of quirky motorcycle maintenance."

Brooks laughed. *"Black Magick and the Art of Motorcycle Maintenance...*You know, like *Zen and the—"*

"Yeah, I know. You've *read* that book?"

"I was married to Nina. Heard of it? Yeah. Read it? No."

Becca closed the saddle bag, her pulse pounding. She tried to steady her breath before turning to face Brooks. Maybe she should tell him what the log meant. She might need his help. Or maybe she was finished here and should just get out.

But before she could decide, his walkie crackled. Northrup's voice came through, charged with urgency: "Brooks, where are you? Get up here, now. Proctor's gone rogue."

Chapter 10

John Proctor raised the piano top board and propped it. The physicist and the unhinged biologist were still downstairs in the game room, humming melodies to each other and trying to sort out chord voicings on a portable electronic keyboard. Northrup had brought it in so they could work on the riddle of the music without the risk of the actual house piano, which derived its power as a portal from its orientation to the angles of the room in which Caleb Wade had placed it.

Proctor found the rope the girl had used to descend still tied to the piano leg. Twice her age and in half the physical condition, he doubted his strength, but he knew this might be his only chance. He had to seize it. At least he wouldn't need to climb back up.

He put on the work gloves Brooks had given him when he'd helped to haul Becca out of the chasm, checked the snug fit of his dagger in his belt, took a deep breath, and scanned his surroundings. This might very well be his last look at the terrestrial realm. It felt strange to be traveling so light, but really, what did he need for such a journey? His sights were set on the far shore, the realm of the gods who would provide for him, if they didn't devour him. He was willing to take that chance, to resign his fate to the guardians of the gate. Better to be judged by them than by any earthly jury.

He hesitated, thinking of what remaining family he would be leaving behind—his sister and nephews in Iraq, to whom Northrup had promised asylum in America. Wouldn't Leyla be justified in judging him? Wouldn't she be right to tell his nephews that their persecution under the hardline Islamic regime could have been assuaged by their uncle, their suffering brought to an end, and the freedom to practice their faith granted by a man who had instead chosen his own liberation over theirs?

It was true he had used them as chess pieces that SPECTRA believed had the power to buy his cooperation. Even after they had tortured him and concluded that he had no part in Darius Marlowe's cosmic terrorism, they had still required collateral before entrusting him with access to the Wade House.

And yet, even after his interrogation, he *still* felt no drive to initiate the foretold apocalypse. He was not a vengeful man. He had glimpsed the magnificence of the infinite, the cold glory of the void, early in life and understood that his communion with and service to the lords whose wisdom was so vast as to render his own equivalent to that of a dust mite—this attainment and no other was worthy of his striving, this relationship the only one that ultimately mattered. If his nephews studied the holy books well, they too would one day come to understand what had driven him to leave the world behind and jettison all terrestrial ties, even family, as ballast from a ship in perilous straits.

What his keepers had failed to grasp in their assessment of him was that he—like the gods he worshipped—bore no hatred in his heart for humankind; he simply found it insignificant, irrelevant.

He ran his hands over his clothes, felt the iron rod in his pocket, and realized that he was procrastinating. Was he afraid? Yes, of course he was. He would have to be mad to face this threshold without fear. He felt a pang of regret at having to leave his books behind, but it would be impractical to travel the terrain that lay ahead with a sack of tomes. It was time to accept that he had learned all he could from study in this life. The time for theory had passed. He stood on the precipice of practice.

With the harness straps adjusted to his girth and the rope trailing from his waist, he stepped around to the keyboard and raised the cover. Before taking his vows and departing for the seminary in Croatia, he had played the organ for the Starry Wisdom Church choir in his duties as attendant to the reverend in Salem.

It had been many years, and his fingers felt awkward on the keys, but he made a deliberate effort not to panic and rush. He would sound no note until he was sure of the chords.

Now or never.

He wondered again if he should have destroyed Wade's book. He'd attempted to, but his hand had faltered at the crucial moment. It seemed a shame to desecrate the document to which he owed his impending exaltation. And what did it matter? The "scholars" on SPECTRAs payroll were fools. No one would glean what *he* had from Caleb Wade's book of shadows.

Another deep breath, and on the exhalation he struck the chords, his scarred and disjointed fingers clawing at the ebony keys.

The keys to transcendence.

The air trembled and he felt a warm, humid draught pass through the cool, dusty room.

Proctor rose and gazed into the piano. Lavender light stretched across the sand below, throwing long shadows from rocks and shells. The Shore of Eternal Twilight. He sat on the edge of the piano, grasped the rope tight, and slipped off into the void. The rope surprised him, flying between his gloved hands and scorching the leather as he descended, struggling to tighten his grip. The smell of burning hide reached his nostrils, and he felt a surge of fear that soon the rope would burn through the gloves and strip the flesh from his palms.

With a jolt, the harness caught him, and he swung like a pendulum out over the breaking waves, his stomach plunging.

The ocean smelled like no earthly ocean; there was salt, yes, but it mingled in the air with other spices—dark, sweet, and dimly familiar. Over the years he had concocted incense recipes from the pages of grimoires with the intention of emulating this scent. He knew now that his efforts had missed the mark. It was a heady, intoxicating atmosphere, and breathing it he overcame his vertigo. Swinging, he fumbled with the harness, found the controlled release, and fearing that he would plummet to his death — but if death came with the mist of this forbidden ocean in his lungs, then so be it — he let out a few feet of rope, then clamped down on the feed and halted with a lurch.

He took a deep breath, assured now that he could control his descent, and gently fed the cable through the pulleys in short bursts, lowering himself to the beach.

The sound of the surf roared in his ears. He drank in the fragrant vapor, eyes closed, reveling in the moment, twisting his sandaled foot into the damp sand. He looked up at the sky, at the impossible piano shaped hole in the low clouds.

Time to move. Time to disappear before they pursued him.

He unclipped the harness and pulled it over his shoulders, then unsheathed his knife and severed the harness from the rope. Had they taken him for such a helpless fool that he couldn't restore the sharp edge they had filed off of the blade?

He plodded up the beach and surveyed the horizon. It was true what he had read about the waterline receding over the years, as if the cosmic ocean were withdrawing from the borderland. Still, not much had changed since the days of the prophets. The rotting hull of the schooner *Emma* still lay on its side in the shallows, the brick and mortar walls of the labyrinth shone in shafts of gray light atop the ridge overlooking the shore. He followed the line of the crumbling wall to where it met the black gates twisting away from the marble pillars they had once been anchored to, held up now by the thorny, poisonous vines that ran rampant among the beach grass.

He wondered if he would find the gates impassable. If he did, perhaps he would climb the wall where great white dunes had massed against it like snowdrifts.

He tugged the burned gloves off and tossed them on the sand, then took the dowsing rod from the pocket of his frock coat.

It felt cold in his hands and buzzed with a gentle vibration. He had felt this same vibration, deep in its core from the first time he'd held it, but it was stronger down here. The rod was made of meteoric iron; a kind of tuning fork forged from the fundamental elements of blood and starlight.

Holding the rod by its curved handles, he paced down the beach, watching the long central shaft, focusing all his efforts on clearing his mind and keeping the rod steady and perpendicular to the ground. It was heavy, and soon his arms were slicked with perspiration. The air was much warmer down here than it had been up above in January. He almost laughed at the realization that he now thought of January as a place he had left behind without an airplane. He wondered what month it was here on the twilit shore, and if there would be seasons in the spheres that lay beyond.

He would only find out if he could find the key to the innermost gate that awaited him at the heart of the labyrinth, the secret heart of the Wade House.

The dowsing rod tugged to the left, leading him up the beach like a dog on a leash. He followed its impulses, careful not to interfere until it jerked violently downward, sending a jolt of pain through his wrists. He slowed his step, turned on his axis, and loosened his grip. The rod dove again as he passed it over a horseshoe crab shell.

Anticipation brimmed in his chest as he knelt in the sand and set the dowsing rod down beside the shell. He was afraid to believe it could be this simple, afraid to hope that he wouldn't find himself held at gunpoint, handcuffed, and hoisted back up through the hole in the sky before searching even half the terrain laid out before him.

John Proctor laid his hand on the spiky umber shell and turned it over. His breath hitched and his eyes brimmed with tears. There it was, locked in the embrace of the crab's legs: the silver key.

He slid a finger under the filigreed grip and pulled. The desiccated crab legs cracked and crumbled and the key came loose in his hand, his pulse pounding against it through his clammy palm.

* * *

Brooks dropped through the hole, the sound of the cable zipping through his harness filling his ears until it was overwhelmed by the sounds of wind and surf. They had quickly fitted him with military grade equipment, the harness set for a swift, controlled descent, leaving his hands free to ready his weapon as the beach raced toward him. The second his feet hit the ground he unclipped the cable and ran for the ridge he had seen on the way down. Footprints marked the hard-packed sand near the touchdown point but disappeared in the looser sand higher up the beach. Climbing the ridge, he lost the reverend's trail altogether in the beach grass. But there could be little doubt of his destination—the only constructed features marking the landscape in this zone: the black gate and stone wall.

Brooks bounded up the slope, struggling to step quickly against the sand collapsing around his shoes, and crested the ridge huffing.

A metallic shriek cut the air; the black iron gate was opening. And was that a black cloak fluttering in the wind before it? From this distance, Brooks couldn't tell, nor could he take an accurate shot. And taking a wild shot would only alert Proctor that the chase was on. He ran for the gate, hoping to close the distance before he was seen.

When he reached the gate, he found it ajar. Beyond, a sand swept corridor stretched away to a marble pedestal topped with a water-filled basin. Proctor stood on the far side, gesticulating over the bowl as he chanted. Brooks raised his weapon and stalked forward, keeping the reverend's tattooed forehead centered on his sight blade as he advanced. He supposed the man could duck and use the marble basin for cover, but there was nowhere else to hide. He was reminded of the birdbath at Allston Asylum, and his stomach fluttered. Beyond Proctor, something shimmered, like a curtain of silver fabric.

"What's your game, John?" Brooks said. "You still trying to conjure monsters from birdbaths? That never worked for you before, why would it now? You may know the spells, but you don't have the voice."

Proctor laughed. "Where I'm going, I won't need it. I will walk amongst them on the streets of their own city. Here, I'm merely paying admission." Proctor drew his knife from its sheath, sliced the palm of his hand, and squeezed a trickle of blood out the bottom of his fist into the water.

Brooks almost moved to tackle him and take the stab wound if necessary, but he remembered what had happened to Becca's friend Rafael when he got too close to that birdbath. The only other option was to shoot and risk sending whatever secrets the reverend kept into oblivion with him. "Admission to what?"

"Did you like the amusement park when you were a boy, Agent Brooks?"

"Sure. Until I figured out the games were rigged."

"My aunt used to take me when the carnival came to Innsmouth. I liked the fun house, the hall of mirrors…"

Brooks advanced slowly while Proctor talked. At this range he couldn't miss.

"This place is the ultimate hall of mirrors. It will lead me beyond the Shore of Eternal Twilight and deliver me unto the city of the Great Old Ones."

"And then what? You'll lead them back out?"

"I've no interest in destroying this world. Don't you see? I just want out of it. It's all I've ever wanted, to go beyond. You can keep your dirty, poisoned Earth. I'm going to a place of starlight and primordial waters. I'll take my chances with dark gods over you white devils every time." Proctor stepped backward toward the shimmering curtain. Brooks saw that it was a waterfall pouring over a marble lintel, a sheet of silver water falling through a slot in the granite floor at Proctor's feet. The reverend backed up toward it and raised an admonishing bloody hand.

"Don't try to follow me," he said. "Without the proper sacrifice, these waters would wash the flesh clean off your bones."

"What about the weapon?" Brooks asked. "You said Ramirez hid a weapon on this beach. Something that would protect us if they came through again. Where is it? *What* is it?"

"It was never a weapon. But I know how you people think, and you would have looked for nothing less."

"What then?"

Proctor drew something from a pocket. Brooks almost put a bullet through his head before it emerged, but he controlled himself, resisted the irrevocable act.

"It's the thing you value least, my friend. A key to the sacred." Proctor turned the silver key in his fingers. The light of the ever-setting sun flared off its angles as he stepped back under the curtain of falling water and disappeared.

Brooks moved around the basin, just close enough to see ribbons of blood twisting in the water. He approached the curtain and raised his hand, but stopped short of touching the falling water, folded his fingers into a fist, and hammered it down against his thigh. *"Fuck!"*

He heard a crash like thunder, and looked back through the crooked iron gates at the shore beyond where foam and spray were raining down on the diminishing beach from a crashing wave. From what he understood of this zone, the tides had been receding for decades, retreating from the ridge the wall was built on. Was the sea now reclaiming that territory? Had Proctor's actions accelerated the process? He approached the gate, and now there could be no doubt: the beach he had just walked was vanishing fast under the encroaching tide. He scanned the sky, found the odd curved hole in the low clouds, and followed the line of his rope to where it now floated beyond the breakers.

Brooks looked again at the curtain of crystal water, and resisted the impulse to dash through it in pursuit of Proctor. He was out of his depth, couldn't know if the man had lied about the lethality of that threshold to the uninitiated. And now his escape route was escaping him. If he had any hope of returning to his own world, he had to act quickly.

He holstered his gun, pushed through the gate, and bounded down the ridge, splashing into the rising surf. A dark wave towered over him on the brink of crashing, and he dove into it. The water felt unnatural, phlegmy on his skin, the taste of it in his nostrils repulsive, but he didn't let it deter him, couldn't, or he would die here. He swam beyond the breakers, and searched the sky for the rope. There—dangling from the cloud ceiling, about twenty yards out. He swam toward it, the water burning his eyes, the pulse of the tide rocking him, pushing him back toward the shore. He fought against the current, and took one last look at the ridge, the wall, and the gate.

A shape walked to the water. A woman? She dipped a toe in the surf and her glistening black body unwound—a shoal of slimy ribbons of flesh slapping into the foam and racing toward him, cutting streamers of agitation on the water's black surface.

Brooks swam harder. His muscles cried out and a stitch seared his side. He caught sight of the rope, undulating in the air nearby, and launched himself at it with two powerful kicks. He seized the rope and wound it once around his body, then pulled the slack in, feeling for the end of it until the metal clamp was in his hand. The icy water numbed his fingers as he fumbled with the hardware.

He sensed the swarm of eels closing in on him, spared a glance toward the beach, and saw a flare of white water cutting the surface like a torpedo. The lead lamprey creature surged forward and latched its needle teeth through his soaked shirt, piercing his chest. Blood sprayed against his neck and his mind went white with pain.

He succeeded in hooking the clamp onto the harness and screamed at the sky, "*UP!* Bring me *up!*"

His body rose from the water. The eel clung to him, sucking blood from his breast. Two more explosions of pain registered from his right calf and left thigh and set him kicking frantically at the leaping, snapping swarm.

The cable tugged him steadily higher and now he could see the surf sweeping white foam below him. With his hands freed by the harness, he squeezed the slimy black monster trying to bore its way to his heart until it released its grip. He cast it at the water below and stared in horror through his ripped shirt at the ring of punctures weeping blood around his nipple. He thrashed in the air, knocking his legs together in an effort to dislodge the two remaining eels, dimly aware that he must look like a fish wriggling on the hook.

After an excruciating eternity, he was passing through the darkness of the piano frame with hands groping at his clothing, catching him under his arms, and hauling him out. He hit the wood floor with a wet slap and someone was beating his legs with something blunt until the teeth let go. Panicked shouts filled the air until the blood drained from his head and gray darkness welled up, and the horrors went away for a while.

Chapter 11

Becca watched the cable zipping out of the piano and winding onto the electric spindle. She could smell the salt water even before the soaked section at the end came over the lip with a spray of mist. He would be close now. She wanted to look into the hole, but the brawny black-clad agents with their boots and gloves and side arms were huddled close around the cable feed, and she would only get in the way. She hung back, biting her thumbnail and feeling helpless.

A tang of spice and rot bloomed in the air and then the men were reaching in, straining against the awkward shape, cursing and directing each other, trying not to knock the leg that propped the lid up. She wondered why they hadn't unscrewed the hinges and taken the damned thing off. Maybe they were afraid to tamper with anything in the house lest they inadvertently open a portal they could never close again.

They hauled Brooks out, kicking and groaning through his gritted teeth. He hit the floor hard, despite their best efforts to set him down easy—his flailing limbs knocking their hands off. At least two eels were latched onto his legs, biting through his soaked black jeans. One of the agents tried pummeling one of the creatures, beating his fist against it in vain. Another drew a tactical knife from a sheath strapped to his leg, setting off a string of anxious protest from Northrup. A third man stepped forward with a length of what looked like piano string, and Becca wondered just how many odd implements of death these guys kept in their kits. She watched him wrap the wire around an eel near the mouth and pull tight, cutting through the black skin of the thing and into its red meat until the creature let go its grip and hit the floor with a slap. The second agent had traded his knife for a baton and was beating it against the remaining eel—hard enough to fracture Brooks' femur if he missed—when it, too, let go.

Brooks coughed brine onto the floor and passed out. When they turned him over, Becca saw blood oozing from a ragged hole in his shirt.

The agent with the piano wire put his ear to Brooks' mouth. "He's breathing."

"Get a stretcher up here," Northrup ordered. "Get him to Medical at base. Now!"

One agent hurried out of the room and down the stairs. Another closed the piano.

Becca moved in and knelt beside Brooks. She took his hand. It was freezing, and his complexion had a bluish hue. Beside her, someone crawled forward on the floor, and turning, she saw that it was Mark Burns. But he hadn't come forward to check on Brooks; he was scooping up one of the eels in his hands, turning it over gingerly, examining it with an expression of rapt fascination on his face.

"*Mayomyzon pieckoensis?*" He probed the creature with his index finger. It contracted like a spasming muscle and Becca yelped.

"No..." He chuckled. "Similar, but no. Look at the hypopharyngeal ridge. A parallel evolution? Is it even a lamprey?"

Becca shuffled away from him on her knees, afraid that the creature would snap his finger off or slip out of his grasp and fasten its rings of teeth into her. Burns seemed beyond concern for his own safety. She was relieved when he rose and carried the thing out of the room. A moment later she heard water running down the hall. Apparently, he had deposited it in the bathtub.

The agent Northrup had sent for the stretcher returned with it, and they soon had Brooks strapped in. A pair of agents carried him from the room with Northrup at their heels, issuing commands into his walkie-talkie.

Becca looked around the room at the blood and water puddled on the floor, and her eyes settled on Dick Hanson. She hadn't noticed him until now. He was standing behind the keyboard, staring down at it, rumpled and sweaty, his sheet music clutched in his hand. He met Becca's gaze, and reading her undisguised fear, said, "He'll be okay." She couldn't tell if he believed it.

The floor shook. Becca threw her arm out to grab for the nearest anchor, but finding nothing, bent her knees and swayed. Her first thought was that they had dropped the stretcher on the stairs, sending a jolt through the floor, but she quickly rejected the notion. The tremor was too strong. Earthquake strong. Combined with the eels and the seawater, she couldn't help feeling that the floor was the deck of a boat, or that the house itself was adrift on whatever subterranean ocean they'd just hoisted Brooks out of.

Her stomach dropped. The wall tilted. Hanson slammed into the piano, buckling over the keyboard and eliciting a dissonant burst of notes. Shards of crystal from the broken chandelier rolled across the floor from the pile they'd been swept into.

Becca hit the floor. She couldn't tell if she'd slipped in a puddle, lost her balance, or both. She looked up at Hanson. He was holding onto the piano, staring at her through the wrong end of a telescope, far away and small as the room warped and stretched into a corridor. Then something passed between them, a reflection in the glossy black lacquer of the piano: a black-clad man with barbed letters tattooed on his face. Becca looked opposite the reflection, expecting to see Proctor. Was that the hem of his frock passing out of the room into the sunlit hall?

Someone seized her arm and pulled her to her feet. She saw it was Hanson and came along. He had somehow covered the distance between them and was leading her from the room, taking advantage of the current pitch of the floor to pull her forward. She knew at any second it might tilt the other way, but for now gravity was in their favor, urging them toward the doorway where a moment ago she'd glimpsed the fleeting black fabric.

But when they rounded the corner and slammed into the banister, there was no sign of Proctor on the stairs below. Plaster dust flurried from the ceiling as cracks fractured the wall like time-lapse vines climbing for the sky. Somewhere, glass shattered. Holding onto each other and the railing, Becca and Hanson began their descent. And then she remembered.

"Mark," she shouted over the din. "We have to go back for Mark."

"Where?"

"The bathroom, I think."

Hanson gazed up the buckling stairs and shook his head. "Too late."

"We can't leave him."

"Are you sure he's up there?"

As if in reply, a keening wail sounded from the second floor, cutting through the rumble. Becca broke from Hanson's grip and climbed the stairs, her feet skipping two out of three steps. The stairs looked closer than they were and she couldn't shake the feeling that she was seeing them through warped lenses. Finally, she dropped to all fours and used her hands to clamber up the rest of the way. Hanson didn't follow. He lingered on the landing, watching her.

She found Mark in the bathroom, kneeling beside the tub, wringing his hands. He looked like a child praying beside a bed, and when his words resolved in her mind out of the stream of syllables issuing urgently from his lips, she realized it was a kind of prayer or petition, though to whom it was directed, she couldn't say: "No, please... Don't go...no, no, no, no, no."

Becca stepped tentatively toward him and put her hand on his shoulder. "Mark, we have to get out of here. The house is falling down."

He shook his head, still staring at the water where a black ribbon was unraveling in inky tendrils. "It's a new species, it's a m-missing piece of the f-fossil record. I need samples, need to...photograph it." He looked at her pleadingly, his eyes wild and bloodshot. "Can you photograph it? Please?"

"I'm sorry, I can't. I don't have my camera. You have to come with me, Mark. You have to come now. The house is falling apart! Now!"

He looked at the ceiling, as if only now comprehending that the unraveling transcended the boundaries of the bathtub. Then he looked back at the water. All that remained of the creature was a gelatinous black lump the size of a grape floating in a black cloud. "No!" He thrust his hands under the water and tried to scoop it up, but came away with ink-stained empty palms, rivulets of black running from his wrists to his elbows.

Becca retched at the putrid, fishy stench. She wanted to make him rinse the stuff off in the sink, feared that it might eat away at his skin, infect him with something, maybe something contagious, something that could worm into his nervous system. But there was no time. The house was breaking apart, the thunder crack of beams splitting and the rumble of foundation stones grinding was deafening. Or was that the sound of *worlds* grinding against each other like gears, cogs in some infernal machine slipping into alignment?

She took a fistful of his clothing, the collar of his cardigan and the t-shirt beneath it, and yanked him to his feet. Thankfully, he didn't slip on the wet tiles, but found his footing and allowed her to usher him out of the bathroom and into the hall.

Another loud crack. Becca looked over her shoulder as the bathroom mirror shattered in a rain of shards dancing in the sink. Arcane letters tattooed on olive skin slid past in the silvered glass.

* * *

"The US Geological Survey recorded a 4.2 magnitude earthquake centered in Concord at 3:23 PM, followed by two small aftershocks," Northrup announced from his leather office chair at the end of the conference table. He let the information hang in the air while lighting a cigarette.

Becca, Dick Hanson, and one of the agents who had taken Brooks out on the stretcher sat in folding metal chairs amid paper cups of burnt coffee. Mark Burns was being interviewed by Nina in a cubicle at the other end of the hut. Northrup had introduced the field agent by name only: Nico Merrit. But dressed and armed as he was, Becca wondered if he was next in line to take Brooks' place as chief security officer. The guy was handsome in spite of—or maybe in part *because* of—a deep scar on his jawline. He was younger than Brooks, with short black hair and dark eyes. He looked strong, but Becca didn't want him at the table if he represented the loss of the one man she trusted to keep her safe in all of this.

"It wasn't just an earthquake," Becca said, arms crossed over her chest.

Northrup knocked a plug of ash into the paper cup at his elbow. "I didn't say it was *just* an earthquake, but it certainly coincided with one. Did something in the house *cause* a quake? Please, you were in the thick of it for longer than anyone, so tell us: what else was it?"

Becca squirmed, tried to find the right words, and sighed. "Perspective got weird."

"Perspective?" Merrit said.

"Space was warped. Like in a funhouse mirror, or when you put on someone else's glasses and the floor looks too close."

"She's right," Hanson said. "You know how the angles of the place are off on a good day? It was like someone cranked the knob on that. Has anyone gone back in? Have they assessed the damage yet?"

Northrup nodded. "It's minimal. Pictures fell off the walls, plaster cracked. No major structural damage noted, but it's night now, and we pulled the inspection team out at sunset. We'll have a better idea in the morning."

"What about broken windows? Cracks in the foundation?" Becca asked. "It sounded like the place was coming down around us."

Northrup shrugged. "We have broken china, toppled furniture. Some of what you heard may have been from...below."

"The reverend caused it, didn't he?" she said.

"We believe so. But we don't know what he set in motion."

"How is Brooks? Is he conscious?"

"We have him on an I.V. antibiotic and pain killer. He's groggy. The doctor says we can interview him shortly."

"Did you check his pockets," Hanson asked. "When you took him off the stretcher, did you search him for the weapon?"

Becca noticed Merrit studying Northrup, as if searching for something in the breath he took before answering.

"Empty," Northrup said. "We have to assume Proctor found it, whatever it is. We'll know more when Brooks can talk."

"So, are we sleeping here tonight?" Becca asked.

"Yes. We'll assess the house by daylight tomorrow and decide how to proceed."

Nina appeared at a corner of the conference cubicle and drummed her fingernails against the metal frame. All heads turned. To Northrup, she said, "He's ready to see you."

Northrup stamped his cigarette out and rose. "How's Burns?" He asked.

Nina glanced at Becca. She looked tired, as if the modular wall was propping her up. "He has moments of lucidity," she said, "which gives me hope that he may come back from this. But mostly, he's still gibbering like a lunatic. Better that than catatonic, I suppose."

"Is Brooks exhibiting any signs of psychosis?"

"No. We're waiting on the pathology report to see if the eels transmitted any neurotoxins to him. Matheson and I recommend that he be monitored carefully for at least three days."

Becca slid her chair back to follow Northrup out of the conference area but he put his hand up. "Not so fast, Philips. I'm seeing him alone first for debriefing. You'll have a turn later, if he's up for it."

* * *

Becca tried to read on the cot in the cubicle they had assigned her but found it too hard to focus. When Django went prowling the hut in search of any friendly tech who might give him a munchkin from the coffee station, she set her book down, fluffed her pillow, and lay back with her eyes closed. A moment later, Nina's voice tugged her back from the edge of sleep.

"Becca? You can see Jason now, if you'd like."

She sat up, blinking.

"Follow me."

Walking beside her, Becca could see the shadows under Nina's eyes showing through a thin layer of makeup; eyes that darted side to side as if scanning for predators, devoid of the calm empathy Becca had once found in them.

Becca touched Nina's arm, causing her to slow her businesslike stride and meet Becca's eyes.

"He'll be okay," Becca said. "Brooks is strong. He'll bounce back from this."

Nina grinned; it somehow made her look sadder. "Well look at you reading *my* worries. How did that happen?"

"Are you okay, Nina?"

Nina blinked, and looked over Becca's head at the track lights. Was her lip trembling? She shook her head, almost imperceptible but for the swaying of her short black hair.

"What is it?" Becca asked, and a manic smile flashed across the psychiatrist's face.

"It's just…everything." She covered her mouth, collected herself, and glanced around before continuing. "I've had a security clearance for less than two weeks and I'm supposed to just…adapt to the idea that everything I've ever known is just a thin crust over a world seething with monsters? Ideas I would have had people committed for... I'm sorry, I'm unloading on you. Shit."

"It's okay. It's a lot."

"I've been, uh, holding it together in front of them, but I guess it's catching up with me." Nina gave Becca's hand a squeeze. "He *is* strong, you're right. So are you. I had no idea the kind of secrets he had to live with until now. I mean, I had *some* idea, but..." She studied Becca's face. "And you actually fought them."

Now Becca looked away. "I don't know that it made a difference, Nina. I mean, here we are, right?"

"Can you do it again?" Nina's gaze settled on the collar of Becca's shirt.

"No. I'm sorry, but no, not the same way. They brought me here to witness and document, to tell them if something was coming through, but if they're counting on me to stop it, I'm afraid we're all fucked. How's that for a pep talk?"

Nina closed her eyes and laughed. "You've always been honest, I'll give you that. Sometimes to a fault." She leaned in closer to Becca and whispered, "Has Nico Merrit asked you any questions?"

"No, I just met him. Why?"

"Rumor has it he was sent by the Joint Chiefs to monitor the situation and override Northrup if it spirals out of control. I don't know if that's true, but—"

"Wait, what do you mean, *override?*"

"They'll only indulge exploration for so long before they decide to just take the house down."

* * *

The medical cubicle looked like all the others, apart from the specific equipment and the presence of an electric hospital bed rather than a cot. Brooks had it in the upright position. He smiled at Becca when she came in.

"What are you grinning at?" she asked him.

"You came to check on me. I didn't know you cared."

She punched his chin in slow motion. "I didn't know if you'd get out of there."

"Sure would have made for a weird death certificate: Eaten by piano."

She laughed, then sobered. "Northrup would probably go with 'drowned.'"

"Drowned in the line of duty in landlocked Concord, Mass."

"How are you feeling? Do the bites hurt?"

"Like a bitch until the painkillers kicked in. Right now, it's just a dull throb."

"I don't know if you heard: Mark tried to keep one alive in the bathtub, but it dissolved."

"Mmm. Maybe it couldn't handle fresh water."

"Or terrestrial physics."

"Yeah. I felt a weird pressure down there. Almost worried if I could get the bends from the cable pulling me up too fast through the *air*. I wonder how Proctor is making out. What's he been in for, seven hours?"

"Something like that."

"Ah, he's probably genetically suited for it."

"I thought I saw his reflection in the piano during the quake. And then again in a broken mirror."

"Really?"

"Yeah. Maybe. I don't know."

"You mention it to Northrup?"

"Not yet."

Brooks grunted.

"I won't ask you to tell me everything you saw down there, but..."

"I didn't see your father. I'm sorry. Proctor escaped into some kind of maze before the flood; probably *caused* the flood. He had a key that he showed me. I think that was what Moe Ramirez hid down there. Not a weapon, but a key. Moe probably thought getting it out of this world altogether would keep it lost, so he took the chance of putting it under the doormat, so to speak. He never thought the music would be reconstructed."

"Keys to a key," Becca said.

Brooks had been staring up at the ribs of the curved ceiling as he spoke. Now he looked at Becca. "You don't seem let down that I didn't find your dad down there. It's because you know he's not in the house. Isn't it?"

"How do you know that?"

"I used to be a cop. I saw how you reacted to the Lincoln log in the saddle bag." He took hold of her wrist, gently, but firmly, letting her know she couldn't wriggle out of the question: "What does it mean to you?"

Becca scanned the shadowy ceiling, then raised an eyebrow at him.

He answered the unspoken question. "I don't think we're bugged here."

She leaned in and, in a threadbare voice, said, "Mount Lincoln in the White Mountains. We used to vacation in a cabin there when I was a kid. I think he wanted someone to think he was lost in the Wade House, so they'd stop looking for him. But he wanted me to know where to find him if I showed up here."

"Why?"

"I don't know. But I don't want to lead anyone to him. At one point you thought there was a cultist in SPECTRA, a mole who helped Darius Marlowe escape his interrogation. Do you still think that?"

"Never ruled it out."

"Then if I go looking for him, I can't tell anyone here what I'm doing."

"You told me."

"Yeah, well...I'm sure you spend your nights praying to the Great Old Ones to help you win big at the casino and get the Sox into the playoffs."

Brooks laughed. "All right. You were smart to keep it to yourself. Just don't try to leave until I'm on my feet again. And don't bring your phone; they might track it."

"Could you give me a ride up there, if we came up with a good story?"

"Maybe. Let's see what happens. Now that Proctor's off the reservation, I'm not sure what our next move will be. Or if they'll even keep me on the case. I know Northrup will want you to do a full scan of the house tomorrow with the drone. I should be up and around by then. Just be patient."

"Okay. Do you know what those things were that bit you?"

Brooks' gaze turned inward and Becca thought he looked even paler than he had when she entered the room and saw him under the cold white LED lamps.

"It walked down the beach," Brooks said, his voice a hoarse whisper. "It was like a woman doing the dance of the seven veils, only the veils were eels and there was no one underneath."

"*Jesus.*"

"No, but I bet it could have walked on the water if it wanted to."

"It sounds like the goddess of the gate, the one I saw in the cave lagoon."

Brooks licked his crusty lips. "Shabat Cycloth. The Lady of a Thousand Hooks."

SPECTRA

SPECIAL PHYSICS EMERGENT COUNTER TERROR RECON AGENCY
NORTHEAST REGIONAL OFFICE, BOSTON, MA.

 PROJECT WADEHOUSE

DREAM RECORD #3
TRANSCRIBED BY N.R.

CONFIDENTIAL

AGENT JASON BROOKS
1/14/22

I'm on the diving board at the public pool where Ma used to bring me and Michael. I was so scared of how high that board was. But it wasn't really that high, I was just small. In the dream, I'm grown up, but the board still seems really high above the water. The pool is crowded as ever. It's a typical summer day, kids screaming and laughing, parents yelling, lifeguard whistles. I bounce, wind up, and dive in and when I hit the blue water, everything goes silent. I escape from all that racket. Only it's not <u>totally</u> silent. I can hear a humming noise. Not electrical, but like someone is humming the words to a song. I can't make out the words.

I open my eyes and look around and there are no other swimmers, not even legs in the shallow end. There <u>is</u> no shallow end. The water is deep. Green and gray. I'm floating in front of a giant pyramid made of the carved bones and the stacked skulls of sea monsters. Not just a heap of bones and skulls with teeth like tusks, but a symmetrical arrangement that looks like a temple. There are giant jewels set in the eye sockets of skulls the size of compact cars.

There's something moving behind the teeth. I can see it? Or do I just know it's there? Floating, climbing, sleeping. That makes no sense. Sleepswimming? It's sleeping and climbing the levels of the temple. I see leathery gray, like an elephant's skin through a bone cavity. Folds of flesh. Then a red eye with an hourglass pupil opens and focuses on me and I let go my mouthful of bubbles, choke on salt water. I realize the sound has been getting louder the whole time. It pounds in my temples, squeezes by brain in rhythm: TUTULOOO, TUTULOOO, TUTULOOO.

SPECIAL PHYSICS EMERGENT COUNTER TERROR RECON AGENCY

Chapter 12

After 3 weeks spent crouching in the shadow of the Wade House, the Base Camp hut was stained with oily streaks from the black flakes. They whispered against the roof, a constant background in the hours since the team had retreated. Becca had learned to distinguish between their susurrus and the grainy chatter of icy snowflakes, which tapered off in the evening after a brief flurry in the afternoon. By full dark, the grounds were once again blanketed in black.

Becca had put off taking Django out for his nightly walk for as long as possible, finally relenting and pulling on a hooded raincoat at half-past eleven. The rustling of the flakes had intensified by then, and as she approached the door and clipped the leash onto the dog's collar, she wondered if the precipitation was surging, or if she was merely more attuned to the sound as she approached the outer shell.

The leash was a new precaution. In the past, she had rarely used one, but now she worried about him bounding off into black oblivion if the cat made another appearance. She was also using it to correct his balance, which had been out of whack since the last encounter. The veterinarian had paid a follow-up visit to Base Camp and diagnosed the imbalance as *vestibular disease*, a temporary condition of the inner ear that usually afflicted older dogs, a sort of canine vertigo. There was no treatment; you could only wait for it to run its course. The vet assured Becca that Django's equilibrium would eventually return. Soon, she hoped. The environment was unreliable enough without an inner imbalance to contend with. But she suspected the house was somehow responsible for that, too.

She pulled the drawstrings dangling from her hood and prepared herself for the repulsive sensation of the ashy flakes against her skin.

When she opened the door, it flew out of her hand and banged against the outer wall, driven by a howling wind. Django braced his paws against the weather, then backed up into the hut, making it clear that he didn't need a walk *that* badly. Becca dropped the leash and reached out to pull the door shut. Leaning into the buffeting wind, she caught sight of a swarm of black flakes swept through the fan of light cast by one of the halogen lamps SPECTRA had installed atop thick, metal poles around the grounds. The sight stopped her breath.

The black snow was flying *upward*. She squinted at it, waiting for the optical illusion to reconcile, but it didn't. Tracking the flakes to their destination, she saw that the chimneys, windows, and even the gaps between shingles appeared to be drawing the flakes from the ground and sucking them in. The house had always been a magnet for the strange precipitation drifting from the sky, but before now it had been a lazy attraction that had left most of the fallout to accumulate in drifts. Now, the attraction had intensified, causing the air around the house to resemble a whirlpool dragging sediment down a drain.

Becca struggled against the wind. She managed to get the door closed, and yelled to a female agent working late in the nearest cubicle, "Call Northrup. There's something he should see."

* * *

When she drifted into shallow wakefulness in the middle of the night, the sound had ceased, and when the team emerged from the hut at daybreak, they found the muddy grounds wiped clean of the black snow, as if it had melted overnight. The Wade House looked more unsettling than ever, looming over the sodden meadow, its gray windows fixed on a gray sky, yellow shingles weeping black rivulets like its mascara had run.

Northrup organized a group of technicians to scan the outside of the house with a variety of devices that Becca didn't recognize. The exploration team was told to hold off while these tests were conducted. Around lunchtime, Northrup declared the interior off-limits due to high levels of radiation and Becca was summoned to fly the drone through it from the Base Camp command center, transmitting video to a high-definition widescreen monitor with Northrup, Hanson, Burns, and Brooks watching.

The fly-through recorded black sludge on the floors and furniture creeping toward mirrors and other reflective surfaces. Becca dragged the drone's tail through the stuff to collect a sample for comparison to the residue left on the outside of the house by the black snow, which had only ever registered low level radiation. Clearly, something had changed when Proctor entered the labyrinth, causing the house to inhale the fallout from the other dimension. Of course, the question troubling everyone now was: would it exhale, and when? And would that bring a tide of monsters?

Structural damage was minimal, as far as they could tell, but Becca was unable to explore the basement, which lay beyond a closed door. All told, it took her a couple of hours to survey 80% of the house, sometimes flying in through broken windows to gain access to rooms with closed doors.

The piano appeared to be inert, with only the soundboard showing under its propped hood. It released a metallic glissando when the drone's wings brushed the strings in passing, giving Becca goose bumps at the distorted sound issuing from the built-in speakers of the remote in her hand.

She felt a wave of relief when it was time to bring the dragonfly out and land it, as if she herself were shaking off the dreadful claustrophobia of the rooms she'd been immersed in through its lenses.

By dinner time, word came back from the lab in Boston that the sludge sample had a different chemical composition from the flakes they had tested: It was an organic substance previously uncatalogued, but bearing a close resemblance to radioactive cephalopod ink collected in the ocean near Fukushima in 2014.

An assistant roamed the cubicles gathering takeout orders from local restaurants. By the time dinner arrived, Becca had recharged with a short nap and was ready to join the others gathered around a monitor on the conference table to study the video she'd recorded.

On the screen, the drone moved down a corridor she recognized as the first floor main hallway when the red drapery that Proctor had tacked over the library entrance came into view. Watching the replay, she recalled how she'd maneuvered the dragonfly over the thick folds of fabric before realizing she could fly it in through the small gap between the curtain and floor.

The library was an inner room with no windows, two stories high and situated at the center of the house. She'd switched on the drone's headlight, but the footage was still murky. Nonetheless, she had captured something of interest.

"There," Northrup said. "Roll it back."

The tech sitting at the keyboard scrubbed the video with a trackball and found the beginning of the segment. He tapped the spacebar and ran it again. The dragonfly's floodlight traveled the length of a bookshelf, spines flicking past until a gray smudge on the wood (possibly incense ash) came racing toward the camera at the same location as a book tilted slightly forward, as if it didn't quite fit the space it had been crammed into. The tech froze the frame.

"What is it?" Brooks asked.

"It's not much," Northrup said. "But enough, I think, to send an agent in a suit in there to fetch that book. It looks like it was of interest to the reverend."

"I'll go," Brooks said.

"No," Nina said. "You're not yet recovered from the last expedition."

"That's why it should be me. For all we know, I already have poison in my system from exposure to this stuff in the realm below. At least this time, I'll be suited up. And anyway, it should be someone with EDEP."

"Listen to Nina," Becca said. "You're still recovering. Exposing you to something new only complicates things. If you suffer side effects from entering the house, how will we know it's from that and not your swim in the ocean, or the lamprey bites?"

"She's right," Northrup said. He pointed at Becca. "Philips it is. You go in, you get the book, you come out. Got it?"

"Got it."

* * *

Thirty minutes later Becca stood outside the hut in a charcoal gray radiation suit. The gloves were a little big and clumsy, but all she needed to do with them was open the front door and pull a book from a shelf. Brooks helped her get the hood on, and checked for gaps. Her breath sounded loud and quick through the valve as he draped her camera strap over her neck.

"You okay?" Brooks asked.

"Fine. It's just a little claustrophobic."

"I mean are you okay about going in there? You don't have to."

"I'm good. Be out in a flash. This isn't so bad. I expected it to be heavier. You sure it's safe?"

"Don't worry, you're dressed in the best. It's nanotech. Lighter than lead, but just as effective. Remember: in and out, that's it. Don't forget to breathe."

Becca nodded, took a deep breath, and trudged up the soggy slope to the veranda. She took a moment to look up at the sky, overcast but clear of snow both black and white. The last remnants of the malignant orb that had hovered over Boston, and that she had destroyed, were no more. It seemed fitting that she should be the one to wade through the sludge formed from the fallout.

Inside, the house was darker than she expected. She clicked on her flashlight and swept the beam over the marbled black patterns snaking across the floor. At the end of the vestibule, she turned the first corner and saw the grandfather clock, its polished brass pendulum still swinging, its gears still ticking loudly enough to hear through the hood.

Brooks' voice sounded in her earpiece, "Can you hear me?"

"Yes. I'm in. You're going to have plenty of samples of this shit. It's all over the bottom of my boots."

"Yeah, we figured. Might just bag and incinerate them. You're not getting stuck to the floor are you?"

"No, I can move. I'm in the second hall now. I can see the library curtain. Just like in the video, most of the sludge is moving in that direction on this floor."

"Okay. Listen, kiddo: if anything looks unstable, you forget about the book and get out. Hear me?"

Something caught her eye and she stopped dead in her tracks. Had she seen a face looking out at her from the tarnished brass of the clock pendulum? Eyes glimpsed as if through the porthole of a ship? She took a step back and stared at the swinging disc. Nothing. Just paranoid jitters.

"Becca? You copy?"

"Yeah, I'm here. I'm going to the library."

Moving down the hall, she heard a female voice shout

(*"Django!"*)

and stopped dead. The air in front of her wavered, the red curtain swayed, and a black and white blur streaked into the parlor, trailing black and brown.

"What was that?" The same voice again. Her *own?* She looked over her shoulder. She was alone.

"A cat, I think." Brooks.

"*What* cat?" The voices ricocheted around her in the oil-streaked corridor.

"A black and white cat. Must've wandered in from the street."

"He's gone. Where did he go?"

"What do you mean *gone?*"

"I thought you trained him not to chase animals."

"We didn't run into any *housecats* in the rainforest. He's fine around—"

"Becca?" Brooks' voice, close and metallic in her earpiece. "Are you in the library?"

She swallowed. "Not yet. I'm going in now."

She came to the heavy red curtain, pulled it aside and shone the light into the dusty room. She had only ever seen the library through the drone's eyes. It was bigger than she'd expected, and well ordered, exhibiting few signs of the Reverend Proctor's residency except for the remains of a few melted candles, what appeared to be a small whetstone, and some spent incense on a charcoal briquette in an iron censer. She wondered if he had even packed a suitcase for Wade House, or if he'd worn the same clothes every day since they'd moved in. A closer inspection revealed his folded cot in a corner, and the faint remains of a chalk circle on the floor. She snapped a few shots of the chalk marks using her SLR with the flash on, the faceplate of her mask beginning to fog from her perspiration, making it difficult to read the settings in the small LCD screen.

The air was thick, the absence of windows conspiring with the heavy curtain to keep all drafts out. She was grateful for the filter in her mask, and could only imagine what the room smelled like. She pictured Caleb Wade sitting at the oak desk burning his noxious candles through the night, year after year as he indulged whatever obsessions had led him to build such a sick house. She looked again at the candle stubs Proctor had left behind. Were they even made of wax? Thoughts of boiled fat welled up in the back of her mind and she shut them down. She had to stay focused. Get the book and get out.

Becca scanned the shelves. It took a moment to get her bearings in the octagonal room, but *there*, opposite where she expected to find it was the ash smudge and the jutting spine. She approached the shelf and withdrew the stubborn volume, finding it to be leather-bound and marred with scorch marks along the bottom edge. Proctor had tried to burn the book, and failing to ignite it, had jammed it into a not-quite-big-enough slot on the shelf in a hasty effort to make it just one more tree in the forest. But where had he found the book in the first place? Under one of the paving stones in the floor? In a desk drawer? She would never know. She cracked the tome open to a random page in the middle and found slanting cursive writing filling every inch down to the singed bottom of the page.

She flipped to the title page and found an elaborately scrolled frame adorned with drawings of a lion, eagle, bull, and man in the four corners. The title, meticulously penned in blackletter calligraphy read: *Ye Shadow Booke of Caleb Wade, Brother of the Craft.*

A chill ran down Becca's spine. She closed the book and trained her flashlight on the cold fireplace. Had Proctor tried to burn the book in there and failed because of the draft drawing the black flakes into the house? It was just one more thing she would never be sure of, but at least the contents of the book might shed some light on the reverend's thoughts, plans, and aspirations, if he had indeed been inspired by it.

She tucked the book under her arm, scanned the upper shelves with the light, and lingered for a moment, wondering if she should explore further. After all, she had what she'd come for, and was under no threat to retreat in haste. Maybe she would find something else of significance. She moved to the spiral stairs that ascended to the second level and gripped the railing with her gloved hand.

A burst of static filled her ear. "Becca. What's your status?"

"I have the book."

"Come out the same way you went in."

"Okay."

She turned and swept the room one last time with the light. It flared back in her eyes from a gilt framed mirror over the mantle. She settled the beam on the slate hearth, letting its ambiance illuminate the glass indirectly. The mirror seemed to reflect another place entirely—not a library, but a long stone corridor speckled with black mold and broken at intervals with dark rectangles where other corridors connected to it.

Mirrors are windows.

Mirrors are doors.

Her grandmother had said that long ago, and Becca had come to understand the meaning of it when for a time, any reflective surface—water, metal, or glass—had become a potential portal to the world next door. Had the reverend been watching the maze through this mirror before he resolved to enter it through the shore beyond the piano? Or had the house's alignment to that other world shifted when he'd entered the maze and unleashed the flood?

Becca approached the fireplace, keeping the light at an oblique angle. She stared down the corridor in the mirror. It was as still as a picture. No, that wasn't entirely true. Light and shadow moved as if with the passing of clouds across sun or moon or whatever celestial body lit this other realm.

She extended her hand toward the glass, expecting to meet no resistance, expecting to pass through or cause a ripple. But the mirror was solid. She tapped her fingertips against it and exhaled, her breath through the mask's air filter loud in her ears. A crackle made her jump. "Becca? You coming out?"

"Yes."

Passing between the red curtain and the doorframe, she felt a moment of disorientation when the hallway she'd stepped into was stripped of its wallpaper and wood floor and became a cold stone corridor like the one she'd glimpsed in the mirror.

A swirl of black fabric disappeared around a corner where the kitchen should have been, and a shadow passed over the hall, dimming even the flashlight beam. When it passed, the hall was the same it had been when she'd entered the library.

The grandfather clock grinding away the seconds was the only sound apart from the pounding surf of her pulse in her ears, her breath in her mask, or was that...distant strains of a chanted melody?

The faded winter sunlight was blinding when she pushed through the front door and staggered down the steps clutching the book to her chest. She had dropped the flashlight inside, where it would remain on the floor, casting its beam down the hall until the batteries died. An agent met her halfway across the meadow and received the book in a leaded pouch.

* * *

"Proctor is in the house." Becca was sitting on the floor of the conference room with Django curled in her lap.

"You saw him?" Brooks paced beside the table at which Northrup, Hanson, and Burns sat. Burns was in his own world, sketching on a legal pad and eating Oreos. The other two looked haggard and tense. Becca had shed the radiation suit and used the hut's portable shower. Now they were waiting for contamination tests to be run on the book.

"I saw him. In and out of the house."

"What, in the yard?" Brooks said.

"No, *flickering* in and out of it. It's like he's in the walls, but not really. He's moving alongside the house at weird angles. I think he's trying to find his way through the maze to the other side. I kept catching glimpses of him in reflective surfaces. I don't know if he could see me, but at one point the hallway shifted and I was in the maze. Like the house lined up with the in-between for a second and I saw him going around a corner. I don't know if I'm making sense..."

"You are," Hanson said. "And it means there's a chance of catching him during one of those alignments before he reaches the center."

"Or a chance of losing one of you to the labyrinth," Northrup said.

"I think it's worth a shot," Brooks said.

"Slow down," Northrup said. "The place is still radioactive. Sending you in wearing a suit that could be punctured in a confrontation isn't ideal. And we don't know all the forces in play here. No one's going in until we at least know what Proctor knows. Not until we know what he found in Wade's book."

Brooks slammed the heel of his hand against the table. His water bottle shuddered and sloshed. Northrup bristled and waited for the argument.

"We can't wait," Brooks said. "You can't wait. If he uses that key..."

Hanson leaned in to finish the thought, "What would you do if he was racing to unleash a bioweapon? You'd send men after him, right? And damn the risk to them."

Northrup shot a glance over the modular wall where Nico Merrit stood watching, listening. His tone remained calm when he spoke. "Knowledge is our greatest advantage, and Becca won that for us. If you go in without a clue, you'll be lost in there. We wait for the book."

"How long until that's cleared?" Brooks asked.

"Not long. Paper doesn't retain radiation. The tests are precautionary."

"Marie Curie's notes are *still* radioactive," Burns said, twisting the top wafer off of an Oreo. Everyone looked at him.

"The paper isn't," Hanson said. "Not really. It's bits of radium she was handling that got stuck between the fibers that register."

"Well, we don't know if the book absorbed enough of that sludge to retain radioactivity," Northrup said. "And paper can't be cleaned without damaging it. We may need to study the book with protective gear, but we don't go into the house blind. The expedition is on hold until we know what we're dealing with. Maybe by then, the sludge will dissolve and the place will be habitable again."

"You think it'll just disappear?" Brooks said.

Northrup shrugged. "The black snow stopped falling. The other side seems to be reclaiming the remains of the incursion.

That's a *good* thing. What we don't want is anything coming out. Remember, we're looking for a way to seal it. Bringing Proctor out may not be advisable. Locking him in with his gods might be better." He shot a look at Becca, expecting an argument about her father, but it didn't come.

"But he has a key," Becca said. "What do you think he plans to do with it? What if he's trying to open the deepest door he can find? What if he intends to let them all loose again through the house?"

Hanson was nodding. "She's right. Our priority should be to stop him at all costs."

"He told me he doesn't want to let anything out," Brooks said. "He doesn't care about this world, only reaching the other. I actually believe him."

Northrup frowned. "It may very well be that he only wants to reach his gods. But what do *they* want?"

Chapter 13

It was snowing again when they drove north. Becca looked at white sky and the wet, black road, and yearned for the jungle. She had tried to escape the weight of winter and the downward spiral that dragged her in every time it came around, draining her of energy, blurring her focus, and undermining her capacity to give a fuck about anything. Intellectually, she knew she should be feeling lighter with every mile Brooks put between the car and that sick house, that so very *wrong* house that hurt her head to even look at. But emotionally, she was succumbing to the old blackness of January in the northern hemisphere. She felt powerless to fight back against it, and that only made her angry with herself. Despite the consistency of her seasonal depression, she felt like she should be over it by now. The medication helped, but it wasn't a miracle cure. And being in New England only made it worse.

Becca rolled a small fleece blanket into a bundle and placed it between her head and the window. She tried to sleep, but found her eyes returning to the overhead signs, the familiar names of North Shore towns. She had approached Northrup and requested leave to use the hiatus for a trip to Miskatonic University, to view her grandmother's collection and see if Catherine had written anything about the Wade House. He had granted it and told her to have the librarians call him directly if she needed him to exert pressure for the release of any restricted items. Becca had almost stopped short of asking for Brooks to accompany her, but decided to go all in at the last minute. By the end of the conversation, she was pretty sure Northrup suspected nothing extracurricular from the pair of them, but he was hard to read.

Now she wondered why she was headed back to Arkham and undisclosed points north when she should be heading to Logan airport and warmer climes. She poked at the radio, in search of something to match her aggressive mood. Nothing fit. The only thing she heard with enough distortion to make her finger hesitate over the scan button for a second was Daughtry, and she couldn't stand that shit. She shut the radio off, itching for a Tool disc. *Aenima* would do just fine. Something cathartic.

"I need to take a little detour on the way to New Hampshire," Brooks said.

"Where?"

"Andover. Just for an hour or so."

"What's in Andover?"

"Tom. You remember Tom?"

"Tom who almost puked on me in a helicopter while the apocalypse broke out? How could I forget?"

"*Jeez*, I thought you had a soft spot for the guy. Maybe you should stay in the car."

"Why are we visiting Tom? We have forty-eight hours to hit Arkham and the White Mountains."

Brooks looked away from the road and scrutinized her. "Are you in a twist because we're going to see your dad? It *was* your idea."

She glared at him. He looked at the road. After a minute, he said, "What is it? What's wrong?"

"Nothing."

He scoffed.

"What?"

"Just, if you don't want to talk about it, fine, tell me to fuck off, but don't say *nothing*. That's such a chick thing to do. I think I know you well enough by now. Don't want to tell me, fine."

Becca looked out the window, then turned to him. "What's wrong is everything. Winter is wrong, New England is wrong. Me working for the government or thinking my dad is worth looking for is wrong. I shouldn't be here and I'm wrong for being involved in any of this. I thought it was over and it's not and if anyone is counting on *me* to deal with it, they've made a mistake. I'm not up to it. This bullshit from beyond has cost me everything. And I don't have anything left to give."

"So why are we going to New Hampshire?"

"We're going because anywhere is better than that house. If I had a home, I'd ask you to take me there, but I don't, so I might as well find out what else my father's been hiding from me and lying about since he rode off into the fucking sunset."

"Well, okay then. Onward."

* * *

Tom Petrie greeted them at the front door of his condo with food stains on his plaid shirt. "Jason," he said with a tone of not unpleasant confusion. "I didn't know you were coming."

"I hope it's okay."

Tom looked beyond the odd couple on his doorstep, scanning the street with a furtive glance. His receding hair looked in need of a trim and in the pale winter light, his eye sockets betrayed the purple shadows earned from sleepless nights.

"We're here alone," Brooks said. "Except for Becca's dog in the car. Do you remember Becca?"

Tom's gaze settled on her, but his polite smile lacked recognition.

"It's okay if you don't," Becca said. "I remember you."

"Did we meet when I met Jason?"

"Yes, Tom, you and Becca both helped out during the crisis," Brooks said.

"Sorry, that time is really fuzzy for me."

"May we come in?" Brooks asked.

Tom stepped aside. "Oh, yeah, please."

The condo was a bi-level with a steep staircase rising from the entryway, a bright, airy kitchen straight ahead, and a carpeted living room with furniture that had seen better days off to the right. It had the split-personality look of a home both carefully baby-proofed and wildly cluttered. Tom led them into the living room and gestured at the couch. Becca sat beside Brooks and took in the room: toddler toys and board books piled on the floor, family photos on the shelves. From the couch, she could also see a rectangular patch on the hallway wall, slightly lighter in hue than the rest of the cream-colored paint, indicating that a picture frame or mirror had been removed, a hook remaining in the drywall near the top of the empty patch.

"I didn't know you were coming," he said again. "Would you like some coffee or tea? Susan's upstairs giving Noah a bath."

"No," Brooks said. "We can't stay long, just stopping by on the way to somewhere else."

Tom fidgeted with his wedding ring, spinning it on his finger.

"I've had you on my mind," Brooks said, "but things have been crazy at work, and I understood your concerns about wanting to talk privately. That's one of the reasons I didn't call before coming. Anyway, I finally had an opportunity to drop in off the books. Is this an okay time? You seem a little anxious."

"Bath time can be a tad stressful is all." Tom's eyes tracked over to Becca, bounced back to Brooks.

"She's cool," Brooks said. "If you could remember her, you'd relax. She's not an agent."

Tom smiled. The same fake smile on display in the family photos. Becca decided she would offer to take some better candid shots of the Petrie family if life ever approached anything like normalcy.

"I figured. She's not dressed like one," Tom said.

Becca took her hands from the pockets of her army jacket and slid them over the thighs of her worn black jeans.

"She's a photographer," Brooks said, "and the only person besides me who didn't take Nepenthe after the crisis to make the extra perception go away."

Tom nodded and swallowed. "I've had a few flashes of memory from that week in September. At least, I think they're memories. But it seems more like remembering fragments of a nightmare, stuff that couldn't really have happened. But you say it did."

"Right," Brooks said. "It did, and trust me, you don't want to remember."

Tom turned to Becca. "Why didn't you take the drug like the rest of us, if you're not with SPECTRA?"

She thought about it for a moment and said, "They gave me a choice. At the time, I didn't want to put blinders on."

"Because of that, she's working with us in a freelance capacity," Brooks said. "But she probably trusts the agency even less than I do. So...you hinted on the phone that you have concerns about your boy, but you're afraid of approaching SPECTRA directly."

Tom nodded. He was pacing the carpet, rubbing his stubbled head. "I just think—and maybe I'm paranoid, but you're on the inside and you haven't reassured me otherwise—I think you have to be careful about getting the government involved where kids are concerned. I mean, I lean kind of libertarian anyway, but even so, I would never risk a government agency stepping in to take Noah away from us, you understand? I could never let that happen." His agitated gaze glanced off of the hallway ceiling, toward the direction of the second floor where his wife and son were. "We can't even talk if that's a possibility," he said.

Brooks shifted in his seat. "What I can assure you, Tom, is that it would never happen through myself or Ms. Philips. We won't betray your confidence, no matter what you tell us."

"I guess that'll have to be good enough because we need help. Susan and I feel very alone in this, and I know better than to search the web looking for other families that might be having similar experiences. I mean, I'm an IT guy, I know they sift for keywords." Tom finally settled in a stuffed chair, facing the couch. "I don't even know where to begin."

"I know where my own concerns begin," Brooks said. "When we talked on the phone around Christmas last year and you told me about some of the gibberish Noah was saying. I didn't want to alarm you, but I recognized those words. They're from a lost language. And back then, he had what? One word in English under his belt? Has there been more of that strange language?"

"Yes. We realized it wasn't just baby talk. He repeats some of the same phrases. There's definitely a syntax to it."

"What else?"

"Sometimes it's more like singing or chanting. You ever hear Tuvan overtone singing? It's like that. From a kid who's barely *two*. Have you ever heard of that? It shouldn't even be physically possible, right?"

"I don't know," Brooks said. "Have you talked to your pediatrician about it?"

"Only very generally. Not like we've given her a demonstration or anything."

"How is he otherwise? Healthy? Developmentally average?"

"Above average. That's the other thing. His drawings—which should be mostly scribbling, barely even stick figures at this point—are...way above his age level. They're kind of disturbing."

"Violent?" Becca asked.

"No. Just weird. Dark. I think they remind me of stuff I've forgotten, I don't know...those nightmare fragments."

"Can we see?" Brooks asked.

"Sure. Follow me."

Tom led them to the kitchen Becca had glimpsed from the entryway. It was clean and neat with new appliances, but the sink tap was wrapped in black duct tape. A crude drawing of a dog and some flowers was tacked to the refrigerator with alphabet magnets. Tom slid a drawer open, clicking the child-lock with his thumb. He removed a sheaf of paper and laid it on the kitchen table. The top sheet depicted a wavy Crayola blue sea with a jagged black mountain rising from it.

"There are a lot of versions of that one," Tom said. "I keep them in the drawer so he doesn't get upset."

"He's frightened by his own drawings?" Becca asked.

"No, he just gets worked up about them if he sees them." Tom pointed to the innocuous dog portrait on the fridge. "That's one of the few we can display. I don't mind him getting excited about dogs." He flipped through the stack of drawings on the table, and withdrew one—a finger painting in smeared shades of green, gray, and purple.

For a couple of seconds, Becca couldn't make sense of it, then Tom rotated the page and the pattern reconciled itself.

She recoiled with a start. A memory of the transformed Darius Marlowe, his face a squirming nest of tentacles flashed in her mind.

Brooks put a hand on her shoulder. "You okay?"

Becca nodded. "What do *you* see?" she said.

"A squidface, like what Marlowe was when he came back from the other side," Brooks said.

"Uh-huh."

Brooks squinted at Becca. "When you saw those reflections of Proctor in the maze, in the house, was he like that?"

"No. I don't think so. It was just glimpses, like looking through warped glass, but his face looked human. I saw his tattoos."

"Who's Proctor?" Tom asked.

Brooks ignored the question.

Becca slid the paper aside with the tip of her finger, revealing the next sheet in the stack. Another crayon drawing, this one a rudimentary arrangement of yellow and purple squares and triangles forming the shape of what might be a house. Becca wondered how much of the oddly aligned geometry had to do with the child's primitive skill level and how much was an accurate portrayal of how that house might appear to his mind's eye in a dream. The white space surrounding the structure was flecked with a storm of black dots.

Brooks frowned at the image, held it up for Tom to see, and asked, "Did he say anything about what this is?"

"He calls it 'the candy house in the snow.' It's one of the ones that's not so disturbing. To me, anyway. But *he* gets worked up about it. Says it's full of candies and the candies are full of smoke. I don't know what that means. Do you?"

"No," Brooks said. "Did he see it in a dream?"

"We think so. We think most of this comes to him in dreams. We'll find him drawing first thing in the morning. Sometimes in the middle of the night, in the dark, if he can find the materials. We've had to get over worrying that he'll choke on a crayon in the middle of the night. Now we leave some in his crib with a pad. I'd never admit that to his doctor, but he was keeping us up all night screaming until we tried it."

Becca thought of the untouched dream journal lying beside her cot in the uninhabitable Wade House. "Tom, when he talks about the candies in the house...do you think he could be saying *candles?*"

"Huh. Maybe."

"You mind if I take a picture of this one with my phone?" Brooks asked.

"Go ahead."

Brooks placed the drawing in better light on the kitchen counter, snapped a shot, and tucked his phone back into the breast pocket of his overcoat. He nodded at the black duct-taped sink tap. "You have a leak?"

"No, we took all the mirrors down. Even the bathroom medicine chest doors. We were seeing things in them when Noah was singing. The faucet was chrome and one time when we were eating dinner, Noah started singing and I swear, I saw something circle the room from the faucet to the toaster to the oven door. I know how it sounds, but Susan saw it too. She screamed. Now, I won't even use a knife when he's in the room. I'm afraid of what I'll see in the blade."

"What *have* you seen?"

"It's hard to describe. Nothing you could name really, nothing you could identify, just gross anatomy, like...veiny membranes and rills of tissue. A web of a hundred eyes like a kaleidoscope, or a fractal made of—"

"Tentacles," Becca said.

Tom's eyes widened. "Yeah. At first I thought I was hallucinating from sleep deprivation. You know, new baby, weird hours. But Susan saw the same things." Tom blew out a breath through pursed lips, his shoulders heaving. He looked on the verge of a breakdown. Then he blinked and ran his hand over his bristly, balding head again. "I haven't been able to talk to anybody about it. This is the first time."

Becca touched his elbow. "It's okay. You're not crazy, the world is. Most of the time we can filter it out, but it's a lot weirder than anyone knows."

"I don't want weird," Tom said. "I want my son to have a normal life."

A crash rumbled through the ceiling from the second floor, followed by a keening cry of alarm. Tom dashed for the stairs with Brooks and Becca fast at his heels.

At the top of the narrow staircase, unable to see past the men, Becca heard splashing water and a child's screams cutting through terrified adult voices. *"What happened, what happened, what happened?"* Tom, babbling, leaving no space for his wife to answer, and her moaning, "No, no, *nononoooo."*

Brooks pushed past Tom, and Becca spilled into the upstairs hallway. He knelt in the bathroom doorframe, taking something from Susan, something wrapped in a towel, and then Becca saw small, pale legs poking out of the bundle and knew it was Noah. At first, Susan looked reluctant to hand the boy over, but Brooks was looking her in the eye, saying something Becca couldn't hear over the child's shrieks, reassuring her, radiating calm and control. There was blood on the towel, blood on the tiles.

Brooks hurried down the hall and placed the bundle on the carpet of the boy's bedroom. "Bandages!" he yelled over his shoulder, over Noah's screams, and Becca suddenly realized that those screams had a shape. They weren't the garbled wailing she'd taken them for at first. Noah, like his parents, was repeating the same thing over and over in an endless loop: *R'LYEEH! R'LYEEH! R'LYEEEEH!*

Tom fumbled with his phone. Susan, on hands and knees in the red water and suds, rummaged through the cabinet under the bathroom sink. She tossed bottles of cleaning fluids, a bag of cotton balls, and a box of tampons away from the puddles, and finding the first aid kit thrust it at Becca in the doorway. Becca ran it to the bedroom, fell to her knees beside Brooks, and undid the latches on the box. She tore open a package of gauze pads and shoved them at Brooks, who was holding the child's bleeding hand while struggling to keep the rest of him from thrashing and squirming away.

"Peroxide," Brooks said, holding the boy's hand up.

Becca found a small brown bottle in the kit, unscrewed the cap with shaking fingers, and splashed some on the tiny, gashed palm. Pink foam bubbled up like a craft volcano and Noah gave out a wail of pure, meaningless pain. Brooks pressed a gauze pad against the wound, and wrapped it.

From the hallway, the parents' frantic voices ricocheted off the tight walls, an argument about calling 911 or taking Noah to the ER. Susan darted into the bedroom and swept her baby off the floor, holding him tight to her chest, patting him and backing away from Brooks into a corner behind the crib. She cooed in Noah's ear until his screams lost voice and became great, rasping breaths.

Tom appeared in the doorway, still holding the phone, looking anxious and useless. "How bad is it? Do we need to take him to the hospital? I haven't called."

Brooks had slipped out of his coat at the height of the mayhem. His arms and blue Oxford shirt were smeared with blood. He nodded. "Let him calm down, maybe give him some Tylenol, then yeah, you should take him in."

"It happened so fast," Susan said. "So fast."

"What happened?" Becca asked her.

"We use bubbles," Susan said. "Lots of bubbles."

"So the water isn't clear," Tom said. "Like any kid, he likes bubbles, but we also use them to cover the water, so there aren't any reflections."

"He made the mountain again," Susan said with a shudder.

"What mountain?" Brooks asked.

"He likes to gather the bubbles into an island and make a mountain," Tom said. "It's another thing he gets excited about. We keep bath time short."

"R'lyeh," Susan said. "That's what he calls the bubble island, R'lyeh."

Tom shushed her, knitting his eyebrows together and nodding toward Noah. Becca held her breath, expecting the boy to respond to the word with another fit. But his head remained on his mother's shoulder, his back rising and falling slowly. The stress appeared to have put him to sleep.

"So he made the mountain," Tom said. "How did he cut himself?"

Susan's jaw worked, but at first no words came out. When they did, they came with tears. "I only looked away for a *minute*, Tommy. I was distracted by who was downstairs. The voices were agitating him. I don't know how he found it."

"Found what?"

"One of my razors," Susan said. "He cut his hand on one of my razors. He didn't even scream until I got him out of the bath. I turned around and the bubble mountain was red and he was painting on the bathtub wall...*painting with his own blood.*" Her breath was short and fast now, on the verge of hyperventilating. Becca worried Noah would sense it and wake up. Brooks must have thought the same thing. He patted the air between them in a keep calm gesture.

"It's okay," Brooks said. "He's okay." He made eye contact with Becca and shot a glance down the hallway. She followed him out of the room, leaving the family alone.

In the bathroom, Becca stepped around the puddles on the floor, looked at the exposed shelves of the medicine cabinet, and ended up staring at the tiled wall above the soapy pink water in the tub.

"Goddamn," Brooks said. He drew his phone from his pocket and snapped a picture, then toggled the drain switch with the heel of his hand. The water gurgled down the drain, leaving a scummy residue in its wake.

The white tiles were emblazoned with a primitive crimson finger painting, a variation on one they had first seen in the kitchen: a bulbous head formed of a smeared palm print with angles that could have been bat wings curving off to the sides, and a beard of long, wavy finger trails running down toward the water.

Chapter 14

"What's R'lyeh?" Becca asked Brooks. They had seen the Petries to the emergency room and were headed north again on 495. "Where have I heard that word before?"

"It's an island," Brooks said. "A sunken island in the South Pacific. We have people on staff who've made entire careers out of studying its legends and lore, and the little bit of documented science they've pieced together from times when it made an appearance."

"Made an appearance? You mean in history?"

"No, I mean times when it surfaced. They don't know what made it sink, but the legends say it's older than the moon, so maybe the moon getting pulled into our orbit had something to do with it. We captured a Japanese submarine during World War II that was studying it up close. That's still classified, so you didn't hear it from me. Anyway, there have been times when the mountain peak of the island has risen above the waves. There's a city on that mountain, and a temple of slanting stones that make no sense."

"Sounds like the whole thing doesn't make sense."

"I mean it defies standard physics."

"Well sure, a sunken island rising from the bottom of the ocean?"

"It's like the Wade House. The geometry of the temple at the peak of R'lyeh is utterly fucked. The few expeditions that have landed there have become hopelessly disoriented. They can't tell if a stone slab is lying flat on the ground or tilted at an angle. Think about it. You're a climber. Imagine not being able to tell how gravity works in relation to a structure when you're looking for somewhere to hook a rope, or find a foothold. Also, the times when the island has risen coincided with sensitive people around the world having dreams about the high priest of the Great Old Ones, Cthulhu."

Becca felt a chill spread down her spine from the crawling flesh of her scalp. That was a name she had heard in whispers as a child, a name she still associated with the darkest secrets of her grandmother's house. "Do you think it's risen again? SPECTRA must monitor it, right? Do you think Noah is tuned into those dreams?"

"That makes the most sense, but I don't know. SPECTRA does monitor it. They watch it like they watch for signs of nuclear weapon use. There are sensors in place looking for submarine geologic activity, satellites devoted to the exact coordinates in the Pacific where it has surfaced before, but from what I hear they haven't been able to find it in years."

Becca chuckled mirthlessly.

"What?"

"They should have hired my grandmother when she was alive."

Brooks looked at her. "Are you sure they didn't?"

Becca's mouth fell open. "Do you know something about that?"

"No, but you might have noticed they don't tell me everything."

* * *

The sun came out as they wound their way north through the Miskatonic River Valley. At a gas station, Becca moved to the back seat to try and nap for a while with her head on Django's side, Brooks' wool overcoat pulled over her as a blanket. "Great," he said, looking at her in the rearview mirror. "Now I have blood on my shirt *and* dog hair on my coat. How professional."

"Occupational hazards, Brooks," Becca replied, shifting her hip against the car seat and finding a comfortable fit. "Wake me up when we get to Franconia Notch."

"We're not stopping in Arkham on the way? Over the river and through the woods to grandmother's house we go?"

"No. Maybe on the way back."

"I know you mainly used it as an excuse for the road trip, but it's actually a good idea to check Catherine's books and notes for references to the house. It could be more important than finding out what your father knows."

"Or finding out what he knows might help clarify what we're looking for at Miskatonic. Besides, it's only a feeling, but I think he won't stay in one place for too long. If he's involved in this and really trying to summon me with a Lincoln log, I think he's in danger. I don't want to waste any time."

"All right. Sweet dreams 'til New Hampshire."

* * *

Becca woke to the smell of wet pine needles and ozone through the car window. Somewhere along the way the snow had turned to rain. The mountaintops in the background remained as white as ever in January, but I-93 was slick and dark and she could hear the spray from the tires. She sat up and looked around. Django thumped his tail and Brooks met her eyes in the rear view mirror. "I told you to wake me up," she said.

"I was going to in a minute. We're almost there. Look familiar?"

It did. There wasn't much on the side of the road, but somehow it looked exactly as she remembered it from childhood vacations: the campground signs and knick-knack shops, the trees, guardrails, even the curve of the winding road. Her dry mouth tasted stale from the nap. She reached between the seats and found her water bottle, took a swig, and replaced it in the console. Rummaging through her bag, she found a tin of mints, popped one in her mouth, and rolled her window down a few inches. The cold air misted her cheeks and the taste of peppermint sharpened her mind. She instinctively craved coffee and almost asked Brooks to stop at a gas station or general store for a cup, but then she thought of how she wanted to feel when she saw her father for the first time in years. She'd already had two cups today and a third would make her jittery, edgy even.

Just the idea of standing face to face with him in a matter of minutes was winding her up. She decided that any lingering fatigue might serve to provide some equilibrium.

"Birch Grove Cabins?" Brooks asked. "Was that the name of the place?"

"Yeah."

"Haven't seen it yet."

"It's coming up," Becca said. "There'll be a turnoff after a blind curve and a creek."

"Your dad used to bring you here camping?"

"My parents did, yeah. Fishing and hiking in the summer, even skiing a couple times in the winter."

"Better days, huh? Were you able to enjoy winter vacations when you were a kid, or were you..."

"Depressed? No, that seemed to kick in with the hormones, after my mother killed herself."

Brooks stared at the road. "Is this the curve you mentioned?"

"Yeah. It'll be on the right."

The Ford bounced on its shocks down a divot-riddled road past squat wooden shacks painted brown to resemble log cabins nestled between the pine and birch trees in the shadow of Mt. Lincoln. Sap-clotted pine needles dusted the tar shingle roofs. A few of the rentals had vehicles parked in front, but most projected the cold stillness of unoccupied units with red-checkered curtains drawn. Brooks pulled the car up to the office beside the VACANCY sign, climbed out with the engine idling, and ducked inside for long enough to flash his ID and request a look at the guest register. Sliding behind the wheel again, he said simply, "Number nine."

"He's here?" Somehow Becca hadn't expected to find him at the end of the trail he'd left.

"Pretty sure. Or someone else using a lousy alias."

"What alias?"

"Stu Redman."

Becca couldn't help smiling. "Dad loved that book. Had a shelf full of second hand hardcovers. I can totally picture the ripped dust jacket with the sword fighter and the bird man."

"Yeah, it's my favorite, too. Tell him to get more creative when he's trying to lay low. For fuck's sake, *everybody's* read King."

* * *

Cabin 9 was one of the empty looking ones. No car, curtains drawn, raised on cinderblocks to keep rot at bay. Becca knocked while Brooks hovered at the bottom of the steps. After a pause and another triple knock, she saw motion through a thin gap in the curtain draped across the front door window. There was a long moment of stillness during which she felt her father's scrutiny, his hesitation. He had summoned her with a clue and she came, but was this really what he wanted, to have to face her after all these years? To involve her even deeper in whatever had drawn him to the Wade House? For a moment she thought he might wait it out, lay low and pretend he wasn't there. But then the muted rattle and scrape of a hook and eyelet gave way to the creaking of hinges in dire need of oil, and the scraggly face of a stranger appeared in the crack, his shallow blue eyes glancing over her face and narrowing as they settled on Brooks.

"Dad," Becca said, calling his gaze back. His eyes were the same, even if the hollow sockets they peered out of were deeper and darker, his eyebrows white and wild, his skin leathery and loose. He shuffled aside and opened the door for her.

He was dressed in a faded graphic tee, flannels and a black hoodie with badly frayed cuffs. His white stubble contrasted against his weathered skin, and when he took a cigarette from a pack atop the cheap, old TV set and lit it, she noticed his fingers were gnarled and callused, with ink stains under the nails. Becca blinked. The skin of his hands seemed to glow faintly from within, like a paper lampshade, subtle, but undeniable.

"You made it," Luke said as if she were late for a holiday meal. And then, to Brooks, "Anybody follow you?"

Brooks shook his head. "May we come in?"

"Make yourself at home."

Brooks stepped inside before Becca. She lingered on the doorstep, half wishing that Luke had come outside rather than inviting them in. It would have been less discreet to talk with him at one of the picnic tables, but reuniting with him under the open sky would have suited her. It would have felt less intimate, more open to escape. She didn't know what she expected from him at this late juncture, but she didn't want to receive it in the stale murky confines of the cabin.

She filled her lungs with a deep draught of fresh air and stepped over the threshold.

The cabin managed to cram a kitchenette, electric heating unit, bed, table, and chairs into two rooms with a closet-sized bathroom. Luke Philips' possessions were scant: a suitcase, a guitar case, and a ragged, overstuffed spiral notebook with loose and folded scraps of paper bulging out on all sides, as if they had been hastily gathered when he'd heard the car pull up.

"Dad, this is Jason Brooks. He's an agent with SPECTRA. Not sure if you know what that is, but you can trust him. We've been through some shit together."

Luke Philips scratched his beard with the two fingers of his right hand not holding his cigarette and Becca thought for a second that he might set his long hair on fire. "Yeah, I know SPECTRA. Lesser of two evils."

"What's the greater?" Brooks asked, pulling a chair out from under the table, spinning it around, and straddling it with his arms folded on the seat back.

"Starry Wisdom, of course. Those fuckers have a hard-on for me."

"I found the log you left in your saddle bag," Becca said.

"Of course you did. You bring my bike?"

Becca scoffed. "Yeah, we trailered it up here and told your *lesser evil* we were returning it to you. Judging by the fact you left a clue instead of a note, I kinda figured you were going for discretion."

"You figured right, sure. I just thought you might ride it up. By yourself."

"In the snow."

"Did it snow?"

"How long have you been holed up in here?" Becca noted the frailty of his frame. "Are you eating?"

Luke tugged his flannel pants up over his bony hips and picked his notebook up off the table. He sat on the bed and waved his cigarette at the vacant chair. "I'm all right. Sit, honey. You remember Walt Rogan? Runs the camp? Maybe not, you were just a kid. Walt cut me a deal where I can stay in the off-season in return for a little handy man work. It's good here. Quiet mostly. Better than the apartment I had in Conway. I couldn't focus on my work there."

Restless, Luke stood up again and rubbed his palms over his thighs, then paced the room, the fingers of his left hand climbing his right forearm like a spider as he took a drag. Becca realized he was absently playing his arm like a guitar, working out fingerings. She wondered if he even knew he was doing it. She wondered what he was on.

"Your work?" Brooks said. "What work is that?"

Luke returned to the bed, picked up his notebook and curled it in his hands. "I might want to talk to my daughter alone about that. Yes, yes I would. Do you mind?"

Brooks looked like he might be rapidly approaching his threshold for bullshit.

"I told you," Becca said. "You can trust him."

"You been in the Wade House?" Luke asked.

"We've spent the past week there," Becca said. "What brought *you* there?"

"Something in your grandmother's library put me on the road to that house. Should have minded my own business."

"When were you in Gran's library? You didn't even show for her funeral."

Luke winced. "I'm talking way back when you were just a girl. This goes back to then, what got me involved." He looked at Brooks, sighed, and committed to tell the tale. "She had a page of music in with all the spells and diagrams. I thought that was weird, so I asked her about it. She told me not to touch it, said it was the most valuable piece in her collection, which for sure made me curious to hear it. Maybe even just to spite her back then. She never took any interest in *my* music back before I gave it up and went into carpentry to support you and your mom. I just wanted to hear it, to understand why she treasured it. Seemed odd she would keep a piece of music and never hear it. So one day when she was away at a conference, I went into her study with my guitar and spent some time working out the prelude. Just the first eight bars."

"Did anything happen?" Becca asked.

Luke laughed. "Well yeah. It took a while to work out the chords—I was never fit for playing classical, but yeah, I must have got it right enough because I started seeing the world behind this one, like through a veil. I'd taken my share of recreationals by then, but this shit was a whole 'nother trip."

"Did she ever find out you played it?"

"I don't think so. Well, not until after your Mom died and I left."

"You told her then? I remember you yelling at her before you left. I wrapped a pillow around my head to shut it out."

"Sorry...I knew you were hurting, but I would have made it worse. You didn't need my rage on top of it all. By then I was using and starting to think I might follow her. I was afraid you'd find me if I did."

Becca's eyes prickled with heat. "So you just...left."

"Yeah. That's what I did. Regretted it, too, for a while, but then I started to think you were maybe better off. Safer without me."

"Safer with the woman you blamed for your wife's suicide."

Luke paced and took another drag. Becca could see his fingers trembling. This was hard for him. Good. He touched her shoulder, his jaw set askew the way hers went when she was sizing up something difficult. She squirmed at his touch and he took his hand back.

"Catherine was different with you," he said. "I think having grandchildren pulled her back from the brink, made her realize she had a chance to do better with you and your cousins than she did with me and my brothers."

"What brink?"

"You know. The abyss she was always staring into. She was fascinated by the dark infinities she found in those books and artifacts. I still say your mother saw something she couldn't accept in that house, and I'll go to my grave not knowing if your grandmother gave her a glimpse on purpose, or if she just opened the wrong door at the wrong time."

Becca had figured most of this out on her own, but it helped to hear him articulate it. She had needed this, needed it for a long time.

"Your Gran never took to your mom, but she loved *you* more than anything. I never thought... *Did* she ever let you see anything...unnatural?" The question frayed into a whisper at the end, like he wanted to simultaneously ask it and never ever ask it.

Becca stared at him, the tears she'd felt rising for her mother and for the little girl she had been now subsumed under her rising anger. She made him wait for his answer.

"What if she did? It's a little late now to take an interest, don't you think? But hey, I'm here, so I didn't check out like Mom. Relieved?"

"Hey now...Yeah, okay. I deserve that, I do."

"You don't get absolved for leaving a piece of a toy to summon me to where we had happier times. Sorry, but you don't. You left me. You fucking rode off with your guitar over your shoulder and didn't look back." And now she *was* crying. Damn him, she was shedding tears for the old waste.

"Did she hurt you?" Luke asked. "Did she hurt your *mind?*"

"No. She was good to me. My mind was..." Becca wiped her nose with a balled up tissue from her pocket, then squeezed it in her fist. "...damaged enough without help."

"I'm sorry, honey. Truly. I didn't know what to do. I stole the music when I left."

Becca stared at him.

He nodded. "She said it was the most valuable thing in the house, so I took it. Figured I'd sell it on the black market if I could make the connections, but mostly I made off with her treasure just to spite her. Then, when I got up here in the mountains, I wanted to hear more of it. I wanted to *see* more, more of what it revealed. I started playing it, working it out in bits and pieces, one phrase at a time. Before I knew it, I was in deep. Not eating, not sleeping, just playing my fingers raw." He turned his palm up and looked at the underside of his right forearm. "Skin started to glow from touching the guitar where the vibrations were strongest. Thighs, too, where the body rested on my lap. Sometimes I'd go translucent for a while and be looking at my own veins and bones." He uttered a cold laugh.

"What's funny?" Brooks asked.

"They call it *The Invisible Symphony.* That's the title. But I didn't know it would make *me* invisible. Thing is, that other world was becoming *more* visible the more I played, and I think I was getting more solid *there*. After a while, I thought I should stay away. I couldn't bring myself to set it on fire, didn't know what would happen if I worked up the nerve to try, but I came to believe I'd taken the most dangerous thing in that house away with me."

Becca pondered the odd title. "All music is invisible."

"True," Luke said. "I think it's a double meaning. It's not just to do with an invisible world. There are hidden variations in the music, inversions of themes implied between the lines. Over the years I puzzled out how to play some of them."

"You re-voiced the chords?" Brooks asked.

"Yeah. Are you a musician?"

"No, but one of the guys on our expedition team at the house is. He figured out to do the same thing with a fragment of music we acquired. Probably a piece of the same score. Do you still have the original, the whole thing?"

Luke nodded. "And every possible permutation right here in my notebook."

"What were you doing at the Wade House?" Becca asked. "Did you go there to play the piano?"

"No. I wanted them to think I did so they'd stop looking for me in this world."

"*They* who?" Becca asked. "Did you even go inside the house? I came back to Massachusetts because I thought you were lost in there. I thought you were in trouble."

"*They* is the Starry Wisdom cult. Catherine sent colleagues looking for me the year after I left, men she thought she could trust because they were academics. She didn't realize the cult was thriving underground at Miskatonic. In the decade since, they've probably got their tentacles up in the government, too. I catch references on TV—odd words dropped into political speeches, newscasts, and Hollywood movies. Secret messages for them that have ears to hear."

"You know you sound paranoid, right?" Becca said.

"Better paranoid than dead. A pair of them came looking for me when I lived in Conway. Well-dressed, clean-cut, no tattoos. Not your typical Starry Wisdom types. But they wore rings with a symbol I recognized from your Gran's books: a triangular rune. I think it represents a triad of musical notes, a chord that opens the gate. Back then I didn't know much, my experiments hadn't progressed much, and I almost admitted to having the score. Hell, I came this close to trying to sell it to them. But they gave me a bad feeling, so I played dumb. They found me again at a different address a few years later. By then I was playing a lot, wearing gloves and long sleeves to hide the glow. That time they beat me up and tossed my apartment, but I had the score rolled up and stashed in a lamp pole, so they didn't find it. I also had a gun under my mattress and when they flipped that, I grabbed it and scared them off."

"They weren't armed?" Brooks asked.

"They had a ritual dagger they threatened me with. You can cut someone up to get information without killing them. But I knew if they came back a third time, it would be with guns. That's when I decided to make it look like I crossed over at the Wade House."

"How did you know the house was important?" Brooks asked.

"I took a chance after Catherine died. When things settled down, I went to Miskatonic. Just walked into the library and showed them my driver's license. Said I wanted to see my mother's books and papers. I don't know if they told anybody I was there. I didn't stay long. Found what I was looking for, snapped some pictures of the pages, and read them when I got home. Unpublished stuff from a manuscript she was writing about the symphony."

"Do you still have the photos?" Brooks asked.

"Yeah, I made print outs. I have them here in my notebook." Luke riffled through the stuffed pages and withdrew a couple of folded, stapled sheets. He handed them to Becca. "She talks about a correspondence between Caleb Wade and a young Parisian architect named Zann. Wade had seen a house designed by Zann while honeymooning in France, and he became obsessed with it. He tracked the architect down and tried to hire him to design a house for him and his bride. His lighting business was the most successful in New England at the time. He's remembered as a candle maker, but he did a lot more than that—all kinds of innovation with gas lamps and even chemical handheld lights. Catherine says he was a kind of physicist, with deep knowledge of the different wavelengths of light and color. Way ahead of his time. But he was especially obsessed with some unconventional theories about what he called 'the psycho-spiritual effects of certain wavelengths on the human organism enhanced by essential salts and olfactory powders.' I don't fully understand that bit, but according to Catherine, Wade believed there was a connection between the theories he had about the manipulation of light with angled mirrors and the odd geometry of Zann's architecture. He thought lighting and architecture could be composed like music to open doors in the mind, and that the process could be enhanced with special incense."

"Zann..." Brooks said. "I've heard that name before. One of the first cases I was assigned to had to do with a physicist named Zann. I wonder if there's a connection."

Luke scratched his beard. When Brooks offered nothing further, he continued. "The correspondence goes on for most of a year, Wade prying Zann for the source of his inspiration and dangling large sums of money for the construction of the house he wants. Zann insists he can only design the house in relation to the landscape. Wade offers an all-expense-paid residency in America. They talk about ley lines and something called *seasonal currents of force.*

"Once he starts to think that Wade might have a thing or two to teach *him,* you can tell Zann gets excited about the project, and he shares more about the source of his designs. Turns out, he had an uncle who played the viol in an orchestra for a while, but he was fired for embellishing the music with his own strange interpretations. This musician, Erich Zann, had his own theories about sound frequencies that parallel Wade's theories about light. And both men were interested in the effects of these vibrations on consciousness. The younger Zann played just enough piano to appreciate the asymmetrical structures in his uncle's music. But his talent was geometry, so he adapted those musical shapes into architecture. *That's* the origin of the Wade House—it's a three-dimensional interpretation of Erich Zann's magnum opus, *The Invisible Symphony.* It's built on Zann's music, illuminated by Caleb Wade. Every window, lamp, and mirror was placed to make the place vibrate in a particular way. The house itself was placed on that hill to vibrate a particular way. I'm curious: did the spooks you work for tell you not to move the furniture so much as an inch?"

"Yeah," Brooks said. "We don't even sleep on the beds."

"But the piano is what they're most concerned about," Becca said. "We've used it as a portal. They're worried that if we move it, that portal will be lost and we won't be able to find it again."

Luke looked at his daughter with horrified awe darkening his features. "Have you gone through it?"

"Once," she said.

"We both have," Brooks said.

"Where did it take you?"

"A different place each time," Becca said. "Depending on what chord was played before opening the lid."

"It worked, then."

"You didn't set foot in the house when you ditched your motorcycle there?" Brooks asked. "You didn't play the piano?"

"I was tempted to, but I was afraid of what might happen if I played the chords I'd puzzled out. I've become a musician over the years, but I'm no magician. The place was sucking in black fallout when I found it. I didn't dare go in alone."

"I don't understand," Becca said. "Why did you spend your life re-writing a piece of music if you don't intend to play it? What aren't you telling us? What are *your* variations on the piece supposed to do? And what was the music supposed to do in its original form?"

Brooks stood up, almost knocking his chair over. He raised a finger for silence, and cocked his ear. Becca heard it, too: a helicopter. Brooks was already at a window, parting the curtain and peering up at the sky. The sound of the rotors grew louder, faded, and then swelled again, shaking the cottage. It wasn't passing over but circling around.

"I think it's one of ours," Brooks said.

Luke moved to his guitar case, clutching his notebook to his chest. He looked like a cornered animal.

"Hide the score," Brooks said. "The original. Make it disappear." Then he sidled through the door and walked down the steps into the cyclone of the descending black bird. A cloud of pine needles, dirt, and ice billowed out over the ground in a radial wave as the helicopter touched down in the barren lot at the center of the circle of cabins.

Becca watched from the doorway, blocking her father from view, listening to his frantic motions as he hid Zann's score. Brooks shielded his eyes and waited for the rotors to slow.

Nico Merrit emerged with his head low and strode across the field toward Brooks. His sidearm was in plain view, but he made no aggressive gestures toward his fellow agent. When he'd cleared the blades, he set his hands on his hips and nodded toward the cabin. "You and Philips taking a romantic weekend getaway, or is her father in there?"

Brooks scratched the back of his head.

"Tell him to pack a bag. I have orders to bring him back to Concord."

Chapter 15

Becca was out of the car before Brooks had put it in park, running for the door of the hut, running to find her father who had never come running for her, Django on her heels.

Inside, she bumped into an agent, nearly knocking him over. "Where is he?" she asked. He pointed down the row of cubicles to the one she had been assigned as a temporary bedroom. She caught her breath and composed herself, striding briskly down the row, the strains of an acoustic guitar reaching her as she approached. The sound, faint at first, grew stronger: a delicate, plaintive minor key sequence, lazily strummed with ornamental arpeggios between the chords.

Luke Philips looked up from the cot where he sat perched with his guitar in his lap, the last chord he'd struck ringing for a second, then abruptly muted when Django thumped his tail against the body of the instrument and licked Luke's hand. Becca hung back, her own hands stuffed in her pockets.

Luke scratched the dog's head and extended his chin for a licking. He looked at Becca. "Your dog?"

"Yeah. His name is Django."

Her father flashed a delighted grin and played a sloppy Django Reinhardt riff before tapering off and setting the guitar down on a folded wool blanket beside him. He continued petting the dog, but it seemed like he was doing it more to soothe himself than the animal as he wrinkled his brow and tried to read Becca's stony expression.

Finally she said, "Have you been here the whole time just chilling? I was worried. I thought they would…"

"Interrogate me?"

"Yeah."

"They did."

She raised an eyebrow.

"Nothing harsh. Mostly the same questions you had for me." His eyes flicked deliberately toward the ceiling, telling her that he knew they were likely under surveillance.

"So what now? Are you free to go?"

"I have been conveniently reunited with my bike, but no. They want to keep me handy for now."

"What for?"

He sighed heavily and his hand reached for the neck of the guitar, an unconscious comfort. He brushed the strings on the headstock and they chimed faintly, reminding Becca of piano notes. "Your man in charge explained that the membrane between the house and the other world was breached by a cultist who tried to pass over, or is maybe still trying to pass over. He said the radiation released by the breach dissipated while you were on your road trip and now they want your team to go back in and try to find him before he can do more damage."

Becca processed the news under her stony façade. It inspired conflicting feelings. She wanted to go in again—that was the explorer in her, the urge to follow strange paths to wherever they led. But a stronger urge told her to flip her finger at the people who had plans for her. Especially if her father agreed with them.

"Are you on the team now? Are you going in now that…" *Now that you have someone to hold your hand on the threshold of madness?*

"No. I'm supposed to sit it out, wait here in case they need me."

"For what exactly?"

"Plan B."

"What's that?"

"If all else fails, I bring the house down."

"Can you?"

He stared at the floor with a grimace. "We'll find out if they tell me to try. They wanted to know if my inversions of the music could seal the portals or nudge the house out of alignment. I don't think I can do that. Might even make things worse trying. But there's one sequence I could try if things can't get any worse that might destabilize the whole thing."

"Well good luck with that," Becca said. She picked her bag up off the floor and slung it over her shoulder.

"Where are you going?" He started to rise from the cot. She held him at bay with a raised hand.

"Don't. Just don't. You don't get to comfort me and reconnect now. Somehow I got caught in the middle of this with *no* guidance. This...*Philips* family business. Things you and Gran never bothered to warn me about. 'Sorry, kid, but the true nature of the cosmos would be too much for you to handle, just be careful you don't step in it.'"

Luke started to respond, but she cut him off.

"But I did step in it. And you know? Now that you're here to help them, I think I'll wipe the black slime off my boots and go back to Brazil. I don't need to end up like Mom, or Catherine, or Moe Ramirez."

He squinted at the name. "*Ramirez.* You knew him?"

"Briefly, yes. Was he a friend of yours? He forgot to mention that during the opening act of Armageddon."

"No. He was Catherine's prize student for a while. Before he dropped out. She said he was wasting a great mind. He accused her of dabbling in things she couldn't control."

Becca scratched at her arm. "She told you that?"

"She told Grandpa. I overheard. She was offended. Probably because she knew he was right."

"Well, I'm done dabbling."

"They need you."

"They don't. They have other people who can see what I see."

"Then why did you come back?"

Becca hated the heat she felt rising in her face, hated his oblivious blindness. She bit her lip, clenched her fists, and waited to get control of her voice. When it spilled out of her, the words were clipped, choked: "For you."

Luke approached her, hesitated, afraid to touch her. "Me?"

"They told me you might be lost in there." She sniffed. "But you're not. So I can go."

"Becca, I'm sorry. I know it's not enough, but I'm sorry for so much."

She folded her arms and exhaled. He touched her hair. She didn't flinch.

"This is bigger than us," he said, "but I'm glad it led you to me. I always wanted to see you. To start making it up to you. But I didn't know how."

Silence welled up between them. The bustle and chatter of agents, techs, and machinery seemed far away, in another dimension.

"You can go to Brazil, New Zealand, Nepal, or wherever," Luke said, "but that gate the reverend is looking for...if something gets out when he opens it, it won't matter where you are. It won't be far enough, honey."

"Don't call me that."

"You can't run from this stuff."

"You would know."

And before she could cave and make it easier for him, she turned and walked off, Django at her heels. She paced a circuit of the hut's outer aisles, not caring where she was headed, only that it was *away*.

Brooks caught sight of her from over a cube wall and stepped into her path. "Hey," he said. "You okay?"

"Yeah. No. I don't know."

"What happened?"

"I just...I don't know what I'm doing here, Jason. We found my father, and honestly, I'm kinda shocked to find that he's probably of more use to SPECTRA than I am."

"I seriously doubt that."

"Have you seen Northrup since we got back?"

"Yeah. All is forgiven with regards to our little trip off the reservation. They're just happy we found your dad before someone else did."

Becca lowered her voice. "If they followed us, then they know we visited Tom too, right?"

Brooks' eyes darted around. "Can't tell yet if anyone is pursuing that. Honestly, it might be best for the family if they are."

Becca considered this. She didn't feel good about the prospect of Tom having to depend on people like Northrup to do what was in Noah's best interest. And would he think she and Brooks had betrayed his trust if a black van showed up to take them in? A moment ago all she could think of was getting herself out of this tangled web, but now she remembered that there were other unwilling people ensnared in it. If she cared about Tom, Susan, and Noah, why didn't she care about everyone else who would suffer if the monsters clawed their way back into the world? Or what if they didn't have to claw their way in because the gate was left swinging wide while she looked the other way because...*why?* Because her daddy had abandoned her and it went against her grain to work for The Man?

"For now we have to focus on the more urgent priority," Brooks said. "The house is clear of radiation. Levels dropped fast. Hopefully that doesn't mean Proctor found the gate at the heart of the maze already and sucked it all down the drain. We have to go on the assumption that we can still stop him. We're going back in tonight. Are you in?"

There was an intensity in his eyes. He really believed he needed her.

She couldn't do this for Luke Philips or Daniel Northrup, not for God and Country—neither of which she'd ever had much faith in and less now than ever—but she could do it for Brooks. She could step up for him because he expected her to. He'd seen another side of her once in a moment of crisis; something she hadn't known was in her until fate demanded it. And hadn't she grown a little then? Hadn't she been braver and more assured since? Who was she trying to kid, thinking she was going to turn her back and run now? Thinking for even a moment that she was going to let Rafael's sacrifice be in vain after all.

"I've come this far," she said. "I'm in."

"Good. Charge the dragonfly." He started to walk away to make his own preparations, thought of something else and turned back. "Hey, Becca?"

"Yeah?"

"You wearing your scarab?"

She nodded.

"Good."

* * *

The expedition team climbed the hill together through the mist of melting frost into the lumbering shadow of the Wade House. The silhouette of the house was cut here and there with planes of light slicing through the mist—not the lamp light one would expect to find emanating from a house, but the cold light of another world arcing out in razored parabolas stretched at odd angles from windows, gaps in the shingles, and cracks between the chimney bricks. Becca walked third in line behind Brooks and Hanson. Behind her Mark took a more winding path, and she paused to make sure he was coming along. She couldn't tell if his meandering could be attributed to fear or distraction. He had mumbled to himself in an incessant stream ever since the night when he'd passed through the closets, and now his babbling was intensifying with proximity to the house.

It was just before midnight when they entered. Brooks went first, finding none of the same dazzling light inside. He used his flashlight in the foyer until he found the wall plate and flipped the switches, bringing the faded brocade wallpaper into view, and with it, a quiet, mundane reorientation to a house that appeared to have changed not at all since they'd last occupied it.

Becca stepped around Brooks and looked down the hall. The architecture was unwavering. The curtain still hung across the entrance to the library. She could see the corner of the grandfather clock perched at the entrance to the parlor and hear its perpetual *kronk-krunk*, could glimpse the cabinet of shattered china in the kitchen beyond the carved walnut arch at the end of the hall; the very spot where she'd caught sight of Reverend Proctor's cloak gliding away down a stone passage the last time she stood here in a radiation suit. But now all appeared normal, and somehow that unnerved her more, set her on edge. The stillness of the house felt like that of a patient predator.

She reached into her coat pocket and withdrew the intricate metal dragonfly, touched its concealed button and set it hovering in the stale air before her face.

"No one opens a door alone," Brooks said. "We'll clear this floor first. Watch for any reflective surfaces. If you see anything, anything at all, even a *flicker* that might be a breach, speak up. Got it?"

Becca and Hanson nodded while Mark wandered ahead toward the velvet curtain.

"*Burns*," Brooks called, "did you hear me? No going alone. That curtain counts as a door."

The biologist brushed his hand over the curtain, but held Brooks' gaze and waited for the rest of the team to catch up. When they did, Brooks ripped the heavy fabric from the doorframe and cast it on the floor, the curtain rod clattering for a second before it was muted in a pool of velvet. Brooks kicked it away and shone his flashlight beam into the dusty library.

"You said you had a look at the labyrinth through the mirror on the mantel in here?" he asked Becca.

"Yes."

Brooks walked through the room, sweeping the beam, and froze when it flared off the square of glass. Holding the light steady, he stalked forward. Mark approached the desk and dragged his fingers through a film of incense ash. Hanson turned on his axis, taking in the height of the octagonal turret room, the shelves winding up into shadow. Becca worked the remote in her hand, flying the drone toward the focus of Brooks' light, the framed mirror.

"Too much glare," she said. "Turn it off for a second."

Brooks killed the flashlight. Hanson sighed at the vista glowing through the glass: a mossy stone passage illuminated by the light of an alien moon.

Mark approached the hearth and raised his hand to touch the glass. Brooks drew a breath to stop him, but changed his mind at the last second, held it, and watched as Mark's fingertips passed through the space where the surface of the mirror should have been with an iridescent shimmer like a bubble popping.

"It's warm," Mark said. "And humid. Like an ocean breeze." He withdrew his hand, rubbed his fingertips together, and craned his neck toward the mirror. This time, Brooks clapped a hand on his shoulder and pulled him back before he could stick his head through for a look around. "No way. Let Becca send the drone."

Mark let Brooks lead him away as Becca stepped up and maneuvered the dragonfly into the rectangle of light. She still had trouble believing the mirror had become a window. The action felt surreal, like flying the little machine through the screen of a television. Once it was in, she focused on the display in her hand, sending the drone down the stone corridor and hooking it left, around the corner of the first passage it came to. On the screen this corridor looked much like the first. No sign of Proctor, but why should there be? He could be anywhere in the labyrinth. Even if she caught a glimpse of him, they wouldn't be able to follow. This portal was too small.

"Bring it back before we lose it," Brooks said.

"That's what I'm thinking," Becca replied. "Not like we can follow it anyway."

"Come on. Let's head upstairs and try some doors," Brooks said. He kicked the curtain aside, and led others down the hall.

Becca took one last look around the library, the dragonfly hovering over her shoulder. "Do you know if they've learned anything from the book?"

"Not much yet," Brooks said. "Most of it's written in a cipher they haven't seen before. Northrup said they're making progress on cracking it, but a full transcription is going to take a while, never mind interpreting the contents. I don't like flying blind in here either, but time is of the essence."

They had come to the foot of the stairs. The rose window on the landing was dark, as was what little of the second floor they could glimpse through the balusters. Becca switched the drone's headlight on and sent it fluttering up the stairs ahead of them, casting a pale puddle of light over the scuffed boards. Her stomach lurched, the moving shadows exacerbating the nausea that had been creeping up on her since reentering the house.

The stairs creaked as they climbed. Becca felt the hairs on the back of her neck rising with each step; a reaction that felt more like the presence of static electricity than fear. Not that she was entirely lacking in fear. She exhaled when Brooks found the switch at the top of the stairs and lit the second-floor lamps, spilling light into the music room and the open bedrooms. She searched every open doorway, half expecting the reverend or something he worshipped to spring out at them, her mouth suddenly dry, her hands clammy on the remote. She dragged her thumb clumsily across the screen, sending the dragonfly careening toward a wall and almost hitting Hanson in the face, but he slapped it out of the air, reflexively.

"Sorry," Becca said.

He scrutinized her. "You all right?"

"Fine." Becca knelt and picked the drone off the floor, then sent it flying into the nearest bedroom. As it disappeared around the corner, reflected light scattered across the wall. Becca selected the stationary hover mode, followed the bug into the chamber, and found it hovering in front of a full-length antique gilt-framed mirror. The light of the LED played over the silver glass, entangled with shafts from within—long, thin rays that rotated lazily, as if filtered through leagues of water. Becca stepped up to the mirror, entranced by the play of light at the center of the shadow-soaked room.

"Don't touch it." Brooks stood beside her. "If you break the membrane, it might flood the room."

Becca stared into the shifting light. It exerted a powerful pull, like a magnet tugging at the iron in her blood. The light was so beautiful. It would be so easy to step through, to swim.

Brooks clenched her wrist and led her from the room. Back in the electric light of the hall, she blinked her burning eyes, realizing it had been minutes since she'd last done so. "That was...hypnotic."

"Yeah, I could tell," Brooks said. "Something about it reminded me of a Venus fly trap."

Reminded of insects, Becca focused on the remote and recalled the dragonfly to the hall. Hanson and Burns had moved on to the room with the fireplace where they had encountered the first closet breach. Brooks called out their names.

"You should see this, Brooks," Hanson shouted back. Passing the music room on the way to catch up, Becca did a double take and Brooks followed her gaze through the entrance. It was the light in the room—not the incandescent ambience that should be spilling in from the electric fixtures, but a distinctly outdoor cast of light, a diffuse, sallow gloaming.

Becca stepped into the room and gasped. The high walls were sheared off in a rough line where ragged plaster gave way to moldy stone, as if the earthquake had exposed the ancient granite bones of the house. Above the stone slabs, a mustard gas sky roiled and heaved, spilling jaundiced light over the glossy piano lid.

"It's breaking through," Becca said. "It's like the other realm is eating away at the house."

"Come on," Brooks said. "We'll come back and send the drone over the wall for an aerial view, but right now let's stay together. They shouldn't be alone in there."

Becca could see the same yellow atmosphere in place of a ceiling before they reached the room at the end of the hall. Passing through the doorframe, she felt the humidity wrap its clammy embrace around her. The room was gone. She and Brooks stood in a stone passage rife with creeping black mold.

There was no sign of the other two. Brooks called their names again.

"Over here!" a thin voice rang back. Becca thought it was Mark's, but it was hard to tell and even harder to locate. Brooks sheathed his flashlight on his belt and drew his gun while Becca sent the drone ahead, searching every intersection for signs of Hanson, Burns, or Proctor.

The first three passages she checked were empty and almost identical but for variations in the mold and the erosion of the stone. She sent the drone into a fourth and her heart leapt. "What the *fuck?*"

Brooks peered over her shoulder at the screen. "Is that a bathroom?"

She nodded. "I think it's the master bath, but the perspective is...through the mirror."

Something rustled in the passage behind them, fleshy and weighty, slithering over stone. They turned and scanned the shadows, found nothing. Becca looked back at the screen in her hand. "Someone's in the bathroom now. Proctor?"

A scream reached their ears, the acoustics of the labyrinth mangling the sound into a ricocheting echo.

"Let's go!" Brooks shoved Becca down the corridor, away from the rustling that sounded more like raspy whispers with every passing millisecond. They turned a corner and stopped short, staring into a collision of planes and angles that made little sense, scenes layered atop one another like photos printed on panes of glass: the octagonal tiles of the second floor bathroom stamped into the granite walls. Mark Burns' body was splayed across a shelf of stone that was also somehow a claw-footed white bathtub, splashed with dark blood. Reverend Proctor spun around, his frock flaring out around him, tattoos arching with the contortions of his battle face, his ritual dagger jutting from the bottom of his clenched fist.

Dick Hanson threw his arms up and buckled backward, getting his belly out of the path of the arcing blade just in time.

Brooks trained his gun on Proctor, but before he could take the shot, Hanson had lunged forward into the wake of the knife, slamming Proctor's overextended shoulder and driving him into the wall. Hanson dragged Proctor's knuckles across the rough granite and seized the dagger by the hilt as it fell free. Proctor flailed and kicked out, but Hanson drove the heel of his hand into the reverend's chin, cracking his head against the stone.

Proctor collapsed and Hanson straddled him, pressing the blade to the reverend's throat and rooting through the man's pockets with his free hand. Proctor's head lolled on his shoulders. He uttered a gravelly moan that climbed in pitch and intensity—a final prayer, or last ditch defense?

Becca took a stumbling step backward, watching the scene play out beyond Brooks' poised weapon. She considered flying the drone into Proctor's face just to interrupt his chant, but before she could, Hanson pressed the blade into Proctor's throat with enough pressure to draw blood and silence the man.

Becca's heart hammered. She tried to focus on Mark, sprawled in the ghostly tub in a pool of his own blood. She stepped around Brooks to reach the body, knelt, and checked for a pulse. Mark stared at her, his eyes glassy but alive, his pulse sluggish under her trembling fingers.

*   *   *

Brooks had Proctor's head lined up on the sight blade of his 9mm. The reverend had stopped chanting but was still conscious. Hanson had proven to be a fierce fighter, and Brooks considered him with fresh eyes. He held the knife to Proctor's throat while searching his clothes. Off to the side, Becca had produced a pocketknife of her own and was cutting a strip of black cotton off her t-shirt. She folded it into a makeshift pad and pressed it to Burns' wound. A sharp laugh pulled Brooks' focus back to Hanson, who was now clenching the gleaming silver key tight in his hand.

Brooks lowered his gun. It was over. They had what they needed. Now the most pressing issue was getting everyone out of the house before they found themselves trapped in the twilight realm. But scanning the area, he saw the bathroom solidifying around them, becoming more present, more materially manifest than the other half of the double-exposure world.

Hanson, sweaty and wild-eyed, smiled at him. Brooks returned the grin and was still wearing it like an idiot with his gun at his hip when Hanson punched the dagger through Proctor's throat. Blood gushed over Hanson's knuckles, and he rose, his right hand gripping the dripping dagger, his left the glowing key. He took a step toward Brooks and held the key up by the shaft, his eye burning through the hole in the grip.

Brooks reeled, brought the gun back up. "Why kill him?"

"He wanted out of this world anyway," Hanson said. "But we couldn't just let him choose his own exit."

Brooks trained his gun on Hanson's chest. "Drop the knife."

Hanson slipped the ritual dagger into his belt.

"It was you, wasn't it?" Brooks said. "You were the one who made sure it was salt water when they waterboarded Darius Marlowe. You *son of a bitch*. Who are you working for?"

Hanson laughed. "I serve no earthly power, Brooks." He brought the key to his lips and blew through the filigreed hole. An undulating whistle pierced the air, climbing to the height of human hearing and beyond. Air, stone, tile, and plaster trembled, rippled.

The whispering sound rushed in from behind. Brooks whirled and brought the gun up, was lashed across the face by something serpentine. A fang lacerated his cheek, blazing a searing trail of pain; no, not a fang, he saw as the fleshy whip retracted, the barb of a stingray tail curling up from the crustacean-armored form of Lung Crawthok. Hanson had called it with the whistle and it was suddenly upon him, rows of claws clacking a vicious syncopated rhythm, face flayed wide and teeth chittering.

Brooks felt a wave of cold fear sluice down his body and for a moment forgot about shooting the thing, frozen by the helpless dread of prey within reach of an overpowering predator. He wobbled, tried to steady his weapon hand. The muscles in his torn cheek burned and spasmed, contorting as the venom from the barb spread, his vision dimming and tunneling. Or was the space around him tunneling and stretching as the two worlds passed out of alignment?

Hanson lunged past him down that tunnel, sounding the whistle as he passed below the harpoon arm of the towering guardian. Brooks fired two shots. One shattered the creature's shell on its thigh, releasing a spray of green paste. Its head swept forward, eclipsing all other sights and a fetid howling wind of pain and rage blasted Brooks in the face. He turned his cheek and saw Becca propping up Mark with her neck under his armpit, pressing the soaked cloth to the gash in his side, trying futilely to drag him away from the monster, her face blanched with terror at the thing.

Burns locked eyes with Brooks, and Brooks could see both of their oncoming deaths in the man's gaze. He turned back to the creature, sensing its claws poised to sweep in on him from the fringes of his diminishing peripheral vision.

And then a body was tumbling past him to the sound of a woman's scream.

Burns had gathered his last reserves of strength and hurled his broken body into the embrace of the pinchers, knocking the monster down the yawning tunnel.

Brooks dropped his gun, felt his consciousness dissolving under the caustic power of the venom. He staggered backward and tripped over something—the edge of the bathtub—and landed in the slippery blood of the man who had sacrificed himself to save them. It was in vain, he thought, as the world contracted to a keyhole of light. The last thing he saw passing through it down the tunnel was the running silhouette of Becca Philips.

Chapter 16

The first thing Brooks saw when he came to was Luke Philips hovering over him, all salt-and-pepper stubble and scraggly hair haloed by painfully bright halogen lights on the tracks that ran the ceiling of the Quonset hut. Luke turned his head and the light flared into Jason's eyes, intensifying the throbbing in his skull. He touched his cheek and felt a thick bandage and medical tape. His face ached in the dull sort of way that told him he'd been given painkillers. His mouth was parched, his tongue a little numb. He looked down at his arm and saw that they were giving him fluids. He groaned. Why did the answer to every injury have to involve plugging him into a saline bag?

"Where is she?" Luke asked. Brooks saw a hand squeeze the man's denim jacket at the biceps and urge him away. Northrup stepped around the worried father and gazed down at Brooks, concern etched in his brow.

"Sorry, Jason. Can you speak?"

Brooks tried to say, *Yeah, I can talk,* but it came out as a sloppy approximation.

"You had a barb stuck in your cheek. Dr. Matheson removed it and stitched you up, but the anesthetic will keep you numb for a while. Unfortunately, we have to send you back in as soon as you're up to it. I'd send someone else, but you're the only one left with EDEP. How's your head?"

"Too soon to tell," Brooks said. He looked at Luke Philips, a man who had only known the whereabouts of his daughter for the past 24 hours, and yet was suddenly very worried about her. Brooks supposed ignorance was bliss compared to knowing your kid was stuck between dimensions.

"What happened in there?" Northrup asked.

Brooks slurred through the story, recounting everything from the overlay of the house with the maze to the discovery of Proctor to Hanson's murder of the reverend, his summoning of the guardian, and escape with the key while Burns threw himself into the path of Lung Crawthok, saving Brooks' life. Luke Philips looked fascinated by the account at first, and then increasingly agitated.

"What about Becca?"

"She followed Hanson down the tunnel. I saw her slip past the guardian while it was…dealing with Burns, but I was fading out by then. If you didn't find her when you found me, then she's still in the maze."

Northrup had remained placid throughout the recap. Now he kneaded his temple with one hand and patted his pocket with the other, instinctively searching for his cigarettes before stopping short of taking one. "If Hanson was a cultist all this time, why did he kill Proctor? Why not work together?"

Brooks sat up. His head throbbed and he let it fall back against the pillow. "Water."

Luke handed him a plastic cup with a straw. Brooks took a sip and relished the icy sensation in his throat before trying to speak again. "I think Proctor told me the truth right before he went into the maze. He doesn't care about letting anything out; he just wants in. And that's not good enough for Hanson. Maybe all *he* cares about is releasing the Old Ones."

"You don't think they were ever working together?" Northrup asked.

"No. Doesn't matter now anyway. The reverend is dead."

"And Becca's in there alone with this traitor who killed him for the key," Luke said.

Brooks looked at Northrup. "What brought you in after us?"

"When you didn't respond on the radio, we sent the backup team in after you. The house was stable by then. They found only you, in the upstairs tub with a good amount of blood. We thought you were dead."

"Burns. It was his blood. I think Hanson attacked him first. Me and Becca got there after. Have you talked to his husband?"

"Not yet. We can't risk drawing public attention to the Wade House until this crisis is resolved."

"Fuckin' Becca..." Brooks shook his head. "She probably went after Hanson more for revenge than anything else. Your daughter has a bit of a temper."

Luke nodded. "I think I know where she gets it from. You want to see mine in full bloom, try telling me I'm not going in there with you when you're back on your feet, which better be soon."

*　*　*

Django wouldn't be held back either. He took the lead and scouted ahead when Brooks reentered the house with Luke Philips shortly after dawn. They found that, for the time being anyway, the structure had resolved into its earthly geometry. The mirrors held only what was in front of them, the closets only dusty shelves. The walls terminated in ceilings, and even the piano, when opened, revealed only strings and hammers. Luke ran a finger over the keys without striking any, and Brooks shook his head sternly. "Not unless we have to."

They let the dog roam freely, counting on his acute sense of smell to alert them to any trace of Becca. His equilibrium had gradually worked itself out, and now he roved the halls and empty rooms with purpose, nose to the floor, snuffling and swishing his tail with a plaintive whine rasping in his throat, but failing to fix on any one spot, or to vocalize with the urgency that would indicate a breach.

"Do you think it's inert because it's daytime?" Luke asked.

"Could be," Brooks said. "Or maybe she found a way to stop the process."

"I don't like it. What if she did something that trapped her?"

"Let's not jump to conclusions. We don't know what's causing the dimensions to go in and out of alignment. Could be tied to day and night; could be based on some other cycle. I doubt my people know as much as they think they do."

Luke looked at the dog. Django cocked his head as if even he were asking, *What now?*

"Come on," Brooks said. "There's one place we haven't explored yet."

Luke raised an eyebrow in a way that reminded Brooks of Becca.

"The basement."

*　*　*

Brooks didn't know what he expected to find in the basement. He had been told there was a candle maker's shop down there, but events on the upper floors had interfered with even a cursory exploration of the sub level. When he opened the door, Django shot past him and ran down the stairs. He yelled after the dog, but there was no calling him back. Brooks found the light switch and flipped it. There was a hum, and the bottom of the stairs flickered into view, dim and gray-washed. Brooks took hold of the railing and slowly descended. His calves still burned from the eel bites, and his stitched cheek throbbed. Luke Philips took the stairs gingerly behind him, the older man apparently plagued by arthritis or old motorcycle injuries. Brooks grinned wryly at what a pathetic front they had to offer in the face of a real threat. Maybe they could count on the dog at least. He unsnapped his holster and loosened his gun.

The walkie on his belt crackled and Northrup's voice came through, distant and metallic: "What's your location? Over."

"Descending to the basement. Over." He expected a reaction, maybe a warning against this course of action, but after a second of silence, Northrup came back with, "I want contact every five. Over."

"Got it. Any luck connecting to the dragonfly? Over."

"No. They keep trying, but all we've got is snow. Over."

Brooks could hear Django's claws clicking on concrete before his head cleared the ceiling. The dog was pacing around a circular pool ringed with black tiles and iron candelabra bearing the dusty remains of spent wax. Benches lining the walls bore spools of wick string, molds, and tools, but Brooks swept his gaze over these before zeroing in on the primary feature of the room: a set of five bronze bells suspended in a pentagonal configuration above the brackish water. The bells, at least 3 feet in diameter, were suspended from a star-shaped iron frame with heavy rope threaded through a set of pulleys and dangling in a line of balled knots beside the dark pool. Chalk sigils on the concrete floor described a path from the tile perimeter to a gaping tunnel mouth in the east wall. The resemblance to a Boston subway tunnel made Brooks' stomach churn.

"All this time you were fucking around with the piano and this was right under your feet," Luke said.

Brooks scowled at him. "What is it?"

"If I had to guess, I'd say it's a summoning portal. More controlled than the piano. This wouldn't be for gaining entrance, but for drawing things out."

"Out of the pool," Brooks said.

"Out of the beyond."

"And into the tunnel."

Chapter 17

Becca walked between curtains of light webbed with scintillating radiance. She was near the heart of the labyrinth; she could smell it: ozone and brine and the flora of another world. The moldy granite walls had given way to pulsing phosphorescence that felt wet to the touch. She had lost sight of Hanson what felt like hours ago, but she wondered if time was the same here as on the other side.

She still had Mark's blood on her hands and smudged across her belly below the ragged line of her ripped shirt. It looked black in the odd light. At least she didn't need electric light to navigate these radiant walls. The drone had fallen out of the air, and the remote had blacked out just seconds after she dashed past the guardian on the threshold, the labyrinth lurching away from the house like a carnival ride. She'd stashed both in her shoulder bag and had been creeping around corners blind ever since, clutching her serrated pocketknife in her fist, and touching the scarab beetle between her breasts for reassurance whenever she felt her nerve might fail her. The burnished gold shone faintly but the ruby remained dark, the wings and legs inanimate.

Becca's skin and bones vibrated in sympathy with the walls of light, and her mind conjured images of her body unraveling in tatters of stray atoms suddenly unconstrained from the pattern that constituted her existence.

She came to a T-junction and instinctively took the left turn. Her pace increased with the gravity of the slope and soon she was confronted with a series of passages opening on both sides. All pulsed with the same green glow, but peering into the third passage on the right, she saw faint black splotches on the floor a few feet ahead. Blood? She took the turn and, coming closer, recognized the stains as the heat signatures of footprints. She was perceiving the infrared spectrum directly.

Were they Hanson's footprints? She was willing to bet on it. After all, they weren't claw shaped and dragging a tail.

The prints started to fade. She picked up her pace. A sound like the ocean in a conch shell swelled around her, and in a little while she could discern something else: a chanted litany emerging from the white noise. Hanson's voice. The walls of the corridor disintegrated into green mist, and she had the sense that she had entered a great chamber. The floor beneath her feet hardened without warning, causing her footsteps to echo.

The chant broke like a rusted chain.

An aperture appeared in the luminous mist, a cyclopean spiral of metal plates converging on a slot from which violet light spilled in a malignant shaft that strained her retinas. Something eclipsed the harsh light, providing momentary relief: the silhouette of a man. He turned to look at her over his shoulder as he notched the key into the slot. "Come for a front row view, have you?"

Becca squeezed the knife in her hand. It felt small compared to the ritual dagger he had tucked in his belt.

"You've witnessed the glory of the lesser emanations. Now you'll see their sexless source, begetter of all abominations, the gate of the spheres: Yog Sothoth."

"Why did you kill Proctor?" She stalked toward him slowly, hoping to get within striking distance while he answered.

Hanson sneered. "Only one man in history can turn this key. What did *he* ever do to earn the honor? All he ever wanted was to escape the world. I've come to transform it. To finish the great work of Caleb Wade." Hanson scoffed at the knife in Becca's hand. "You should run, girl. That won't avail you against what's coming."

"It'll do fine against you."

"Not for long. You're about to become the sole witness to my apotheosis. I'll be deemed worthy of entrance to the kingdom. The lady of a thousand hooks will speed my passage, and space and time will be my servants."

"How do you know you're not shit under your gods' fingernails?"

"Because *I hold the key*. The key to the lock that Zann built this house around. The key he stole from Wade when he realized the implications. That crazy shattered nigger went all the way to Paris to dig it up, and what did he do with it? He hid it right on the fucking doorstep." Hanson shook with laughter and held the shining silver key in front of his face.

Becca felt a flutter at her heart and caught her breath. Had the scarab stirred?

"I hope you live to tell the tale," Hanson said, turning the key. "This moment deserves a witness. But then, I suppose history comes to an end here."

The plates shifted, whirling outward with a sound of scraping iron and the churning of massive cogs. The slot of ultraviolet light at the center of the portal spread, became a many-rayed star, a wheel of curling teeth, a dilating eye. The filigreed silver key floated at the core, suspended in the maelstrom. Becca knew she should attack, but bathed in that mind-shattering light, the will drained from her nerves.

Hanson was chanting again, his mantra cresting, resonating and ricocheting around the misty chamber.

The scarab twitched and Becca dropped the knife. She reached to touch it but it scampered over the collar of her shirt, fleeing the corrosive radiance of the emerging hell realm.

Squinting at the undulating substance suspended in the eye of the portal, Becca couldn't tell if it was water refusing to spill despite the lack of a boundary, or something more viscous. Hanson answered the question with a fingertip. The liquid light broke in a sluggish wave, the placenta of a new world spilling over Becca's scuffed boots.

Her paralysis broke. She recoiled from the flood and turned to run, but found herself surrounded by curtains of green mist on all sides with no clear exit. Nonetheless, she backed away from the portal, the anger that had driven her pursuit leaching out of her, leaving only cold dread and an animal urge to flee.

Hanson let the flood pour over him, his arms spread, basking in the foul wave. Something floated toward him, a spinning globe, oily and iridescent. It passed through the portal, absorbing the key, which flared, released tendrils of electricity, and dissolved.

The first sphere was followed by a trail of others, clinging in a floating mass, separating and joining. As they rolled over the lip of the aperture toward her, Becca felt probed by a vast and alien intelligence.

Hanson screamed.

A swarm of lamprey eels thrashed in the portal, a tumult of black flesh whirling around him. He twisted away, and Becca could see that some of the eels on the outer arms of the spiral had fastened their fangs in his upturned wrists, and were dragging him bleeding into the devouring embrace of Shabat Cycloth.

The scream wavered and was subsumed in a tidal rush of white noise. Fluid—or was it a wash of photons?—crashed out of the portal as Hanson was sucked into it, sweeping Becca off her feet, and carrying her away on a vile tide.

* * *

The rope burrowed rough splinters into Luke's palm, but it pulled easier than he expected, given the size of the iron bell. The resulting tone vibrated in the core of his body, resounded through the stone chamber, and reverberated down the tunnel.

The surface of the pool rippled with a pattern of concentric circles. He waited for the water to settle, then moved on to the next rope, girding himself against the impending explosion of sound as he rang the second bell. The tone of this one was higher in pitch, as he had expected, but no less bowel shaking. He could see the discomfort on Brooks' face across the pool. The agent held his gun and flashlight low, both aimed at the water.

The second bell vibrated the water in a triangular pattern. Again, Luke waited for the ripples to settle before trying the next node in the sequence, which affected a series of overlapping spirals. He knew that sound waves could form intricate patterns in sand poured over glass but had never seen acoustics behave in quite this way. The growing sense that he was communicating with an unseen listener in a language of geometric signals unnerved him. He was sending those signals blind. And what might answer?

By the fourth note, he had what he wanted: knowledge of the scale the bells were arranged for, an exotic asymmetrical mode.

As the fifth and final note faded, Brooks said, "I think that's enough for now."

"Me too."

Django paced at the threshold of the tunnel arch, snuffling at the damp stone floor.

Brooks thumbed the talk button on his radio: "Brooks to base, over."

"Base here, over."

"You guys know anything about a tunnel in the basement?"

There was a long pause, then: "Scans show no tunnel."

Brooks stepped under the arch and swept the beam of his flashlight over the ceiling. "It appears to be lined with lead. That might have kept it off your scans, but I wonder what the original purpose of the shielding was. Over."

Luke walked a careful circuit around the pool and approached Brooks, glancing over his shoulder at the still water. "Could have been to keep entities from escaping through the ground before reaching the end of the tunnel," he said, his words laced with echo.

Brooks nodded and clicked the radio. "We're gonna walk it a bit, see where it leads. Over."

Northrup's voice came back this time, "Be careful and keep talking to me. Over."

The tunnel seemed to go on for about a quarter of a mile, the walls slimy and streaked with corrosion where water had seeped through seams in the lead sheets. Django diligently wove back and forth ahead of the men, nose to the ground. Mushrooms sprouted occasionally in the corners where the flagstone floor joined the leaded arch, but there were no other signs of organic life. The oppressive silence had begun to work on their resolve to find the end when Django started whining and pacing frantic circles in front of them. A moment later, Brooks could smell it too: fresh air and pine.

The tunnel inclined upward for the last stretch before coming to an abrupt end at a lead covered wall. Sunlight dappled the floor. Looking up they could see fragments of gray sky through a stone slab cut like a drain grate with oddly shaped holes—an occult configuration of whorls and fractured star shapes. Small leaves and pine needles littered a puddle of rainwater on the floor below the grate. Django spun, sat, looked up, and whined at the smell of the woods above.

The grate was probably ten feet above the flagstone floor. Brooks sized up Luke Philips, and said, "You're lighter than me. Climb on my shoulders and tell me what you can see." He dropped to one knee while Luke mounted the back of his neck, then stood up. They wobbled for a few seconds while Brooks stabilized the weight, but then a bolt of pain shot through his thigh and he hissed sharply through gritted teeth.

"My stitches..." He said. "Can you grab hold and take your weight off?"

Luke reached up and slipped his fingers through a cluster of holes, raising himself off Brooks' shoulders by his fingertips. Brooks made a final effort to push him up high enough for a glimpse through the grate. Luke held on for a few seconds, his face and clothes speckled with daylight, before giving out and dangling at a full stretch. He let go and landed hard on his feet in front of Brooks.

"Did you see anything?"

"Yeah. Standing stones with symbols carved on them."

"I know the place," Brooks said. "Becca found it the day we moved into the house." He played his flashlight beam around the circumference of the stone grate. "Doesn't look like anything could pass through that but mice."

"I wouldn't be so sure," Luke said. He pointed at the figured holes in the slab. "Could be those are meant to filter whatever raw energy passes down this tunnel. Like the angles of the house, it might be designed to let certain things through."

Brooks nodded. "Well, I don't see *us* getting through." He thumbed the walkie. "Northrup: we're headed back. Over."

Luke touched Brooks' arm. "You hear that?"

Brooks tilted his head. "Something in the water."

* * *

Emerging from the arch at the end of the tunnel, Brooks stopped dead. A shadow was rising from the bottom of the churning pool. He trained his gun on it, but before it surfaced, Django shot past him and dropped to his haunches at the edge of the tile coping, yelping frantically. It was a human body. The filmy gray water concealed the details until it had almost surfaced, but Brooks knew who it was even before he could make out the flowing strands of long, dark hair or the army jacket. Moving fast, he slipped out of his coat and emptied his belt, tossing his holstered weapon, flashlight, and radio to the floor. Luke stared at the rising body, stammering, trying to form a sentence as Brooks jumped into the pool.

The water slammed his senses with its slimy caress and foul odor. He swam to the body,

then dove under the surface to come up from under it, turning it around and wrapping his arm across the chest. There was no struggle in response, only dead weight. He kicked hard, propelling toward the edge and using the momentum to lift Becca's head above the water.

Django was panicking, filling the cavernous space with his barking. Luke seized Becca under the arms, and hauled her out onto the tile. The skinny old man's strength surprised Brooks. Becca was out cold and heavy in her soaking jeans, boots, and jacket. Dried blood was still smeared across her belly below her torn shirt.

"She's not breathing," Luke said. "Do something! *She's not breathing!*"

Brooks climbed out of the water and crawled on his hands and knees to Becca's side, gasping for breath and wishing the damned dog would shut up. He checked for a pulse and couldn't find one. Her skin was so cold. No time to waste. He tugged her jacket out of the way, layered his hands over her sternum, and started compressions.

"Give me space!" he shouted. "Get the damn dog out of the way!"

Luke wrapped his arms around Django and dragged him back from his frantic efforts to lick Becca's face.

"If you can reach the walkie without letting go of him, call for backup. Paramedic. Say *paramedic.*"

"Philips to base. Do you copy?"

He almost forgot to release the PTT button. When he did, the walkie let out a squeal that modulated and stuttered like a fax machine getting raped by some alien intelligence. He tried again, but even with the button depressed this time, the exotic interference garbled on.

"It's not working." He squeezed the button and yelled over the noise, "Paramedic! We need a paramedic in the cellar!"

Brooks remained vaguely aware of Luke's struggles with the dog and the radio, but he shoved these distractions aside, focused on his counting, on keeping the compressions steady and rhythmic.

Bubbles stirred the surface of the pool again, gently at first, then roiling to a boil.

"Something's coming," Luke said.

"I know. Get my gun."

Luke let go of the dog and grabbed the gun. Django, in guardian mode, lunged at the water's edge and let loose a barrage of aggressive barks.

"Is there a safety?" Luke asked, frantic.

"It's off."

The boiling water cast a web of violet light across the ceiling.

Becca's chest heaved with a ragged breath and she coughed out a spray of brackish water. Her eyes, suddenly open, staring wide and wild past Brooks, told him all he needed to know. Whatever had followed her out of the labyrinth was rising from the water behind him.

Luke raised the gun in his trembling interlaced hands.

Brooks turned to face the pool.

A cloud of iridescent spheres hovered over the water, crackling with flitting blue flames. His mind struggled to resolve the thing into some recognizable pattern and failed after touching on every state of matter and rejecting them all. The only irrefutable characteristic was the aura of baleful intelligence the spheres radiated, permeating his consciousness and eroding his courage. He knew, in the same way that Django—retreating in a looping trail of urine—knew that he was in the presence of a force against which he stood no chance.

A shot thundered from the gun and one of the spheres flickered. Plaster flurried from the ceiling onto the black water. Brooks looked at Luke. "That's useless," he said. He scanned the workbenches and his gaze fixed on a shelf where glass bottles of lamp oil were arranged in neat rows. Brooks shuffled behind Becca, seized her under her arms, and dragged her away from the water. "Get a bottle of oil," he called to Luke. "And rags if you can find some. Over there!"

Luke didn't waste any time asking why. He ran for the bench. As the spheres rose toward the ceiling, Becca brought her hand to her chest and touched the scarab through her shirt. Brooks had taken note of the chain right away before starting CPR on her. She slipped it out and examined the gem in the beetle's pincers. Was it starting to glow, or only reflecting the strange light of the spheres? Brooks couldn't tell.

Luke returned with a moth-eaten blanket and a bottle of oil. Brooks took the bottle and screwed the cap off. He doused the blanket, splashing oil over the floor, and filling the room with bitter fumes that at least had the benefit of temporarily overpowering the swamp stench wafting off of their clothes.

"You got a light?" Brooks asked. "We need to keep it from escaping the house. Fire at the mouth of the tunnel might do it."

Luke dug in his jacket pocket and produced a disposable lighter.

Becca tried to speak but was seized by a coughing fit. When it passed, she said, "What's down the tunnel?"

"It leads to the stone circle in the woods," Brooks said.

"Let it go," she said. "Let the thing go there."

"Why?"

"It's a cage...made to contain it. So Wade could summon and constrain them...commune with them."

"How do you know that?" Luke asked.

"A bird told me," she said. "Gate and cage. Hanson opened the gate. Now drive it into the cage."

Brooks seized Luke's shoulder. "The bells," he said. "That's what they're for. To drive what he summoned away from the pool and down the tunnel. Can you do it?"

* * *

Luke ran for the ropes, slowing as he neared the pool and the nebula rotating in the air above it. He mentally ran through the variations on the symphony, the chord inversions he had experimented with over the years, and tried to correlate them to the scale he had sounded on the iron bells. His hairline prickled with sweat. Then it came to him. *Harmony.* He would strike a triad of the purest harmony available to him, something that vibrated right by the physics of *this* world, something that just might antagonize an entity from the other.

Gathering three ropes in his hands, he stepped back and threw his weight against the bells.

The chord rolled over the water and resounded in the domed ceiling. The result was immediately visible. The caged light bulbs exploded in a shower of glass and sparks. The cloud of spheres distorted into jagged shards of blazing plasma, then contracted like a lanced worm and shot away from the pool, coagulating again before gliding through the great stone arch and vanishing down the black throat of the tunnel.

With the eldritch light of Yog Sothoth banished from the chamber, darkness fell around them, almost complete, but for a dim red glow slowly blooming to a ruby blaze at Becca's heart.

The Fire of Cairo had awakened.

Chapter 18

Becca stood and tugged off her soaking wet jacket. Her boots were heavy and her head ached, but she managed to take a few steps, holding her hand out to ward off the support Brooks offered. Django licked her fingers as she looked around and got her bearings. She took a few swaying steps toward the tunnel from which the last remnants of sickly violet light flickered.

"Whoa, whoa, whoa," Brooks said. "Where are you going?"

"After it," she said.

He lit his flashlight and trained it on the tunnel mouth. A faint rumble echoed from the yawning black hole. "We don't even know what that was. Just be glad you're alive and let's get out of here."

"It's what escaped when Hanson opened the portal," Becca said. "Yog Sothoth."

"*Yog Sothoth,*" Luke whispered in awe.

"What?" Brooks said.

"It's the only one that needs to escape. It can manifest the other gods as emanations."

Becca's lower lip was already shivering in the drafty air. "I might be able to stop it," she said. "Like last time. The scarab is stirring."

Luke stared at the red glow through her shirt. "Catherine's beetle?" he said.

Becca nodded. "I think proximity to the Great Old Ones wakes it. It was made to banish them. I have to try."

Brooks checked his gun, ejecting the magazine and slotting it back into the grip. "I'm coming with you. But not that way. Luke and I scouted it out. There's no way out at the end of the tunnel. Not for humans, anyway. And you don't want to be trapped in the circle with that thing. We'll go above ground. You say it's a trap, right? A cage? It should hold it at least until we get there. Luke, you man the bells in case it tries to retreat. Don't let it."

"Okay. Can I borrow your flashlight?" Brooks handed it over and Luke hurried to the workshop in the corner, the light bobbing ahead of him. He returned with another wool blanket, wrapped it around Becca's shoulders and kissed her temple before she could resist. "You be careful, baby girl."

"You too." She looked at him, wanting to say more, but unable to find the words, unsure of where to even begin. His fear was written all over his face. She squeezed his fingers, and let Brooks help her up the stairs.

* * *

The house looked as normal as it ever did; the only odd angles on display were the ones inherent to the architecture. Rooms, doorways, and halls were all where they belonged with no double-exposure overlap from the other realm. They detoured through their respective rooms, dripping on the wood floors and frantically rummaging for dry clothes before reconvening in the kitchen and pushing through the back door into the cold. On the veranda, Brooks tried the walkie-talkie again.

"Brooks to base, do you read? Over."

"Northrup here. What the fuck's going on, Brooks?"

"Something got out," Brooks said. "Yog Sothoth. We lost radio contact to interference. Luke drove it down the tunnel with bells. He's still in the house. I'm going with Becca to the stone circle where the tunnel lets out. She's gonna try to destroy it with the scarab. I've got her back. Over."

There was a moment of silence. Brooks wondered if the radio had failed. Then static and Northrup's reply: "Wait. Give me a minute to think. You need backup. Don't rush in. Over."

"I don't know how much time we have," Brooks said.

The radio whistled with feedback. "Our instruments, the readings are all over the place," Northrup said. "Nothing is stable. The house, the woods... The book breakers say the stone circle was never meant to constrain Yog Sothoth. It may not hold. Over."

"That's what Luke said. I advise setting up a perimeter around the house and woods from the distance of a decent blast radius. Evacuate the hut and try to contain anything that comes out of the house or the woods if we fail. Over."

"On it. Good luck, Jason. Over and out."

*   *   *

Above the treetops, a shaft of darkness pierced the gray afternoon sky, like the negative image of a high-powered floodlight. Frozen grass crunched under Becca's soggy boots. She pulled the blanket her father had given her tight around her shoulders, a poor substitute for the saturated jacket she'd abandoned. Her shoulder bag swung at her side, the damp canvas hardening as it iced. She had done what she could to dry her hair with a towel before leaving the house, but it was still freezing.

Brooks walked with a mild limp, the sutured gash on his face an angry red against his pale, freckled skin.

"You sure you're up for this?" Becca asked.

He laughed in spite of his evident pain and misery. *"Me?* Am *I* up for it, asks the girl I just resuscitated? You're something else, Philips."

"Well, you *have* taken some pretty good beatings lately."

"I'm fine. And hey, this only sucks so bad because we're damp." He looked at his watch. "Forty-two degrees in January. Could be worse."

"Life, the universe, and everything," she said.

"Huh?"

"Never mind." She opened the frozen flap of her bag and dug out a piece of beef jerky for Django. The dog eagerly accepted the treat, scoffing it down as they approached the woods.

"A vegetarian carrying jerky?"

"Raf gave him a taste for it."

"Oh...sorry."

"It's okay. I don't mind being reminded of him."

Brooks nudged her with his elbow. "You ever sneak a little nibble of that stuff when you're lost in a trans-dimensional maze?"

Becca shoved him back and laughed. "Fuck off." She picked through the bag and took out the drone remote. "What do you think, toast?"

"Try it."

"Mark said he used it for marine biology. Said it was waterproof. But unless they built it for Navy SEALS..." She thumbed the power switch. To her surprise, the display lit, accompanied by the sound of the dragonfly buzzing in her bag. "Well I'll be damned. The government can do that, but they can't get a web site to work."

She switched the remote off and put it back in the bag. "Think they'll let me keep it if we survive this?"

Brooks shrugged. "Maybe you lost it in the maze."

They had come to the edge of the woods. A low mist rolled between the trees, carrying another wave of the foul odor they'd encountered at the pool. The lowering sun burned through the haze, crowning the pine spires with orange fire. Becca remembered the path she had taken to the stone circle, but even if she didn't, retracing it now would have been easy given the subsonic waves pulsing through the ground from their destination, setting the dead leaves trembling and small animals fleeing in panic. Django paced in circles, put his snout to the ground, and pawed at his ears, whining.

"I should've left him in the basement with Luke," Becca said. "I don't think he'll come any further." She dropped to one knee and stroked Django's fur. "You can go, boy. It's okay, go." She pointed up the rise toward the house. "Go on. I'll be right back."

Django cocked his head and whimpered, then licked Becca's face and took a few tentative retreating steps. He kept looking back to see if she was coming, prancing in nervous circles. At last, he trotted back toward the house. She hoped he would go straight to Base Camp where someone would let him in and look after him.

When she turned around, Brooks was holding a small gun by the barrel, offering the grip to her. His main sidearm was still holstered at his hip. This must have been a backup he kept concealed somewhere.

"Take it," he said. "I doubt it'll do you much good, but I'll feel better knowing you have it."

Becca took the gun and examined it. "Will it fire after taking a swim?"

"Try it."

She aimed at a tree and squeezed the trigger. The report was loud, but not as loud as the shot Brooks had fired in the stone chamber at the top of the Bunker Hill Monument. She thought she saw the place where the bullet bored into the oak, chipping the bark, but couldn't be sure. She thumbed the safety on and wedged the pistol into her jeans pocket where the protruding handgrip was concealed by the blanket she wore around her shoulders like a poncho, feeling like a child playing gunslinger.

A little farther up the trail, they came to a place where the woods were flooded with brackish water laced with ashy silt. At first they tried to find places where the ground humped above the flood, or thick tree roots and rocks to enable a zigzagging course toward the shaft of blackness smudged in the sky, but the effort was futile, and soon they were soaked up to their shins, shivering harder than before.

The low pulse droned through the water, and now, as they approached the standing stones, a peal of metallic harmonics sliced the air and rang painfully in their ears. Becca noticed that even her vision was distorted by the vibrations, but now she could see the granite slabs between the trees. She cut toward them with Brooks keeping pace until they were back on the trail they'd abandoned for the last few yards, the megalithic ring towering before them in the orange limned indigo sky—black silhouettes encircling a morphing storm of flesh and fire.

A hemisphere of pale green energy arched over the stones, constraining the entity for now. Each time one of the spheres collided with the boundary, the light crackled and flared, sending the errant bubble spinning back toward the clustered mass at the center.

The stone grate in the ground at the center of the circle had been shattered by the god's eruption from the tunnel. Giant shards of rock lay scattered among the standing slabs, partially submerged in the tide of black water bubbling out of the hole.

Becca whirled on Brooks in alarm. "If the tunnel is flooded from the pool, then the bells...*Luke.*"

Brooks opened his mouth to say something reassuring about how Luke would have fled the basement when the water started rising, but before he could steel his mind to speak against the painful cacophony radiating from the circle, a pair of cyclones rose from the wreckage of the grate, summoned by the languid touch of drooping tendrils of violet flame. Becca took a step backward, tugging at Brooks' wrist. Whatever the cyclones were, if that storm of malign intelligence at the center of the circle was calling them up, they couldn't be good.

Her stomach clenched instinctively just a second before the twisters burst. The inky splash congealed and she could make out the shapes of the glistening eels that had formed it. They exploded outward in a rain of black scraps, splattering against the standing stones or burning on contact with the green energy field, leaving the unveiled forms of two humans and two monsters where the cyclones had been.

Shabat Cycloth cradled the pale, naked form of Richard Hanson, if that was even his name. Maybe he had received a new name from his initiators now that he had been baptized on the threshold of their world, dipped in their dimension and returned to the terrestrial. His skin looked raw, his eyes aflame with an order of madness so pure it demanded that the world conform to its warped parameters. The dark goddess deposited him gently on the ground where he uncoiled from the fetal position and revealed the sole object curled in his fist—Reverend Proctor's silver dagger.

Her consort, Lung Crawthok, clenched a soaking wet Luke Philips in the cage of claws that ran the length of the monster's armored underside. Its stingray tail undulated between muscled humanoid legs and its eyes blazed—green stars piercing the dusk. The razor sharp hook of the harpoon it brandished in its right hand was poised at its captive's temple.

Becca moaned at the sight.

"What do they want, Hanson?" Brooks called across the circle.

Hanson laughed. Despite his nakedness, the cold and damp didn't seem to bother him. His pale skin was shot through with dark veins and his face was stubbled with a beard of writhing maggot-like nodes. Or were they nascent tentacles just starting to bud? A pustule popped with a bloody spray and sprouted another as he stalked to the perimeter of the circle, fingering the baroque pommel of the dagger.

"What they always want," Hanson said. "Passage. Dominion."

Brooks raised his gun. Becca wondered if bullets could pass through the energy dome constraining the creatures.

"And they'll get it," Hanson said. "No matter what you do." He gazed upward. "This won't hold for long."

"Why take a hostage then?" Brooks said. "And what do they need you for?"

"Me? I'm a translator, but I don't mind helping to flay him." He stared at Becca. "If you make me."

"What's in it for you?" Brooks asked.

Hanson smiled and Becca recoiled. His gums had receded and his teeth looked loose. God only knew what would grow in to replace them.

"I am becoming my reward," Hanson hissed.

Becca's hand had drifted to the scarab pendant. She squeezed it between her thumb and the knuckle of her forefinger, glancing down at the dull red glow pulsing at the heart of the ruby in the beetle's pincers.

Hanson took a step toward Lung Crawthok and pressed the point of the dagger to Luke Philips' pale potbelly, where it hung out the bottom of his t-shirt in contrast to the rest of his skinny frame. The tip indented the flesh, not sharp enough to draw blood without the force of speed, but Luke drew a short breath nonetheless, anticipating the plunge.

"I wouldn't do that," Hanson said to Becca. "Take the beetle off and throw it into the circle."

Becca hesitated.

"I said take it off and throw it in the fucking circle!"

Becca let her shoulder bag slip to the ground. She reached under her hair and undid the necklace clasp, then caught the pooling chain and scarab in her hand. She studied it, fingers trembling from the cold, but more from the fear that she was about to do something irrevocable.

The dome of light crackled against the sky, on the brink of fracturing under the strain of the burgeoning spheres.

"Don't even think about whispering the mantra," Hanson said. "If your lips form so much as a syllable, Daddy gets gutted. Now toss it over."

Becca looked at Brooks. If he was going to shoot, he would've done it by now. She could read the frustration in his eyes, knew he didn't want her to surrender the only weapon that might stand a chance against the forces in play. She also knew that if she weren't here, Brooks would take the gamble on her father's life. He'd shoot and test his luck. But she *was* here, and for her sake he was treading carefully.

Becca threw the scarab at the energy field. It soared between a pair of the standing stones, and for a moment she dared believe it might take flight, but it landed on the icy broken granite with an impotent tinkle.

The creature responded immediately. Luke Philips no longer mattered. The rows of claws released him and he fell into the gurgling black water, his temple striking a chunk of fractured rock as he collapsed.

"Dad!" Becca cried, stepping forward but stopping at the perimeter of the shield. "Pull him out of the water!" she yelled at Hanson. "I gave you what you wanted. Pull him out!"

Lung Crawthok took a lumbering step toward the scarab, raised the harpoon and drove it down. The iron flue sparked against the granite and the scarab jumped, golden wings fluttering, the ruby skimming away across the water and landing in the mud where Luke's hair was splayed in a filthy tangle. Raindrops danced in the dark water around his body—a scattering at first, then a dance of white water as the clouds opened up.

The guardian brought the shaft down again, pinning the metal beetle to the rock and sending a segment of its shell skittering off. Becca stared in horror at the damage. Her heart ached with sympathetic pain. But it was an object. Not alive. And her father still lay unmoving at the monster's feet.

She pulled the gun out from under the blanket, trained it on Hanson, cold fire coursing through her eyes and down the barrel when she said, "Get him out of there, you son of a bitch. Get him away from that thing or I'll blow your fucking head off."

Hanson knelt beside Luke and rolled the body over.

"Drop the knife," Becca said, wondering why Brooks hadn't taken a shot yet, but not willing to risk taking her eyes off Hanson.

Hanson turned the knife over in his hand, admiring the three-sided blade, watching the rain patter off of the blackened silver alloy. He sneered at Becca. "He knows too many permutations."

Everything seemed to happen at once after that. Time slowed to a crawl. Becca's blood surged with adrenaline, and her vision tunneled. She sensed Hanson's movement before he started to raise the dagger and fired, sending a spray of black blood out the back of his skull before the weapon reached its zenith above her father's chest. Hanson fell over backward and the sky cracked, the barometric pressure plunging, the electrical tension in the atmosphere suddenly dissipating as if the earth had popped its ears. The energy dome was gone—had she done that with her bullet?

No, it was the expanding power of Yog Sothoth throwing off the feeble cage. The congress of spheres rose above the treetops, ascending toward the bruised clouds, trailing tendrils of oily vapor. She saw flashes of other forms in that roiling cloud: a goat with eyes like spiders, a black pharaoh with blue fire in his hair, a great serpent with a jeweled crown.

A flash of silver streaked past Becca's face: the dragonfly drone. It flitted between the standing stones and perched on a shard of rock beside Luke's face. His eyes opened, blinking at the rain.

Something bumped Becca's shoulder and she looked into Brooks' urgent eyes. He was shoving something into her hands— the remote—trying to trade it for the hot gun in her hand.

"Take it! Get the gem," Brooks said. "It's all we've got. I can't do it."

Suddenly she understood but didn't know if she could do it either, if she had the skill to maneuver the drone with that level of precision. But then the screen was in her hands, the Fire of Cairo glowing in the glass. She thumbed the wheels of light, her fingers stiff and clumsy with fear. The dragonfly stuttered, dipped, clicked its forelegs at the ruby and missed. Becca looked up from the remote, fixed her eyes on the drone and its prize, and with a deep breath, tried again on the exhalation. She let her fingers find the sequence, banishing thought and fear from her mind for just a moment. She was one with the dragonfly, picking up the gem, clenching it in serrated silver claws.

Luke groaned and Becca looked up just in time to see the harpoon come down and run him through, pinning his frail, broken body to the muddy ground.

She screamed and dropped the remote, took two halting steps toward the horror.

Luke drew a ragged inhalation and spoke the mantra on his dying breath: *"Yehi Aur."*

The dragonfly hovered over his face, and the gem blazed to life.

Becca dropped to her knees, scrambled in the dirt for the remote, and finding it, thumbed the elevation control. The drone arced into the sky, blazing a trail of phosphorous red light, a flare fired into the heart of Yog Sothoth.

The clouds trembled, then convulsed.

The monsters on the ground joined voices in a wavering howl of agony before the spheres above them reacted. Their cry died on the rain-lashed wind and for a second Becca thought she had failed. Then the world strobed red and white as a series of concussions rolled across the sky. The spheres shattered, throwing scraps of fleshy black shrapnel at the ground.

The twin guardians whirled in tatters of oily smoke, screaming against disintegration, fighting to retain coherence and failing, their remains rising to join the noxious cloud drifting over the wood toward the house on the hill.

Becca dropped the remote and ran into the circle. She knelt beside Luke and wiped his dirty gray hair from his brow, a flood of hot tears swelling under her cheeks, prickling her eyes, and spilling down her nose.

The flood of filthy water from the tunnel had abated. Brooks stepped into the circle and picked up the remote. "It's being sucked into the chimneys," he said. "The wreckage of the gods…sucked down the drain…you did it."

Becca heard him, but didn't care, not yet. She gazed into her father's glassy blue eyes, searching for a final glimmer of waning light. Eyes that no longer blinked at the rain.

Chapter 19

Becca clung to Luke's body as the smoke cleared, the residue sucked down cracks and fissures around her. She thought she could hear the bells ringing underground, but maybe that was her imagination. A burning ember slowly fell from the sky and came to hover beside her: the dragonfly bearing the Fire of Cairo. The drone flitted from side to side, as if studying her, then darted down the tunnel in pursuit of the last remnants of the incursion. Or *were* they the last? Becca gazed skyward. It was almost dark now, but she glimpsed a lone scrap of translucent blackness hanging on the breeze like a flag that had escaped its tether. A crow climbing the sky flew through it as she watched. The bird shivered and plunged, a blur of charcoal smeared across the sky. It recovered at the tree line, pounded its wings hard to regain altitude, and then flew off east toward the city and the sea.

Brooks crouched beside Becca in the mud, laid his hand on her back. "I'm sorry," he said.

Becca rested her head in the hollow of his shoulder and let herself sob. When she looked up, the rain was tapering off, and she could hear voices approaching through the woods.

"Thanks for taking me to find him," she said.

Brooks furrowed his brow and Becca wondered if he'd expected her to be angry with him for his role in her father's death, for entangling him in the crisis. Luke had entangled himself long ago, and had died trying to make a difference. She didn't know if the threat was vanquished, but for now, she had to believe he had succeeded.

"He knew the incantation," Brooks said, "for the gem."

"Yeah. He knew more than I ever expected."

Becca looked at the remote in Brooks' hand. She nodded at it. "You're not controlling it? It flew down the hole like it was on a mission."

"I know. I think the gem is controlling it," Brooks thumbed the display button. "It seems to have a mind of its own."

Becca took the blanket from her shoulders and laid it over Luke's face and upper body. Then she crawled, shivering, through the mud to the granite slab where the golden scarab lay in pieces. She gathered them in her palm and searched the ground for the section of shell that had skittered away under the harpoon blow. The weapon had vanished with its wielder, but she found the last fragment of the beetle and deposited the handful into her muddy canvas rucksack.

The voices were growing louder now. Flashlight beams bobbed at the edge of the wood. "Over here!" Brooks called. "I hope you brought coats or we're gonna die of hypothermia before the debriefing."

Django barked, broke away from the team he had led through the woods, and bounded over to Becca.

Brooks passed her the remote.

*   *   *

The dragonfly chased the receding black vapor through the tunnel. It shot out of the stone arch and traced a circle around the pool, grazing the wicks of candles and oil lamps with the flaming gem and setting them ablaze. The cellar walls and vaulted ceiling pulsed with golden light as the drone sped up the stairs to the first floor. It dipped to touch drapes and set eager flames searing up their length, burning dust, shattering glass, and inviting the wind in to feed the blaze. It swept through every room, visiting flame upon every wick and shattered globe where oil soaked the rugs and floorboards. It swooped low and scorched a trail of flame down the length of the Persian carpet runner in the central hallway. At the library, it paused for a second to give the video feed a lingering look at the bountiful fuel awaiting its kiss— crumbling paper, parchment and vellum, polished wood, and cracked leather—before winding around the turret room and, climbing in a great blazing spiral, leaving a blistering inferno in its wake as it shot out onto the second floor.

It buzzed the piano strings, setting them vibrating, then climbed the wall of the music room, charring the peeling wallpaper. Downstairs, the wood and glass of the grandfather clock popped and shattered as the fire raged. The velvet furniture cooked, and the gilt-framed mirror over the mantel imploded, sucking in smoke and swirling scraps of burning paper like moths fluttering through an open window.

* * *

At the edge of the wood, Becca could hear the wail of sirens. She walked beside Brooks, bundled in a Mylar emergency blanket. She had refused a ride on a stretcher, but had gratefully accepted a pair of wool socks. Her feet ached with blisters and what felt like the beginning of frostbite from her wet boots. Django trotted a few feet ahead of her, while the agents who had found them brought up the rear, flashlights sweeping the ground. Full night had fallen. Flashes of orange fire shone through the trees, and the smell of burning wood was thick on the cold air. Becca could see her breath mingling with the layers of smoke and fog rising from the house and the marshes, and pooling around the base of the hill.

The ground shuddered as a support beam let go and a section of roof collapsed, sending up a spray of sparks. But as she drew nearer, Becca saw that the Wade House wasn't crumbling in the way that a burning building should. It was folding in on itself, like origami executed on a burning sheet of paper by invisible hands trying various permutations, rejecting some, embracing others, and collapsing matter into the spaces between space, leaving her with the impression that the fire was doing a more mundane kind of damage than this other process set in motion by the awakened gem.

Becca caught glimpses of stone passages as the walls fell away, a patch between the blazing timbers where she could swear she saw birds flying in a yellow sky, not ashes swirling in fire-illuminated smoke.

At the base of the hill, the flashers of fire engines rolled over the dead grass, dirty snow, and the gray arch of the hut. Raised voices cut the air, and she saw that the security officers were arguing with the fire lieutenant, denying the trucks access. Northrup strode toward the gate in his long black overcoat, a glowing phone held to his ear.

"Let it burn," Brooks said beside her.

"Looks like they're trying to," she said. "Good."

And yet, she was drawn to the house. The heat of the fire warming her face, thawing her hands, was glorious. In the woods, in the cellar, she'd thought she would never feel heat again.

Brooks put his arm around her and led her away from the blaze, toward the hut. "Come on. Let's get some tea into you."

Chapter 20

The crow that was no longer merely a crow, having passed through a scrap of a god floating on the wind, flew southeast at daybreak, gliding over the gray ice of Walden Pond and skirting Rt. 117 as the rising sun burned the mist off of the woodlands. In Waltham, the bird that was not a bird rested on a parapet atop the tower of Usen Castle, then swooped down over the flooded train tracks, and followed the Charles River to Cambridge, where it alighted at last on the great white sphinx facing the gothic cathedral at Mt. Auburn Cemetery.

The sphinx, a memorial to the Civil War, reminded the crow of his favorite incarnation. Commissioned by Dr. Jacob Bigelow and unveiled in 1872, the statue is one of the most unusual monuments ever crafted in tribute to that bloody chapter of New World history, intended to represent the union of African strength and Anglo intellect in the fusion of the lion's body and the white woman's face draped in Egyptian headdress. But to the crow, the iconography spoke of home, of riddles among the pyramids, and of a day to come when the blood-infused oceans of the world would pay tribute to all of mankind's unity in slavery to the Great Old Ones, who would soon inherit the Earth.

The bird hopped down from its perch onto the grass, pecked at the ground for a worm, and then flapped its wings, ascending to the height of a man in the shadow of the trees, and *becoming* one before stepping out onto the path.

Having shed his wings, the Black Pharaoh walked, cloaked in the early dark of a January afternoon. He liked to walk when he could, and where he walked, the people of the city looked away, and the wild animals of the riverbank bowed their heads.

By 9:30 P.M. he had reached Harvard Square, where the streets still thrummed with the psychic residue of the subway massacre carried out by Darius Marlowe in the autumn of 2019. He breathed in the aura of stale suffering, the lingering overtones of primal fear, and savored the taste.

He walked among the students, tourists, and skate punks beneath strings of holiday lights. The crowd parted and made way for him.

Around the corner of the Coop, across the street from the Old Burying Ground, the sound he sought reached his ears, and he slowed his stride. His red robes blazed, reflecting his pleasure like shivering plumage. Blue fire crackled in his knotted hair, and his kingly lips spread in a smile.

The strains of a guitar filtered through the bundled crowd and echoed off the buildings. The pharaoh drew near, and dipped his slender brown fingers into a pocket of his robe.

A musician in a black pea coat, ripped jeans, and fingerless gloves stood in front of the entrance to the T, tapping his foot on the red bricks and thumping his battered acoustic guitar with the dull determination of one whose long night in the cold has numbed his extremities. He gazed out past the crowd at the news kiosk across the street, and sang "Across the Universe" by the Beatles in a soulful, crooning voice, raspy at the edges. His features were steep and dark, his hair curly, his skin olive. He was young, probably in his early twenties, possibly of Eastern European descent.

The open guitar case that lay on the bricks beside the busker's microphone stand was littered with a scattering of quarters and crumpled dollar bills. Beside it, a little battery powered amp worked at its upper limits to cut through the traffic and crowd noise, the chords and voice ringing from its tiny speaker laced with metallic reverb on the brink of feedback.

The Black Pharaoh bent over the guitar case, and the musician blinked his dark lashes, and swayed as if buffeted by an icy wind. The long-fingered hand emerged from the crimson robe and tossed a coin onto the balding blue velvet interior.

The song faltered, the musician gazed at the coin and shivered. Then his hands recovered and strummed a slow cadence, winding down the rhythm into a final resolving chord.

He slung his guitar across his hip, knelt beside the case, and stared at the coin. A few stray snowflakes drifted down and settled on the velvet lining. The pharaoh hovered over the busker's shoulder only half sharing his world, a swarm of strange colors that repelled human perception, a wavering flame of should-not-exist.

It was a strange coin: big as a silver dollar and forged of meteoric iron, its surface pitted and engraved with a tentacled head encircled by tiny sigils and a phrase the musician couldn't read, an inscription in tribute to the High Priest who would one day rise from his dreaming in the deep on wings of dark song.

The singer's name was Tristan Furlong. The pharaoh plucked it from his mind as Tristan plucked the coin from the case. A snowflake touched the metal and melted. The coin was as hot as if plucked from desert sand, and it felt good in his cold fingers. It brought feeling back to them. And as he absorbed the heat of the strange coin, he absorbed something more—something red-robed and regal, austere and ancient, fierce, furious, and older than death.

He could feel his throat opening up the way it did after vocal warm-ups, and then passing beyond comfort into a range of sudden pain, the very bone and cartilage of his voice box reconfiguring, excruciating, but only for a moment.

The pharaoh stood and stretched. He liked his new garment. Tristan Furlong's body was young, strong, and handsome. Clothed in this form, he would make a fine Pied Piper, leading the Children of the Voice in a song to raise R'lyeh.

He slid the coin into the tight pocket of his black jeans and spat a phlegmy dollop of blood at the ground. The pharaoh blazed; a diamond of consciousness wrapped in rags of humanity, born from a ray of Yog Sothoth, praise to the congress of spheres. Stronger than he had been in ages; strong enough to mold the clay of his host.

He set the guitar in its case, fastened the clasps and tried to remember where he'd parked his rusty car. It was time to pack up and point north. Time to make for the mountains. There was new music to learn, old work to be done.

Chapter 21

Becca came down with a raging fever the morning after the Wade House burned to the ground, as if the house had transferred some of its heat to her in its collapse. In actuality, she knew it was the time she'd spent soaking wet in the cold that had done her in. They treated her with antibiotics at Base Camp, and in three days she was on her feet again. Django never left her side, and Brooks and Nina checked in often, bringing her National Geographic magazines and vegetable curry soup.

The few possessions she had that weren't in storage in her mentor Neil Hafner's attic in Brookline were barely enough to fill her canvas shoulder bag when she packed, and most of those were water damaged. She threw out a pocket notebook of camera settings, field notes, and random thoughts when she realized the bloated pages would never come unstuck from each other without ripping. Her smart phone was dead, but who did she have to call, anyway? In the end, the only things of real value she had were her camera and the broken gold scarab. Even shattered and lacking the magic gem, the scarab was still a family heirloom. She reluctantly turned it over to SPECTRA's occult scholars and technicians for study, and, she hoped, repair. She tried to remind herself that it was better than bringing it to some jeweler on Newbury Street. She gave them the phone, too, on the off chance they could extract her snapshots from it.

* * *

On February 2, Becca rode her father's motorcycle to his funeral in Arkham. She had spent a few days learning to drive it in the quiet wooded hills surrounding the scorched timbers of the Wade House. She quickly got the hang of it and figured the lessons he'd given her as a child on an old secondhand moped they'd owned for a while were to thank for the knack. She took it slow, scanning the road for patches of black ice, and getting a feel for the balance of the bike.

She knew it was reckless for a beginner to take up motorcycle driving in the dead of winter, but no more reckless than most of the things she had done in recent years. And it made her feel close to him, which mattered a whole lot more to her now that he was truly gone, the years she might've spent learning to forgive him stolen. Becca knew now that there was no more forgiveness to excavate from her heart; it had all come flooding up when he'd whispered the Hebrew words for *let there be light* with his dying breath.

Now here she was, coming into Arkham, winding up the lane and through the gates of Christchurch Cemetery beneath the stark maple trees, past the mourners come to honor other dead, aware of the noise of the motorcycle and yet not quite giving a fuck because the noise itself was a tribute to Luke Philips. The day was cold and overcast, but bright.

She had a feeling of déjà vu as she put down the kickstand, killed the engine, and walked away from the bike, thighs still humming, glancing over her shoulder and seeing it where she had once desperately wanted to find it at her grandmother's funeral.

Had that only been two years ago? It felt like so much longer. So much had happened since. She'd been wearing a dress on that day when they gathered to put Catherine in the ground, the only one she owned. Today, dressed in jeans and a leather jacket, she felt more herself than she had then, even though she was still plagued by the same old handicaps, haunted by the same old ghosts. She didn't know if there was an afterlife — although she'd seen evidence of many things that were far stranger—but her father had haunted her for years while he was alive, and now she knew he would continue to haunt her in the company of the other dead she had loved: her mother, her grandparents, and Rafael.

She walked to the grave slowly, her legs getting a feel for the ground under boots after the long ride. She knew she'd have to buy a car eventually if she was going to stay in New England. The expense wouldn't be a problem, not with the compensation SPECTRA owed her for her first job with them. She expected that would go a pretty long way, even though she had no idea what to call it on her taxes. Freelance videography? Consulting? Brooks or Northrup would have some advice. Anyway, she thought she would likely stay in New England for a while, and when spring came, maybe she'd even buy a motorcycle sidecar for Django.

"What are you smiling at? It's a funeral." Brooks looked pretty dapper in a suit and tie under his black trench coat.

"Nothing. Just thinking of getting a sidecar for that thing."

"For Django?" Brooks laughed.

"Did he behave himself on the ride up?"

"Yeah, he's a perfect co-pilot. You better go say hello to him though, or he's not gonna settle down."

Becca could hear the familiar whimpering, and looked around for Brooks' car. The window was cracked a few inches and glazed with slobber, Django's rubbery black nose poking out of the gap. She ambled over with soothing words, and offered her fingers for him to lick before heading back to the graveside.

The arrangements had fallen to Becca. Her uncle Alan had stated flat out that he had no interest in attending his prodigal brother's funeral, that Luke had never been there for his nieces, and they had said their goodbyes long ago. He didn't even want to know the circumstance of Luke's death. Angry at first, Becca had started to push back, but ultimately realized the impossibility of telling the story in a way that would make any sense to him. Even if she could do so without violating the national security oath she'd signed, she could hardly tell anything close to the truth without violating the accepted laws of nature. In the end, she gave up and told the funeral director to forgo a wake and prepare a closed coffin affair at the graveside with no preacher. After all, what could a preacher know about the worlds Luke Philips had seen, or the demons he had wrestled?

Neil—whom she had always considered more of an uncle than Alan—*did* show up. She was grateful for his presence at the cemetery, but when he offered to say a few words, she politely declined. Instead, they observed a moment of silence beside the coffin suspended over the grave. Neil looked older and more weathered than she thought he should. Scarcely two years had passed since she'd last seen him, but maybe living through the Boston crisis with her had made the slope steeper for him.

"I wish I knew how to play a song," Becca said. "That would fit him better than a sermon."

"I have his guitar in the trunk," Brooks said. "Do *you* play?" he asked Neil.

"No. Sorry. I wish."

"I don't even know which one he'd like," Becca said.

Neil handed her a single rose he'd brought along and she laid it on the coffin. It reminded her of the ones on her solitary dress. It was all too much, too familiar, and she wanted to go. She was too tired to cry.

She nodded at the lift operator, and he pressed the switch. There was a low hum and the coffin descended, revealing the modest headstone.

LUKE ROBERT PHILIPS
Nov 14, 1970 - Jan 26, 2021

"That's a nice touch," Brooks said. "How's the real thing?"

Becca dipped a finger under the collar of her plaid shirt and the golden scarab emerged on its chain. It still bore deep scratches and the bezel in the pincers was empty, but the shell and wings had been repaired, and the tarnish polished off enough to make it shine in the muted sunlight.

Brooks scrunched his chin and nodded, impressed. "Those artifacts geeks did a good job."

"Yeah," Becca said. "It feels good to wear it, but I don't know if it'll ever fly again."

"Maybe not," Brooks said. "But hey, let's hope it never needs to."

Neil looked back and forth between the two with naked curiosity.

"Do you think the drone still has the gem?" Becca asked. "On the other side?"

A thorough sifting of the Wade House ashes hadn't turned up the dragonfly or the ruby, and the remote had lost contact. The piano had been reduced to cinders and blackened metal, and no signs of other portals were uncovered in the wreckage. The pool in the cellar, cracked and drained, led nowhere.

"I don't know," Brooks said. "Let's hope it's wreaking havoc over there." He sighed. "I'd like to say maybe it'll fly out and find you someday, but no. Let's hope nothing ever gets out again."

Becca nodded, tucked the scarab back inside her shirt, and buttoned it.

Chapter 22

When Becca called to let Walt Rogan, the proprietor of Birch Grove Cabins, know that her father had passed away suddenly, the old man claimed to remember her from her childhood vacations and said that Luke had talked about her often while doing maintenance chores in the hours when he wasn't holed up with his guitar. Becca didn't know if she believed either of those claims, but when Rogan was done offering his condolences she asked if she could collect Luke's things and take over the rental for a while. He had readily agreed.

Becca arrived on the Harley in the late afternoon of Thursday, February 3, and claimed a key from Rogan at the rental office. Brooks trailed the bike to the White Mountains, arriving right behind her with Django riding shotgun and Luke's guitar in the trunk of his government issue Ford.

The cabin smelled stale. Becca set the guitar case in the corner while Django sniffed around, probably detecting mice. She looked at the rumpled bedclothes and sighed. Her first thought was that she should find a laundromat and wash them. Her second was that maybe she wasn't ready yet to wash the last lingering traces of him from the place where she would be sleeping for the foreseeable future while she figured out her next move.

"You gonna be okay?" Brooks asked from the doorway. She could tell he was hesitant to leave her, and she felt a flush of affection for the stoic ex-cop. They had been through a lot together now. He was starting to feel like the brother she'd never had.

Becca nodded. "Thanks for giving Django a ride."

"Sure. You've got my number if you need anything. *Oh,* almost forgot." He reached into his coat pocket and produced a new phone, two models up from the one she'd taken a swim with. "SPECTRA was able to recover your data. Transferred it to this. On the house." He handed it to her.

"Cool. Thanks. It doesn't come with a drone, huh?"

Brooks laughed. "Afraid not."

"Damn. I was starting to get a feel for the thing."

"Hey, take care of yourself, Becca." He turned to go.

"Jason." She pulled him into a tight hug and kissed him on the cheek. His stubble was rough, and before she'd let him go, he was blushing like only the Irish can.

Brooks patted her back, dropped into a squat and gave Django a vigorous scratching between the ears before stepping out onto the front steps of the little cabin, closing the flimsy door behind him, and heading for the black sedan without looking back.

Becca wondered when she would see him again.

She switched on the new phone. When the startup screen finished loading, she tapped on the photo icon to make sure her little archive was intact. Everything looked the same as it had, but she noticed one new video. It was the most recent item in the file grid, and the thumbnail was a picture of her father's face.

She hadn't taken any pictures of Luke. As an afterthought, she wished she had taken at least one, but she hadn't. Nor had she shot any video of him. A tingle of unease passed through her and she noticed her breath had gone shallow. Her first instinct was to turn the phone off. She didn't know if she was ready for whatever this was, this final message from the man she had lost once and then again.

So she waited. She sat on the bed with the phone in her lap and the dog curled up beside her and waited because she knew that as long as she didn't watch it, there would be a piece of him in the world that wasn't yet spent, that wasn't yet discovered by her, and she could save that and savor it, and put it away for someday.

But then she turned the screen on again and stared at the thumbnail. Was the light haloing his long gray hair one of the track lights in the Quonset hut? She thought it was. He must have shot this while waiting in her bunk cubicle after SPECTRA brought him in on the helicopter, while she and Brooks were still driving back to Concord.

Her trembling finger hovered over the glass. She took a deep breath and tapped the PLAY arrow.

Luke Philips worked his jaw and cleared his throat. His ginger salt-and-pepper beard dominated the screen. His face, hovering over the lens at close range, looked nervous. His eyes darted side to side before he spoke, and when he did, his voice was little more than a whisper.

"Okay, so… they were nice enough to me in the helicopter, and after a little chat with the man in charge, I think I understand what they're trying to do here. I don't know if they have any chance of really stopping what's been set in motion, but it's worth a try and I'm willing to help. Like you're helping. I admire what you're trying to do, Becca, and I know your mother would've been proud of your bravery. Catherine too, the wiser part of her, would be proud. But baby… Don't underestimate the forces at work here.

"I don't know how much time we have. Don't know if we'll get a chance to talk before the shit hits the fan. They're talking about going back into the house, to try and find the reverend that took the key and stop him before he can open the gate. I don't know if you can trust these people, but I'm in because…who *else* do we have to trust?"

He glanced up toward the ceiling, then leaned in close to the microphone and whispered, "You know where I put the original score. The versions in my notebook are just fragments, pieces of the puzzle. I've rearranged them, tried to make them form a different picture. It's hard to explain. It almost makes sense to me when I'm playing the music, or dreaming it. I used to think that if I rewrote it the right way, changed the melody, or the chord structures...I used to think if I inverted it, put the bass line in the upper register...I might realign the spheres, open up a door for angels instead of those monstrous gods. I thought there might be a utopia beyond the gate, if it was aligned to a different point on the cosmic compass."

Luke laughed and the audio distorted. He breathed in deep through his nose and continued, "World peace through music. Isn't that what the hippies wanted? I should know better. The house, the *Invisible Symphony*... It's all a bad trip. There's no redeeming any of it, so you listen: destroy it. It holds no secrets worth decoding. No amount of tinkering is going to take the cancer out of that music. If the wrong people get hold of it—game over. There's a choral section at the end, at the climax. It was written for mutants, for people with a different physiology, from an earlier time in human evolution. If people could sing it, could produce those notes the way they're written... There are *unwritten* notes, invisible on the page that would resonate out of the ones that *are* written. Becca, that music must never find its voice.

"If you make it out of here and I don't— get the scroll and make sure no one follows you. Burn it in the fire pit like I should've done but didn't have the nerve to.

"Okay, honey. I love you. I made a shitty dad, but I always loved you."

His finger loomed over the screen, and then the video froze and collapsed to just another thumbnail on the grid.

Becca set the phone down on a pillow, slid off of the bed and went to the door. She zipped her coat up with her father's words ricocheting around in her head. *Mutants. Different physiology.* She descended the steps, and circled the cabin, scanning the trees, searching the shadows, looking for a glint of binocular glass, or the barrel of a parabolic microphone.

If people could sing it...

She searched the clouds for low flying aircraft, and cursed herself for not listening to the video through earbuds, but the chances that SPECTRA agents had already seen and archived it while transferring her data were high. Even if they hadn't watched it yet, they had surely kept a copy that was right now slumbering on a classified server, waiting for someone to take notice.

She thought of Tom's son, Noah, and his secret language and listened to the silent sky.

There were no black helicopters on the wind, circling Mt. Lincoln, no cultists closing in on the Birch Grove Cabins tonight, brandishing ritual daggers.

Becca went back inside, drew the curtains, and approached the floor lamp. Palms sweating, she unscrewed the aluminum tube where the two sections connected in the center. Luke had rolled the score up and slid it into the lamp while the SPECTRA helicopter touched down. Becca had watched him do it.

But there was no paper visible in the dark tube. She turned it over and shook it at the floor, but nothing fell out. Becca dropped both ends of the lamp. The bulb shattered. The *Invisible Symphony* was gone.

Acknowledgments

My heartfelt thanks to the following people who helped make this a better book: Jen Salt, Chuck Killorin, Jill Sweeney-Bosa, Jeff Miller, Nick Nafpliotis, Meghan Chapman, Christopher C. Payne, and my editor, Vincenzo Bilof, who pushed me hard in the eleventh hour. Thanks also to Mike Davis and the Lovecraft eZine community for countless acts of kindness and support.

DOUGLAS WYNNE is the author of the novels *The Devil of Echo Lake,* *Steel Breeze,* and *Red Equinox.* He lives in Massachusetts with his wife and son and a houseful of animals just a stone's throw from H.P. Lovecraft's fictional town of Arkham. You can find him on the web at www.dougwynne.com

RED EQUINOX

DOUGLAS WYNNE

CPSIA information can be obtained at www.ICGtesting.com
Printed in the USA
LVOW08s1624111016

508320LV00002B/348/P